*A Candlelight
Regency Special*

CANDLELIGHT REGENCIES

MISS CLARINGDON'S CONDITION

Laureen Kwock

A CANDLELIGHT REGENCY SPECIAL

Published by
Dell Publishing Co., Inc.
1 Dag Hammarskjold Plaza
New York, New York 10017

Dell ® TM 681510, Dell Publishing Co., Inc.

ISBN 0-440-11467-5

Printed in the United States of America
First printing—October 1981

1

Sir Arthur Claringdon stormed into his wife's sitting room with the latest copy of the *Gazette* clutched in his fist. The mustache he had cultivated and worn with such distinction over the years quivered as he fixed a baleful eye on his wife and daughter embroidering together on a winged couch.

Lady Claringdon, his wife of twenty-seven years, was unaccustomed to such violence in her private rooms, and her keen eyes held an unmistakable reproof.

"Arthur, whatever is the matter with you?"

Their daughter, Clarissa, was quicker at recognizing the crumpled remains of the newspaper, and her warm chuckle filled the room.

"Papa has been reading the marriage announcements again," she said to her mother. "And I wish you would convince him not to anymore. They always put him out of temper."

"Do they indeed?" Sir Arthur asked witheringly. He flung the paper down on the carpet, the veins of his forehead standing out wildly.

"I should like a word with you, Clarissa."

Clarissa's gray eyes traveled speculatively over her father's face. His normally florid complexion had already taken on the color best suited to ripe tomatoes.

"Just a word, sir?" she murmured. "And not, I hope, another stuffy speech on the joys of matrimony?"

Sir Arthur gritted his teeth. His disposition had already been rendered peevish by the information that Sir Edwin Smiley's daughter—squint and all—had lured a baron to the altar, and he was in no mood to appreciate his own unmarried daughter's jests.

"What do you know about my views of marriage?" he demanded, sinking into an armchair by the fire.

Clarissa's brows shot up in astonishment.

"I know everything about your views," she declared. "You acquaint me with them almost every week. True, the pattern shifts slightly on occasion, but as a rule you confine yourself to two points. Either you stress the sacredness of the holy bond, or you urge me to set up my nursery quickly before the infirmity of my advanced years sets in."

Sir Arthur glowered as she bestowed a most unfilial smile on him.

"Sometimes you try my patience, Clarissa."

"And you try mine, sir," she retorted. "The way you go on about marriage as though I had sixty years in my dish."

Sir Arthur adjusted the folds of his snowy white cravat.

"And what, pray, do you hold against the institution of marriage?"

Clarissa's eyes widened. "Nothing, Papa, except that the whole idea of marriage strikes me as absurd!"

"Absurd is it?!" Sir Arthur roared and slammed his fist down hard on a side table, narrowly missing a jade horse. Lady Claringdon averted her eyes. Peace might be at hand on the Continent in this May of 1814, but it was sorely absent from her sitting room.

Sir Arthur worked his jaw back and forth as he groped for words.

"Absurd you call it," he said finally. "Do you know how many London belles would leap at any of the offers you scorn so rudely?"

"A full score or more, sir," Clarissa replied promptly. "I vow their number increases each time you speak of it to me."

Sir Arthur snorted. At fifty he was every inch the indulgent father from the bottoms of his well-heeled Hessians to the crown of his thinning hair. He had shown no initial displeasure when Clarissa had passed her previous Seasons without accepting any offer of marriage, but in this her fifth Season as an acclaimed Beauty he had begun to fidget. She was now twenty-three, and she still showed no interest in the marital state.

Sir Arthur stared moodily into his daughter's merry face, trying to determine the reason for this unfortunate situation, but try as he might no flaw could he uncover in her appearance. The figure clad now in a green silk gown was slim but well formed and the envy of other marriage minded damsels frequenting Almack's. Her face held more liveliness than classic beauty perhaps, with a generous mouth, two riveting gray eyes, and a head of bouncy red curls that never obeyed a hairdresser's comb. Sir Arthur dug deeper into his armchair. That hair did not fool him for a second. His daughter might resemble a lovely widgeon, but she was *not*. And no one knew this better than Sir Arthur himself.

But she was twenty-three! Again and again he returned to this appalling bit of news. She must wed and soon. This folly had gone on long enough.

Sir Arthur fortified himself with a pinch of snuff, a new blend from the Berry Brothers which he could not decide if he enjoyed or not. He snapped the lid of the enameled box shut, narrowly missing a fingernail in the process, and summoned Clarissa from her smiling scrutiny of a rather gloomy new seascape by Mr. Constable.

"I have no quarrel with your being particular, Clarissa," he said mildly. "But if you keep up these missish ways you shall soon find yourself an old maid."

"Oh, Papa."

"What did you call young Hedges who offered you one of the richest alignments in the kingdom?"

"I believe it was a clumsy monkey, sir."

"Yes, and well ashamed you should be of that."

"And so I should if the matter got out," Clarissa said quickly. "But I only told you and Mama in private, and neither of you would repeat that remark in public."

"Our manners do you credit," Sir Arthur said caustically. "But for your information no man of Hedges's wealth can be dismissed as a monkey, no matter how clumsy you perceive him."

"But, Papa, you have not danced with him."

Clarissa's merry laugh filled the room. Lady Claringdon hid a tiny smile. Sir Arthur, muttering a little about ungrateful daughters, plucked another name from the list of eligibles in the ton.

"What of Lord Pedlow? Does he possess some flaw, too?"

"Just one," Clarissa answered.

"Which is?"

"His mother."

Lady Claringdon, long acquainted with the eccentricities of the dowager Countess Pedlow, fell into a fit of choking, and Clarissa was obliged to pound her firmly on the back until the spasm passed.

"Anyone marrying into that family would be forced to fetch and carry to her and I could not."

Sir Arthur cast his mind wildly about and settled on his perennial favorite.

"What of Charles Alsgood?"

Clarissa's face softened momentarily. "Charles is the greatest friend, Papa. But I grew up with him. He is almost a brother to me, and I am not about to marry my brother."

"No, but I heartily wish you would marry someone," Sir Arthur said peevishly. Clarissa swept up from her mother's side and stalked the room like a lioness.

"But why should I?" she asked. "All your talk of marriage quite puts me out of patience, sir. You speak as though I am at my last prayers."

"I want you married, Clarissa, and soon!"

Clarissa's eyes flashed a warning. Sir Arthur met it with a dogged thrust of his quivering mustache. To Lady Claringdon, the encounter resembled a meeting between a bantam cock and a mule.

Clarissa turned away first.

"I see. Is there some schedule I must follow, sir?" she asked quietly. Perhaps, Lady Claringdon thought, pricking up her ears, a shade too quietly.

Sir Arthur beamed. "I shall give you plenty of time," he promised. "Shall we say 'til the end of this Season?"

"You are too generous, sir. And whom shall I marry?"

Sir Arthur threw up his hands. "How should I know? If not Hedges or Pedlow then someone of your own choosing. I am as tired of this topic as you profess to be. I am warning you, Clarissa. I want you wed, or I shall wash my hands of you."

"But that is an even greater absurdity," Clarissa declared. "Just think of the scandal. I should be obliged to beg for work, genteel work to begin with, but after that, who can say. And I shall tell all who ask that you abandoned me!"

"Really, Clarissa, I wish you will stop talking fustian," Lady Claringdon interrupted, abandoning her pretense at embroidery for the first time that evening. "Your father has no intention of throwing you out on the street, and, Arthur, these threats are most unseemly."

Sir Arthur squared his shoulders and avoided his wife's gaze.

"I'm sorry, my dear," he murmured, "but these are not just threats." He glanced over again at their daughter. "No one has said anything hitherto about throwing you out, Clarissa. And I shan't. But I might just send you down to Claring!"

He accentuated this threat with a nod that ended in the lower regions of his Mathematical tie. "No more London socializing," he went on. "Think about that. You shall miss the czar next month and Wellington after that and all the festivities for the two of them."

Clarissa yawned prettily behind a dainty hand. "If I had wanted to see Wellington," she replied, "I'd have gone to France with everyone else. So I shouldn't worry about him. But the czar is another matter." She reflected privately on this potential loss. "People do claim he is so handsome, and I confess, I should like to see for myself since I have met his sister, and she is no beauty."

These words were spoken coolly, but the idea of being sequestered in the family's country estate during the height of Season did not set well in Clarissa's dish. But then neither did marriage. And to remain in London while her father had marriage on his brain would never bring her a moment's peace.

"If you keep me confined in the Cotswolds," she pointed out, unable to resist one last skirmish with her father, "people shall think me disgraced, and evil minds shall say that I am *breeding!*"

"Oh, Clarissa!" Lady Claringdon wailed.

"That's *it,* by Jupiter!" Sir Arthur exploded out of his chair. "Breeding, is it?"

"Yes," Clarissa announced. "Or at the very least they shall say I am seduced. You know the prattle boxes in the ton. Think how awkward it would be for Mama. She could not show her face in public without some odious scene. But you have worse in store, Papa," she assured him. "Since you and Carlton should be obliged to defend my honor, and since neither of you is especially skilled in pistols or swords, I can foresee only black cloth for the females of the family."

"Can you indeed?" Sir Arthur fingered his mustache with icy courtesy. "I vow I have never heard a worse tale in my entire life, and I shan't listen to it a moment longer."

"As you wish," Clarissa said, rising and heading toward the doorway.

A roar from her father stopped her at once.

"And where do you think you're going?" he demanded.

Clarissa turned. "To pack, of course. The Cotswolds are said to be quite lovely in the spring."

When the last glimpse of green silk was gone, Sir Arthur flung himself back into his chair and tugged wildly at the cravat choking him.

"Madame, your daughter . . ."

He got no further. Lady Claringdon cut him off quickly.

"My daughter is yours as well. And pray tell me what is she to do in the Cotswolds?"

"*Do?*" Sir Arthur barked. "She shall think of marriage, of course!"

"I doubt that. Clarissa is as mulish as she is lovely."

Sir Arthur waved a pudgy hand. "She shall come around." A new thought struck him as he watched his wife search for her scissors. "Don't you want her married, Constance?"

A frown puckered Lady Claringdon's brow. "Of course I do. But to force her into marriage this way . . ."

"Force her?" Sir Arthur expostulated. "I'd like to see anyone force Clarissa to do anything she doesn't want to do. Dash it all, Constance, it's high time for her to be settled. We both know that. I'm a reasonable man. She can

11

take her pick of the litter. I merely ask that she make up her mind."

"But how is she to decide," Lady Claringdon asked, snipping off a thread with a pointed scissors, "when she is in the country, and the litter lies in London?"

Mr. Sidney Montcrieff smothered a yawn with the palm of his right hand while his left searched the confines of his plum waistcoat for his fob. Surely, he thought as he frowned at the timepiece in his hand, this watch was in error. Only two o'clock? He could have sworn the hour was much later. Yawning again ever so slightly, he pushed himself away from the faro table and began to pocket his winnings.

"Good heavens, Sidney. You can't be leaving yet," Tyrus Morely cried out with alarm as he watched his night's losses disappear onto Montcrieff's person. "The night's barely begun."

"The night, Tyrus, is already morning," Sidney answered with a good-humored glint in his eye.

"Stay another round, Montcrieff." The voice of Lord Wentworth, another loser, advised.

Sidney shook his head.

"Really," Morely said with the petulance for which he was famed, "you have been winning half the night. Stay another hour longer."

"Not an hour or a half hour or another minute."

Sidney's voice took on the ring of iron, causing Lord Wentworth, in his heyday the winner of a number of notorious duels, to look askance at Morely. A pleasant chap, Montcrieff, but one who could be a regular bearjaw when provoked. He dealt another negligent glance across the green baize table toward Morely. That was sufficient. Tyrus, never a gentleman of inordinate courage and no

12

doubt recalling some of Sidney's wizardry with swords, had already desisted his whining.

"Perhaps with Sidney gone we can all enjoy better luck!" Charles Alsgood spoke up peacefully from his corner of the cardroom.

"A good point, Charles," Sidney said gratefully. He walked quietly through the noisy halls toward the entrance way, stopping only at the door to view the unfortunate Mr. Philip Kentmere with his pockets obviously to let. A sympathetic smile flitted across Sidney's face. Would the lad never learn?

The cool air stung his cheeks as he stepped from White's to find the streets shimmering from the light drizzle that had fallen during his hours at the club. Sidney inhaled a deep breath, feeling too restless for a carriage ride home. He decided to walk.

Here and there on his journey a carriage passed him, but the streets, even though it was late, seemed oddly deserted. Napoleon's exile had much to do with that, he thought as he crossed Jermyn Street. With the Bourbons restored to power half of London had flocked to Paris. In private Sidney doubted whether Louis, no matter how great a friend of the Regent, would do anything worthwhile for France, just as he doubted whether any island could hold Bonaparte for long.

These reflections lasted only until he reached Piccadilly when the face of Lady Vye suddenly popped into his mind. Sidney sighed with pleasure as he dwelled on the beautiful widow who of late had occupied many of his days and evenings. He gave his Malacca cane a twirl, then frowned in annoyance. A pity he could not call on Lady Vye this morning.

It was not the late hour which caused this obstacle, but the scrap of information retained in his memory that Lady Vye had recently flown into a pet with him. Their latest quarrel centered upon a bracelet consisting of twenty-four perfectly matched emeralds. She had taken a fancy to it, a fancy he did not share.

No . . . Sidney shook his head. It would not do to call on Lady Vye in the middle of the night unannounced. There was no telling whom she might be entertaining. And Lady Vye herself professed a profound dislike of all surprises except those hailing from Messrs. Rundell & Bridges.

Sidney headed up Berkeley Street, but only two steps had he taken when he felt a jab in the back of his greatcoat. He stopped, as rigid as a nail. All thoughts of widows, lovely and ugly, vanished into the cool air.

"Your purse, milord," a voice muttered behind him.

"My purse?" Sidney turned slowly, staring into the shadows behind, where he dimly perceived the robber.

A pistol jabbed at him again. "Don't move again, unless you want this. Your purse."

"Certainly," Sidney said, bored. One hand reached into the folds of his coat while the other tightened on the knob of his cane. He held out the requested purse. The robber, eyes glinting a little, reached for it; no sooner did he spy this movement then Sidney crashed his cane down hard on top of the criminal's head. A startled oath rang out. The pistol toppled from the robber's hand and onto the ground. Quickly Sidney kicked it out toward the middle of the street. The robber, weaponless now, recognized too late the size and skill of one of Gentleman Jack's prize pupils. He fled, but not before enduring another blow with the well-aimed cane.

Sidney eyed his cane sadly. Broken, a pity. He was rather fond of it. He strolled over toward the pistol and carried it home with him to Hill Street.

"Bender? What are *you* doing up?" he asked, astonished at finding his butler sitting in the hallway.

14

"A message has arrived, sir," Bender explained, taking Sidney's hat, coat, cane, and gun without a change of expression.

"Complete with messenger," a voice added.

Montcrieff turned to find his young cousin Lawrence, Earl of Lytton, smiling genially at him.

"I told Bender I could be trusted with the family silver, Sidney." The earl stopped, noticing the pistol in the butler's possession. "Firearms? Napoleon has not left Elba, has he?"

A muscle twitched in Sidney's cheek. "No, my dear Larry. Bonaparte by all accounts remains on his island."

"Then is this the latest rage? To go about London armed? If so, I wish you might have warned me. I have no pistol in my possession."

"Nor do I as a rule. I stole this object from a ruffian."

Lytton's face shone with envy. "Did you, by Jove? You have all the luck, Sidney. Still you're mighty cool about it."

"Certainly, I broke a cane in the process. My favorite one at that," Sidney explained. He led the way into the blue saloon that bore unmistakable traces of his cousin's visit—a half-empty decanter of Madeira, an empty glass, and an untidy newspaper. Obviously the wine had fallen into company with the earl. "Never mind my scuffle, why do you drop by at this time of the morning?"

"Important message," his cousin answered. "And it wouldn't be so early in the morning if you had not taken a devilish long time getting home."

Sidney smiled at the rebuke. "I beg pardon. I was at White's."

"Winning?"

Sidney shrugged, feeling no inclination to boast about something as common to him as breathing.

"Would you care for a glass, Sidney?" Lytton asked.

"Since you shall drink it up without my help, yes, Lytton, to be sure."

The earl poured the drinks, laughing a little. The resemblance between the two men was cursory at best, though they both did possess the Montcrieff jaw, a legacy from their fathers, who had been brothers. Lytton, however, was the shorter by several inches, with hazel eyes usually brimming with laughter, and golden hair. Sidney, gray-eyed and darker, leaned toward the copper tresses of his mother.

"Aren't you glad the war is over so we can have decent wine again?" Lytton asked, dropping himself back into the chair he had occupied so well during most of the night.

Sidney rolled the Madeira on his tongue. "You did not descend upon me to praise the wine nor to talk of Napoleon. Hadn't you better cut line and tell me the rap?"

"My word, Sidney. Must there always be a scrape?"

Sidney swung one leg over the other. "I beg pardon, Lytton. It's simply that of the last three times I set eyes on you, twice the situation warranted I go bail for you. Am I to understand this is a social visit? If so, be advised that late morning is the appropriate hour to call in town."

"My manners are every bit as perfect as yours, Sidney," the earl protested. "And I have half a mind not to tell you the news."

Sidney stifled a yawn. "Pray, what news might that be?" he asked politely.

"Cousin Edward's fortune, it's yours!"

2

At Lytton's words a frown creased Sidney's brow.

"Are you quite certain, Larry?" he asked mildly. "I thought Edward's estate lay in shambles. He died over in India, wasn't it?"

"The estate was confused," Lytton agreed, warming his hands by the fire. "But the matter has been sorted out on both continents with one result. You are the winner, Sidney."

"How odd." Sidney stared into the fire, puzzled.

"Well, I must say you don't look deuced happy over my news," Lytton said, rather put out that his announcement had not brought some glow of satisfaction to his cousin's countenance.

Sidney drained his Madeira. "Perhaps it's because the news is not such good news to me."

Lytton stood thunderstruck for a moment. "Ten thousand pounds is not your notion of good news?" he asked. It was plain to his lordship that Sidney at thirty-two hovered on the brink of senility. "I know you're well pursed, coz, but to turn up your nose in your fashion at ten thousand pounds. . . . And you haven't forgotten Bengal Court, have you?"

A polite shudder shook Sidney. No one in his right mind could forget Bengal Court, Edward's country home built for use as a modest abode, and except for the fickleness of fate it might have remained that way. Dispatched to the subcontinent on military duty, Edward had discovered a taste for the Orient. His Cotswolds home had borne ample proof to his infatuation with elephant tusks, brass trays, and if memory served Sidney correctly, a variety of mummified monkey paws gracing the hallways.

Sidney unwound his lanky body and reached for the decanter. "I remember the property," he said now. "Even in my father's day it was badly run-down. Edward was more occupied in subduing Calcutta than in seeing to his own property kept up in style. And if his later years followed his early ones I predict those ten thousand pounds shall go quickly toward bringing the property up to snuff. Unless the fortune falls short, in which case I shall have to part with my own blunt!"

Lytton pursed his lips and whistled softly. "So that's how the matter sits. No wonder you want no part of it."

Sidney rubbed his chin. "Do you know I only saw Edward twice in my lifetime? I don't begrudge the honor, but why the devil did he select me?"

The earl shrugged. "I think Joseph shall soon be asking that same question when he hears the news."

At the mention of Joseph, their cousin some distance removed, Sidney let out a bark of laughter. Joseph's attempts to win Edward's favor was legion in the family annals. It had included numerous trips to the Cotswolds with wife and progeny in tow during those infrequent times when Edward was home from India.

"I'd give a monkey to see his face," Sidney admitted.

"Then come with me tomorrow," Lytton said, putting his glass down on a pier table. "I mean to relate the happy news to him in person. I hope he shows more reaction than you have."

"This tendency of yours to play town crier is most

18

unseemly, Larry," Sidney said patiently. "And how the devil did you hear the news anyway?"

Lytton grinned. "Henriks, Edward's solicitor. His younger brother was a chum from Oxford, and Henriks knew I'd no pretensions to Bengal Court. He was just happy to have the thing nice and tidy. It seems nothing is more complicated than to die abroad."

"I shall keep it in mind when my time comes."

Another grin crossed Lytton's cheerful face. "By the way, Aunt Agatha comes along with the house, you must know."

Sidney's shoulders shook with laughter. "Does she, by Jove? This windfall gets better and better. I had half forgotten her. Can she still be alive?"

"Oh, yes, and breathing fire still," Lytton said. He stifled a yawn. "Anyway, one can't really forget Aunt Agatha. She scared me half to death when I was a child and still does."

"You are not alone there," Sidney said. "I distinctly recall that on the occasion we met she called me a pasty-faced brat." He did some mental computation and stared at the earl with frank amazement. "She must be sixty or older."

"Older, I should think," Lytton answered. "But Agatha needn't trouble you. Unless you mean to live in Bengal Court."

Sidney laughed. To live at Bengal Court would try the patience of a monk, which he was not. "No, Larry. I don't intend to live there. But I shall be obliged to see to the estates, and that shall mean a trip to the country which I loathe. And to leave London now would be inconvenient, shall we say?"

Lytton picked up the decanter of Madeira. The cut crystal shone in the firelight.

"Is it the Lady Vye who worries you?" he asked innocently.

Sidney was not drawn in by that angelic look. "How the devil do you know so much?" he asked affably. "And don't nauseate me with more tales of Oxford chums. Or can it be that you stand acquainted with Lady Vye herself."

"I don't know her," Lytton said quickly, taking pains to put distance between himself and his cousin's *chère-amie*. "But if you do squire her around, talk shall follow. Isn't that what you've always told me?"

"That does have the ring of my own syllables."

The earl cocked his head. "Is she as beautiful as they say?"

"More," Sidney said absentmindedly.

"The rumor mill has it she is quite eager to be married. You aren't in love with her, are you?"

Sidney turned as white as his collar points. "Not in the least, Larry. You know me better than to think I would contemplate a trip to the altar with anyone, let alone Lady Vye. For the moment she is amusing and to leave her company for that of Aunt Agatha . . . well . . . ." He sought refuge in his glass.

"I am sorry, Sidney," Lytton said as another yawn shook him. "I didn't expect my news to bring down so much calamity at once." He rose from his chair. "I should be getting home."

"Stay the night," Sidney suggested. "Most of it is gone."

"Now that's mighty civil of you," Lytton said, fighting and then surrendering to another yawn. "Can't think why I am so tired. It must be your Madeira. I shall sleep here but only long enough to rise and give the word to Joseph tomorrow."

At eleven the next morning Sidney stood frowning in

his library. The great mahogany map cabinet was open in front of him, and the map of Bengal Court lay spread on the table. This dusty document had been thrust upon him by Henriks who had called an hour earlier to urge the matter be settled at once. Too much delay had already been allowed to elapse since Edward's death six months ago.

Sidney heaved a sigh and dropped his quizzing glass. A visit to Bengal Court seemed inescapable now, but when would be the least inconvenient time to quit the city? He was still grappling with this problem when a new one arrived in the green room: Mr. Joseph Cranley, accompanied by his wife, Mary.

Uttering a silent oath that he be preserved from any more relations gathering under his roof, Sidney shook hands with his balding cousin and accepted the sherry that Bender was pouring. As he sampled the sherry he observed Joseph with customary distaste. Pushing forty now, his cousin was running to fat, and before much longer it would be corsets such as the Regent himself wore. It puzzled Sidney more than it should that Joseph, a purse pincher *extraordinaire,* stopped short of nothing in satisfying the demands of his stomach.

"Well, Joseph," Sidney said as they settled into mahogany chairs. "And Mary too. How do the children go on, Mary?"

At this opening, Mary, a flaccid woman with a face burdened with freckles, embarked on a long episode that dealt with her twins and the measles that had afflicted them of late. To Sidney's profound relief she was cut short just as the tale seemed to reach epidemic proportions.

"We have more important things to discuss with Sidney than children," Joseph said irritably.

Mary, who lived for her offspring, thought that this

21

smacked of heresy, but she retreated haughtily into her ratafia.

"What are these important matters, Joseph?" Sidney asked, taking reluctant command of the conversation again.

"Matters to do with Cousin Edward."

"Edward?" Sidney pulled an imaginary thread from his exquisite waistcoat and surveyed it with scrupulous care. "Well, I hope the matter is unimportant, Joseph. Edward's dead. Hadn't you heard? It happened out in India, a dreadful country."

Joseph turned the color of his puce coat. "I know that Edward is dead," he said. "It's his estate. Has he left it to you?"

Sidney, by nature a stickler for honesty, hesitated not a trifle. Somehow Joseph had already heard the news.

"Yes," he admitted. He held up both hands to stem the flood of accusations sure to come his way. "Pray, don't ask me why. I don't know myself. But since he is dead and presumably buried in that godforsaken place he was so fond of, neither of us can quarrel with him again."

"How can you be so heartless!" Mary cried out from the couch. "Sweet, gentle Edward."

This reading of their late cousin's character was so far-fetched that Sidney stood poised on his own carpet with his mouth agape. By no stretch of the imagination could Edward be called gentle, and as for sweet . . . !

"And Aunt Agatha?" Joseph asked, seizing this pause to reenter the fray. "What do you propose to do with her?"

"Do?" Sidney asked, irritation appearing on his handsome face for the first time. "I shall do nothing, Joseph. Aunt Agatha is sixty if she's a day and has long reached her maturity without my aid."

"She won't like your inheriting."

"She don't signify."

"You're wrong there, Sidney," Lytton remarked, strolling into the saloon in time to hear this last remark. "Grandaunts always signify, particularly a griffin like Aunt Agatha. Good morning, Joseph, and Mary. How nice. I was meaning to call on you earlier but must have overslept. I apologize for not coming down sooner, Sidney, but I had a devil of a time with this neckcloth." He stood back to examine Sidney's own in the morning light. "How do you get yours looking like that?"

"It's all in the wrist, Larry."

"Well, I wish you would show me sometime. I crushed four of yours before this fifth fell into place."

Smiling, Sidney turned his lordship's attention away from his toilette and toward their cousins.

"Joseph and Mary came over to felicitate me. They . . . ah . . . heard the news."

Lytton pivoted and beamed at Joseph. "Did they? How nice. For myself I should have Sidney drawn and quartered. Do you know how much Edward has left him?"

"No," Joseph said thickly.

The earl turned toward Sidney. "How much was it, cousin? You know my atrocious head for figures."

"Ten thousand pounds or thereabouts," Sidney said, looking bored.

"But you are forgetting the property," Lytton chided. "Indeed a very tidy sum. Don't you think, Joseph?"

Tight-lipped, Joseph rose to his feet. "I don't think, my dear Lawrence, but I do know when I am being roasted. Come, Mary. We must be off. If there's anything I can't abide in the morning, it's dandyism."

"Oh, I can see that simply by viewing your shirt points," Lytton replied sunnily.

Joseph sniffed. "Remember me to Aunt Agatha, Sidney."

"Only if you insist," Sidney said promptly. "You have

been staying in her town residence so long, Joseph, that being remembered to her might bring about her London return."

Joseph preened a little. "I can handle Aunt Agatha and any other old woman who crosses my path."

"Well, if I come across any, I'll send them your way," Sidney promised. He gazed toward his butler. "Bender? My cousins are just leaving."

As soon as Bender had escorted Mary and Joseph out of the room, Sidney collapsed in his wing chair. Living in London was not without its hazards.

"How long were you saddled with those two?" Lytton asked with quick sympathy.

Sidney gestured helplessly. "I've no idea. It seemed an eternity."

"He's as jealous as a cat."

"As long as it's not a Bengal cat!"

Sidney met his cousin's brimming eyes and then threw back his head and laughed.

"Did you see his face?" Lytton asked, recovering first.

"Yes. . . . But let's forget old Joseph. There's nothing he can do over Bengal Court even if he wanted to." He gazed at his cousin fondly. "What are your plans for this week, Larry?"

"Plans?" The earl paused in thought. "There's Almack's on Wednesday and maybe a trip to the opera. Why do you ask?"

"Come to Bengal Court with me."

"What of Lady Vye?" Lytton asked.

Sidney's face wrinkled in distaste. "The sooner I rid myself of the nuisance of Bengal Court the more time I can devote to Lady Vye's amusement and my own."

"And I am to bear your company in the country?"

"Not if you dislike it," Sidney said at once. "It shall be boring, I know, so if you'd rather not . . ."

"Oh, I don't mind," Lytton answered. He grinned. "In fact, I'm flattered."

"Good." Sidney rubbed his palms together. "Now all I need do is drive around to Grosvenor Square and beg Lady Vye's pardon for my absence from London this week."

As Sidney gave the order for his curricle to be fetched, another carriage began its turn around St. James Square headed in a northerly direction. From inside the vehicle Clarissa stared out gloomily, plying herself with an ivory fan. The carriage halted briefly at Bruton Street, and she descended to inform the renowned modiste Madame Fanchon that she was canceling all of her dress fittings for the weeks to come.

Madame Fanchon, wise in the whims of the Quality she served, accepted this without a blink, merely informing Clarissa that the fittings could be continued whenever *mademoiselle* wished. Clarissa returned to her carriage, and the journey resumed with the vehicle swinging up through Berkeley Square where again it halted, this time at the Mount Street residence of her brother.

As luck would have it, Carlton himself was just about to enter No. 12 when he caught sight of his father's carriage. He waited, hat and gloves in hand, while his sister stepped down. Smiling a fond welcome, he kissed her soundly on both cheeks. Clarissa's spirits, at an ebb since receiving her gaol sentence to Claring, rose upon seeing her handsome brother. She linked her arm through his, and together they crossed the threshold into his residence.

Carlton, like Clarissa, had inherited his mother's piercing gray eyes, curly red hair, and languid grace. But he had also been blessed with her placid disposition, enabling him to ride out even the most insufferable of bores while Clarissa's volatility was a direct gift from their father.

"New dress, Clarissa?" he asked now, admiring the high-necked French muslin she wore. "It becomes you greatly."

"Thank you, Carlton," she said absently. "It's the Paris fashion on account of the Bourbons. Next year I suppose we'll all don Russian mantles."

"I hope not," Carlton said with a grin. "It would clash badly with my waistcoats."

By nature Carlton Claringdon did not boast any extraordinary sense of perception. In any battle of wits his sister would have been the victor, but it was obvious even to him that something was amiss with Clarissa this fine spring morning. Wisely, he led her up the stairs, still chatting about waistcoats and neckcloths and into the comfortable parlor of his wife, Beatrice.

Trixie, who had been frowning over a sketchpad, looked up at her husband and sister-in-law and flew to her feet.

"Clarissa! Such a nice surprise."

"It may be the last surprise for some time, Trixie," Clarissa said, embracing her sister-in-law. Trixie drew away and searched Clarissa's face.

"But what is the matter, my dear?" she asked, leading her toward the couch. "I've never seen you look so low."

"Nor I," Carlton declared, drawing his brows together in a frown. "So will you tell us before we burst?"

Suppressing a gurgle of laughter, Clarissa told them what had transpired the previous night. Trixie shook her blond head in bewildered sympathy, but Carlton spoke first, all sign of amusement gone from his handsome face.

"To Claring in the middle of Season? No, Clarissa, even Father would never do such a thing."

"He is doing just that."

Carlton paced a moment on his prized Persian rug. "But think of all the expense of your gowns . . ."

"He doesn't care about that, Carlton. He and I are too

26

busy arguing to worry about clothes." Clarissa heaved a heartfelt sigh.

"But that is hardly news, Clarissa," Trixie said, then stopped short, the color rising in her cheeks. "Oh, I do beg your pardon."

"A pox on that pardon," Carlton said rudely. "Trixie is right. Your quarrels with Father are nothing new. You two have been fighting forever."

"Not that long," Clarissa corrected. "Just since my come-out. He is determined that I shall marry within this Season."

"Are you so opposed to the idea?" Carlton probed gently. A dutiful son and fond brother, he found these family quarrels troublesome.

"It is not a disagreeable state, Clarissa. I do assure you," Trixie added with such earnestness that Clarissa's ready sense of the ridiculous rose at once.

"I am exceedingly relieved to hear that," she replied with a twinkle in her eye. "But I wish to marry whom I shall and not have Papa forever arranging matches with those I have no interest in!"

"Anyone I know?" Carlton asked, intrigued.

"You know them all," Clarissa declared. "There's Pedlow to start with, and Hedges. . . ." She ticked off her suitors one by one on the fingers of a dainty hand.

"All of them found wanting, Clarissa?" Trixie asked when Clarissa had come to a halt.

"I'm afraid so," Clarissa said with a sad nod.

"But you can't go to Claring," Carlton insisted. "You shall be bored within a day."

"Even less, I fear," Clarissa said. She rose from the couch and walked agitatedly for a few minutes. "Don't you see, that's just what Papa wants. When I do get bored I shall beg to come home or so he thinks. But I don't intend to let him win so easily, and you must help me, Trixie."

Trixie, who had been trailing Clarissa across the room, spoke up at once, her face turning a delightful pink.

"But anything, Clarissa. Would you like me to intercede on your behalf? Speak with your father? I don't think he shall listen to me, but perhaps Carlton, with his long experience in the family—"

"No," Clarissa interrupted her. "It's not that kind of favor I want." She squeezed Trixie's hands in hers. "You told me once of a friend near Claring, a woman our age. To help pass the time and to keep from being bored, I thought I would make her acquaintance. Will you write me a short note?"

"Nothing could be simpler," Trixie declared. "I daresay Emily shall be glad to meet you for I have talked of you so often to her." Her face momentarily clouded as she searched her memory. "Now where did I put her last letter? I know . . . and I shall fetch it in a trice." Quickly Trixie left the room. Clarissa watched her, a thoughtful expression on her face, then she turned to her brother with a rueful smile.

"You are lucky to have Trixie, Carlton."

"I know," he said. Brother and sister gazed at each other in mute understanding. "Do you really believe that Emily will ease the tedium of the countryside?" Carlton asked, breaking the silence that had fallen.

"She must," Clarissa said, resolving to be optimistic. She patted her brother fondly on his sleeve. "Don't look so gloomy. I shan't give in to Papa."

"That's what worries me. You're as stubborn as he is."

"Oh, no," she boasted. "I'm much worse."

Carlton chuckled. "When I lived at home he was just as eager for me to wed," he reminded her.

28

"Yes," Clarissa agreed. "And I recall *you* resisted every effort of his until you met Trixie one day on your own."

"At Hookam's Library," Carlton said, remembering. "One glimpse of her, and I took the plunge immediately." His face glowed with such happiness that a momentary sadness overwhelmed Clarissa.

"Does it happen that quickly, Carlton?" she asked without thinking.

"Does what happen?"

"Love."

"Love?" Carlton stepped back, the better to observe his sister. "Good Jupiter, Clarissa, you must know for yourself. Surely you've fallen in love once or twice in your life." He peered at her anxiously. "You're not just out of a schoolroom."

"I know that! But the truth is I've never been in love," Clarissa admitted. "Which is why I shan't marry until I do fall in love. And who can fall in love with such specimens as Papa thrusts at me!"

"Here is the note!" Trixie said, coming back into the room. "I penned it quickly. I know you'll like Emily, Clarissa." Her soft blue eyes filled with tears as Clarissa placed the note in her reticule. "I do hope your father relents, and you shall not have to stay long at Claring."

"If Papa has his way," Clarissa said with unfailing good cheer, "I shall spend my dotage there!"

3

Two days later on a gray, windswept Thursday morning —perfect for a hanging!—Clarissa departed from St. James Square for Claring accompanied by Henry, her groom, and Polly, her abigail. Since Claring lay twenty miles short of Cheltenham, it would take the greater part of a day's journey to reach, and she had insisted on an early start.

Sir Arthur himself saw his daughter off, grumbling a little about the early hour.

"You may return, Clarissa," he said gruffly, eyeing her recalcitrant face, "whenever you see fit to obey my wishes."

"In that case, Papa," she replied, kissing his hand, " 'twould be best not to return and wed some monkey."

Lady Claringdon, who had hoped for a settlement in this latest domestic war, quickly intervened, enfolding her daughter in a scented embrace and speeding her into the safety of the carriage.

Several hours later all pleasure in Clarissa's quarrel with her father was rapidly disappearing in the rolling dust and heat of the countryside. The travel chaise, though light sprung and cushioned, was no protection against the holes and bumps that cluttered the road. The bones of her body sent up waves of protest as the chaise rattled on, and she spent most of her time jolted and shaken in her seat, clutching her reticule and calling out for Henry to slow down the pace for pity's sake.

Dust rose with each mile. Clarissa fanned herself wearily and resorted to her vinaigrette. On the seat opposite, Polly, refreshed by a light nuncheon of ham and cheese, dozed. Her gentle snores punctuated the early afternoon.

Moodily, Clarissa parted the curtain at the window, staring out into the gray stone countryside. The green hills were just beginning to peek out from the spring thaw. Now and then she glimpsed a woolly ewe and a baby lamb, certain clues that Claring was not far off.

Peacefully, she settled back into her seat and gazed across fondly at her abigail. Maybe Polly held the answer to the day's tedium. Clarissa closed her eyes the better to emulate her woman, but though the carriage rocked and lulled Polly to sleep, it only gave her the headache!

She forced her lids open and rubbed her throbbing temples with slender fingers, all the while thinking of her father. This was all his doing. He had forced her into this ridiculous exile by speaking of marriage so often that anyone would have thought she were on the shelf.

A frown pierced Clarissa's troubled brow.

But if I do stay at Claring for long, I shall be on the shelf, she thought, warily considering her future. She took a sniff of her hartshorn. The heat was still insufferable, but now a new dilemma faced her.

Whatever was she to do at Claring? Never before had she worried about amusing herself in the country. Customarily Sir Arthur and Lady Claringdon would have invited a score of friends and relatives to share their visit, and a full house was *de rigeur*. But on this occasion Clarissa would be all alone.

Sighing, Clarissa tried to remember what amusements Cheltenham offered. The chief of these, it appeared to her now, revolved around its famous springs, and since she was no invalid, she had a profound distaste for watering holes. There would be Assemblies probably, but she felt in no mood to attend them alone. She shook her head. She would be bored within a day, just as Carlton had predicted and just as her father hoped.

The carriage hit another rut in the road. Clarissa hugged a cushion to her bosom. Better boredom in the country, she thought to herself as she gritted her teeth, than marriage in the town!

The afternoon was growing warm and sticky when Henry drove the carriage down the estate road. On either side of the lane poplars towered like green arrows pointing toward heaven. A smile played on the curve of Clarissa's lips. How often she and Carlton had raced on this very road as youngsters. Reaching out, she shook Polly awake.

"Wake up, Polly," she whispered softly. "We're home."

Polly's eyes flew open. "London?" she asked tremulously, not daring to hope that her mistress had finally come to her senses.

"Not London. Claring," Clarissa countered gently.

Polly shuddered and closed her eyes again.

Henry drew the carriage to a stop and opened the door. Clarissa stepped down, shaking off the layers of dust that had accumulated on the ruffle of her travel dress. As always the first sight of Claring took her breath away. The gray stone mansion had weathered all the elements thrown at it during this hardest of past winters and stood resolute and tall like the proud Elizabethan it was. Now as Clarissa approached the great oak door she found Mrs. Quill, Claring's housekeeper, hurrying to greet her and wearing a flustered expression that bespoke utter confusion.

"Miss Clarissa! I had no word that you were coming," she said, clucking her tongue, bobbing a curtsy, and leading the way into the hall. She accentuated her words of apology by peeling off first one holland cover and then another from the chairs lining the corridor.

"Don't trouble yourself, Mrs. Quill," Clarissa said, shocked to find the house so closed up. "I am just relieved to be on firm ground again."

"Yes, miss," Mrs. Quill said. "And will Lady Claringdon and Sir Arthur be joining you later?"

Clarissa shrugged. "I think not." She forestalled any further questions with a request for dinner. "I trust the kitchen is not shut up?"

"Oh, no," Mrs. Quill said at once. "Quill shall make your supper directly, and I can bring it to your room, or. . . ." Here she directed an agonized look down the hall. "Or would you be wanting it in the main dining room?"

"A tray will be fine," Clarissa said, correctly surmising the state of the main dining room.

"I am sorry," Mrs. Quill repeated. "I had no idea . . ."

"No more apologies," Clarissa insisted. Her eyes swept over the faithful retainer and the coverings on the chairs. "Indeed, I have brought all this upon myself."

She mounted the marble stairs to her bedchamber where she found Polly already occupied unpacking her dressing case and airing the bedding.

"I didn't think my father would go this far, Polly," she said with a sigh as she loosened the strings of her travel cloak. "He's obviously not warned the Quills about my arrival. But I daresay we shall survive. Mrs. Quill will get the house shining, and soon we will be quite comfortable."

Never famous for her optimism, Polly looked dourly at her young mistress.

"Shall I unpack all your trunks, Miss Clarissa?"

"Yes, all of them," Clarissa said. "After all, I am here a year or more."

"Don't even think such a thing!" her abigail protested.

33

"A whole year here? Do say the word, and we'll get ourselves back to London where we belong."

Clarissa stared at Polly with astonishment. "Go running back to London to do my father's bidding?" she asked. "Polly, I am not such a coward."

"But you can't stay here alone."

"I'm not alone," Clarissa pointed out. "I have you here and the Quills and Henry and John at the stables. Unless you all mean to desert me."

Polly picked up a pillow and thumped it with two fists. "There's no need to tease yourself on that score," she said severely. "But if you must marry sometime, Miss Clarissa —and you can't wish to be an old maid, can you?—then why not marry now and please your father as well . . ."

Clarissa threw up her hands in disgust. "Polly, I beg you not to start on that topic too. I have had my ears filled with nonsense about marriage! All I desire tonight is a warm bath and a hot supper."

"I shall draw your bath directly," Polly said stiffly, "but you still might think to write to your father. He'll be worried about you and glad to hear you've arrived safe and sound."

"I shall do no such thing," declared Sir Arthur Claringdon's daughter. "If Papa wants news of me, he can come and visit me himself!"

Five miles east of Claring at Bengal Court Lady Agatha Beale lay on her great four-poster. A silver bowl of lavender water stood on a table next to her alongside a porcelain elephant. She paused in her afternoon's repose to eye this beast with considerable loathing. Decorated with touches of silver, gold, and red, the creature never failed to give her nightmares.

A light tap on her door brought relief from her contemplation of the animal. The door opened wide, and her niece Elizabeth Standworthy entered. Elizabeth, tall and stately and at thirty-seven very married, twice a year felt conscience-stricken about her old aunt cooped up in a drafty, gloomy mansion. These thoughts led inevitably to her visits to Bengal Court, which lasted only until she was once again convinced that Agatha was fully capable of fending for herself, and was well protected by an army of servants who would have slain anything for her.

"How do you feel, Aunt?" she asked now, coming over to the bed. "Rested, I hope?"

Agatha, on the verge of reply, noticed a letter in Elizabeth's hand.

"What have you there?" she demanded.

"A note from Sidney."

"Montcrieff is writing to me?" Agatha broke the seal and scanned the few lines Sidney had penned days earlier. "It says he shall arrive here tomorrow, Friday at the latest, to take over the estate."

She crushed the missive in her fist and threw it feebly toward the fire. "How did this get here?"

"One of his men brought it. He's down below. Do you wish to see him?"

"Good God! What need do I have to question messengers? Montcrieff's on his way, so be it. And bad luck to him and me."

Elizabeth looked worried. "Aunt Agatha," she implored, "you must not say such things. How can you talk about a man you have not seen any part of these past thirty years?"

"Good heavens," Agatha replied, sitting up on the side of her bed. "I have not known any one these past thirty years, let alone Montcrieff!"

Agatha had in fact been only twenty-five when she startled the polite world of which she was a leading member and announced her plans to marry one Geoffrey Beale and settle in the Cotswolds permanently. Those who knew her best had predicted that she would last only a fortnight, but the time had stretched to thirty-five years.

The Honorable Geoffrey Beale had cooperated long enough in his wife's venture to sire a son before he had promptly fallen dead of apoplexy in the middle of a country fair. This had given Agatha a convenient road back to the city in the guise of a widow if she so chose, but oddly she had not.

At sixty Agatha was short, spare, and totally at a loss to explain why her son—whom she had never been particularly fond of—had left his fortune and the shambles of his estate to a loose screw like Sidney Montcrieff.

"Who would you have preferred?" Elizabeth asked, listening to the familiar tirade, and helping her aunt down the polished stairs. "Lytton, perhaps?"

"Lytton?" Agatha barked. "A strawberry brat if ever I saw one."

"Then Joseph?"

"No. Not Joseph or his sallow-faced wife and their passel of brats who run through my house in London as though they owned it!"

"Then what quarrel do you hold with Sidney?" Elizabeth asked as they successfully completed the stairs. "I am not well acquainted with him, but he seems charming and handsome from what I have heard."

"And have you also heard that he is a rake?" Agatha asked ominously.

Elizabeth's worry deepened. "I hope you shall not say such things to him when he arrives, Aunt. He may take offense."

"Let him," Agatha declared. "What can he do? Throw me out?"

"Edward did leave him the estate," Elizabeth said tactfully.

"I know." Agatha shook her cane. "And the other thing I know is that the sooner Montcrieff finishes up his business here and returns to London and his flock of ladybirds, the happier I shall be."

Some twenty-four hours later Sidney Montcrieff bent over in the road and pushed back his high-crowned beaver hat, a new purchase from Mr. Locke's, the better to examine the left rear wheel of his travel chaise.

"Broken, Sidney?" Lytton asked over his shoulder.

"See for yourself," Sidney murmured, dusting his hands. This journey to Bengal Court was turning into even more of a nuisance than he had originally anticipated. They were already a day behind schedule thanks to the pleas of Lord Wentworth, who had suddenly seen the need to redeem some of the notes hastily wagered in faro several nights ago, and also due to Lady Vye's ungovernable temper.

Sidney's lip curled slightly as he thought of Lady Vye again. He had forgotten about her blasted dinner party scheduled for later in the week, and she had taken his absence as a personal affront.

"I shall be the laughing stock of the ton!" she had screamed in her dressing room.

"Surely, my dear Eleanor, the ton will understand that I cannot make one tiny dinner party."

"But it's *my* party!" Lady Vye tossed her raven hair back, showing off bare shoulders and a pair of ruby earrings which Sidney had definitely not purchased for her. "They shall say you left because you did not wish to attend."

"That shows you what paperskulls they are," Sidney said mildly. "But we know better."

He took her hand and tried to kiss it, but Lady Vye was in no mood to be easily coaxed.

"I tell you, Sidney," she said, lapsing into a too familiar pout, "if you do go to this Indian mansion you have inherited, do not think that I shall be waiting patiently for you to return."

"Indeed, madame," Sidney said crushingly, "I have never once labored under the misconception that you waited peacefully for my return at any time, not even when I resided in town."

Lady Vye pressed a palm to her heaving bosom. "Now you insult me. You are horrid!"

Sidney was rapidly reaching the end of his patience. He was quite willing to meet her halfway, but evidently she wanted more than apologies.

"I am horrid, yes. But you take my horrid jewels when I offer them to you," he pointed out with a cool smile.

At the mention of jewelry Lady Vye's eyes flashed, but she held her tongue. Sidney took advantage of this momentary lull to reexamine the gloss of his Hessians. It was not difficult to read either the shine of his boots or the face of Lady Vye. She was undeniably beautiful in a diaphanous wrapper showing her skin to perfection, but she was also as acquisitive as a squirrel, and like most squirrels she was attracted to jewelry.

This had amused him at first, but now it was rapidly boring him. If she planned to force him into a contest of wills—over Bengal Court of all idiocies!—she would lose. He chuckled. Unfortunately, Lady Vye, who had been avidly awaiting some pronouncement on her favorite topic of jewelry, misinterpreted his amusement.

"You laugh at me," she said coldly. "It amuses you to leave me with this impossible dinner party."

"My dear, you forget yourself," Sidney said. "I have explained the matter twice as best I can. I know fashion dictates women to be shatterbrained, but I fear you carry the pose too far."

Lady Vye's face darkened, but she swayed her hips saucily as she moved across the room toward Sidney. He watched her approach, inhaling her intoxicating perfume. One light hand curled up and tugged at his cravat.

"I might be persuaded to forgive you, Sidney," she purred.

"And I am certain the persuasion lies with Rundell and Bridges," he said, rescuing his cravat. "I'm sorry, Eleanor, about missing your party, and I shall miss you too. But I shan't buy you that bracelet."

Lady Vye's cheeks blazed with disappointed fury.

"You are an odious creature!" she shouted, turning her back to him. "Go to your Indian mansion, but don't look for me on your return."

Sidney rose. "My dear Eleanor, I have no intention of looking anywhere for you at any time."

He drove off from Grosvenor Square asking divine Providence to spare him from any further attachments to society's ladies.

Now he straightened up and caught sight of Stewart, his groom, fast approaching.

"How long are we laid up?" he asked, determined to hear the worst.

Stewart's usually gloomy face turned even gloomier. "Two hours, maybe three, sir."

"Blast!" Sidney flung his caped driving coat back over his shoulder. "You must fix it, I suppose? If darkness comes, we shall lay up somewhere for the night."

"We passed a posting house not far back," Lytton said, overhearing. "We might walk there, though it shall be deuced uncomfortable."

While Sidney was considering the discomforts ahead, a small boy appeared. "Excuse me, sir," he said, performing a creditable bow to both Lytton's and Sidney's amusement. "I beg your pardons. My father's the vicar here, and we couldn't help but notice your set-to. I say, it is the most awful luck, isn't it?"

"Yes," Sidney said, smiling ruefully. The boy, who looked to be about twelve, with a shock of untidy red hair, seemed to be horse mad, judging by the way he petted the horses.

"You like horses, lad?"

"Oh, yes, sir," the boy exclaimed with sparkling eyes. "Though I've never seen such a pair."

"What's your name?"

"Felix Boatwright, sir," he announced then stopped. "I do beg your pardon. Here I stand gabblemongering and what is Father going to say? Our house is just down the lane here, if you care to stay until the wheel is repaired."

It was impossible to decline such an invitation and impossible to dislike so cheerful a messenger. By the time they had reached the vicarage, a splendid and solid gray stone with ivy on its outer walls, both Sidney and Lytton stood on excellent terms with young Felix.

Five minutes later they were seated in front of a rousing fire in the parlor, in the pleasant company of the Boatwrights and their friend, Miss Emily Manville. A glass of the vicar's finest sherry had been thrust into Sidney's hand, and a plate of Mrs. Boatwright's sweetest biscuits lay in the other.

Sidney sipped and chewed, finding the Boatwrights every bit as welcoming as their son. Charles Boatwright, the vicar, commiserating now on the appalling condition of country roads, was tall and distinguished with a twinkle in his brown eyes. His wife, Fiona, blessed with a warmth reminiscent of Felix's, was just as sweet as her fine biscuits. Sidney relaxed in his armchair. And her husband's sherry was excellent.

While Sidney was forming these opinions of the Boatwrights, the earl was busy forming one of his own. It concerned Miss Emily Manville. While the Montcrieff party had been struck down on the road, Miss Manville had been enjoying a short visit with Mrs. Boatwright and had been present in the parlor when Felix ushered in the two gentlemen. On the verge of taking her leave, Emily was pressed to stay by Mrs. Boatwright who knew an opportunity when it presented itself unbidden in her own home. Not for the world would the vicar's wife have allowed Emily to escape without making the acquaintance of two of the ton's leading members!

Lord Lytton, though not—as he put it—in the petticoat line, was accustomed, as most gentlemen were, to the charms of society's grandest ladies. So far none had enticed him for long. Upon introduction to Miss Manville, however, he felt a flutter deep in his chest, and his breath escaped in a rush, not dissimilar to the feeling that overcame him when he took his fences with a rush. Here was an entirely different sort of Beauty.

As he accepted his glass of sherry from their host, the earl observed Emily's flawless skin, simple white muslin day dress, and blond hair done up in braids. It was scarcely the toilette that would have enticed Brummel, but Lytton thought the results utterly enchanting.

He sat down next to Emily on the sofa and received from her a shy smile of welcome. Encouraged, he cleared his throat and began to speak, but after uttering one syllable he found to his stupefaction that his mind had gone blank, and that assuredly had never happened before! In vain he searched for the pleasantries and tidbits with which he had beguiled so many wits, including Lady Jersey herself, but it was nigh impossible. The earl's tongue—blast the instrument!—seemed to its owner to have withered on the spot.

"Biscuit?" Miss Manville inquired.

The earl, jolted from his quandary, noticed the plate held out in front of him. Good heavens! She would think him a veritable coxcomb. He took the nearest biscuit on the plate and gnashed it between his teeth while Miss Manville put the plate down on the table in front of them.

"Are you on your way to Cheltenham spa?" she asked.

"No," Lytton gurgled. "Bengal Court."

"Oh, yes. I've heard of that estate," Emily said, smiling. For the first time Lytton noticed her eyes. They were a dark blue, the color akin to sapphires or the sea. In fact, Lytton thought, stuffing another biscuit into his mouth, a man might drown just looking into those eyes.

Fortunately for the earl's health and well-being—he could never swim—he was not obliged to test the waters with this statement.

Emily refused Fiona's offer of another glass of lemonade and insisted that she must leave.

"But must you go?" Lytton asked, quickly rising from the couch he had shared with her. "We have been chatting here so nicely."

Since the earl had spoken a total of twelve words, Emily's astonishment was considerable, but she was too well-bred to show it.

"I really must be going," she said with a shy smile. "It was an honor to meet you, my lord, and you, Mr. Montcrieff."

"Perhaps you will allow us to visit your school sometime," Lytton said.

"Indeed you must," Mrs. Boatwright exclaimed, pleased that her little plan was progressing so smoothly. "I shall tell you how to reach it, my lord."

After Emily had left, Sidney turned toward the vicar.

"A charming young lady."

"We think highly of her," Mrs. Boatwright said, casting another look of approval, this time at Sidney.

The vicar, who wondered inwardly at his wife's audacity—though well meant of course!—explained quickly, "Emily has ideas on education. She handles the schooling for several of the parish families."

"And her own family?" Sidney inquired solicitously.

Mrs. Boatwright's cheerful face clouded.

"She has none, sir. Her parents are dead. She lives quite alone."

Sidney made a sympathetic sound. To be cast alone in the world was never pleasant, but it was hardly the fate for someone like Miss Manville.

"You are serious?" Lytton spoke up. "She is much too young to be on her own, especially here in the country."

"I know that too well, my lord," the vicar said. "I have offered to have her introduced in London. My brother, General Boatwright, would sponsor her for a Season. But she claims to have no liking for the town."

"But it is difficult for someone as gently bred as Emily to make her way in the country," Mrs. Boatwright said, offering another plate of biscuits to the earl.

"I shouldn't wonder about that!" his lordship declared, chewing on another biscuit.

Sidney leaned a negligent elbow on the armchair and cocked his head at his cousin, but no further word issued from the earl's throat. He seemed to be locked into some secret world of his own, a world that would no doubt include Miss Manville, Sidney thought. He frowned a little. If they had been alone he would have put the question to his cousin at once, but since they were guests he tactfully changed the subject.

"How long have you been in this parish, sir?"

"Twenty years," the vicar replied with some satisfaction.

"Then you must know my aunt, Lady Agatha, and my late cousin Edward?"

"Your cousin I knew sparingly," the vicar explained, replenishing Sidney's sherry glass, "since he was always in India. But your aunt I am well acquainted with." His eye held an appreciative twinkle. "Do you know she professes herself an atheist these days?"

"Does she, by Jove?" Sidney laughed, much diverted. "You did not tell me that, Lytton."

"She wasn't an atheist when I saw her last," Lytton said peaceably.

A comfortable hour passed on such topics as atheism, religion, and the whims of elderly gentlewomen. But finally Sidney grew aware of the darkening sky and rose to his feet.

"But you cannot go back out there," Mrs. Boatwright said with genuine alarm. "You must stay the night. Charles, do you not agree?"

The vicarage, although comfortable for the Boatwrights, was a modest establishment, and the vicar was in no way assured that such out and outers as the Montcrieff cousins must stay anywhere so Spartan. However, he had enjoyed his hours with them, finding the pair far from toplofty, and did not hesitate to add his voice to his wife's invitation.

Sidney had no intention of overstaying his welcome. However disagreeable a posting house must be, it should be faced quickly as must Aunt Agatha later. But he had reckoned without the power of Felix.

The lad had been seated quietly in the room, but at his father's words jumped up in excitement. "Oh sirs, do stay," he said, bestowing such a look of longing at Sidney and then Lytton. "We can have so much fun!"

Sidney's lip twitched, and he met the earl's eye. To refuse would be like kicking a puppy.

"We shall be glad to stay," he said gratefully and wondered to himself how long the guest beds in the vicarage would be.

4

On Saturday morning Clarissa rose from her bed and hummed a little tune to herself. Two days of fresh country air and Mr. Quill's excellent cuisine combined to send her dismals packing. Besides, she told herself, as she selected a cream cambric gown from those that Polly laid out for her inspection, she never could tolerate watering pots, and she was not going to turn into one herself!

It was too stupid to be downhearted. Claring, with its abundant lakes, green meadows, and bridle paths, was no dungeon. And there was no reason for her to play the Tragedy Jane.

"Besides," she confided to Polly who dressed her, "I fully expect a letter from Father soon, begging me to return."

"Well, I just hope you're right, Miss Clarissa," Polly said doubtfully.

"You shall see," Clarissa said confidently.

She entertained this last thought through her dressing, then descended the stairs. Mrs. Quill waited at the bottom.

"Good morning, miss," the housekeeper said in answer to Clarissa's cheerful greeting. "You're feeling better, I fancy?"

45

"Much better," Clarissa said, going into the sunlit breakfast room where heaping trays of blueberry muffins, hot cereals, and a large country ham waited her pleasure.

"Mrs. Quill," she asked as the housekeeper followed her in, "have you heard why I am sent down?"

Mrs. Quill's gaze dropped from the ham to her young mistress, and she struggled briefly with her conscience. She nodded.

"Displeased your father, or so they say."

"You have a way with words," Clarissa complimented her and reached for the chocolate pot. The liquid tasted sweet and warm on her tongue.

"But I did more than displease Papa, Mrs. Quill. I enraged him."

Mrs. Quill clucked her tongue sympathetically as she held out a basket of fresh muffins. "Still, he'll be lonely without you."

"You have been talking to Polly," Clarissa said, taking a muffin and buttering it lightly. "I assure you, Papa will get along famously without me to scold."

"But what about your mother?" Mrs. Quill asked, uncovering a dish of stewed apples and pears.

"Well, I do miss Mama," Clarissa confessed. "And Papa, too, if the truth be known. But I have no alternative." She put her half-eaten muffin down on her plate and reflected. "If only he would write and tell me to come back, all would be well."

"Perhaps if you wrote and suggested it, your parents could join you here. You could patch up your quarrel, and it would be just like old times."

Clarissa shook her head defiantly. "You don't understand. It's Papa who must apologize to me. He would marry me off to some hideous old rake."

"Oh, no," Mrs. Quill said, quite shocked.

"Well, nearly that," Clarissa conceded, leaving Mrs.

Quill to ruminate briefly on the changes in her employers. Clarissa finished her breakfast. The whole day stretched ahead. How would she fill it?

"Mrs. Quill?" she asked, "does Emily Manville still reside hereabouts?"

"Oh, yes," Mrs. Quill answered. "Do you know her?"

"She's a friend of Trixie's," Clarissa explained. "I promised to call on her."

"I'm sure she'd like that," Mrs. Quill said distractedly. "She doesn't get many callers these days."

Mrs. Quill, however, was entirely wrong. This Saturday morning found Emily entertaining two callers in her modest parlor, and such an illustrious pair! Emily's blue eyes had widened the minute she glimpsed Sidney and Lytton in her entrance hall.

Lytton's knock had been first answered by Owen, Emily's ancient butler whose devotion to her was augmented by his deafness. The earl was obliged to shout his name and his cousin's so loudly that Miss Manville, several doors down in her study, came on the run.

Sidney, who had refrained from the shouting duel, bowed over Emily's hand, murmured apologies for their spontaneous call, and followed her into the small parlor, sharing her bewilderment.

Sidney had passed a tolerable night in a narrow bed, borne with the farewells at the vicarage, and, once seated in his carriage, wanted nothing more arduous than to reach Bengal Court and face the set-down certain to come from his aunt. But what must Lytton do—at his age!—but order the carriage in on the Manville estate.

"I know you shan't mind, Sidney," his lordship had said before stepping down to tangle wits with Owen, or perhaps, Sidney thought, his wits were already tangled to begin with.

With his topboots stretched out toward the fire, Sidney glanced around him. Miss Manville's residence was modest as befitted a female in straightened circumstances. Sidney did not need the aid of his quizzing glass to notice the peeling paintwork and sparse furnishings, yet the parlor was cheerful and airy with a small pianoforte standing in the corner. Only what in the name of heaven was he doing here? For enlightenment he stared out of the corner of his eye at Lytton, but his cousin scarcely noticed. The earl's eyes were fixed on Miss Manville, now busying herself with a tray of tea and milk. Sidney, lounging at his ease, observed her quietly. His first impression of her still endured: a lovely bluestocking. Lytton would have his hands full if he intended to pursue this game, but did he?

Sidney turned his gaze back toward Lytton and then quickly looked away with brimming eyes. By Jupiter, there was no mistaking the telltale signs of a Brummel in love. The disheveled hair. The spots of color on both cheeks. And by heaven, the inarticulate tongue. Sidney burrowed his lanky body deeper into Miss Manville's chair. Not to mention the quantities of tea Lytton was spilling over his frilled shirt.

For a brief moment Sidney was tempted to flee the parlor. He had no longing to be on hand when Lytton went a-courting. But the idea of escape, however attractive, was impossible. Sidney's own understanding of conventions might be imperfect, but of the three in the parlor he constituted the chaperone. His shoulders quaked. No need to ask what Lady Vye would have thought of such a situation!

"You find scarlet fever amusing, Mr. Montcrieff?" Emily broke off her earnest speech on this most dreaded disease and fastened an incredulous eye on him.

"I'm sorry," Sidney said, replacing his teacup on the table. "I was not attending."

"Then attend to this," Lytton said with some acerbity. "Miss Manville has offered to show us her schoolroom. Are you interested?"

In private, Sidney would have favored Lord Lytton with his low opinion of tours in general and those of schoolrooms in particular. But he could not do so now without dashing the eagerness in Miss Manville's eyes. Rather graciously, he felt, Sidney rose to his feet.

The schoolroom lay across the main hall, set up with benches, writing blocks, bookshelves, and similar contraptions of schooling. A map of the continents hung on one large wall. A faint odor of disuse lingered in the air.

"We are on holiday until the fall," Emily explained. "That is why everything looks so barren. I assure you with squirming students this room becomes much too small."

Sidney smiled. "I can well imagine." He twirled the globe on her desk. "How many of these squirmers do you teach?"

"At the moment just five."

"But they are a lucky five to have such a handsome schoolroom," Lytton said. "Don't you agree, Sidney?"

While handsome might have been doing it too brown, Sidney thought the room pleasanter than those he had had the misfortune to inhabit in his own youth and said so. Emily smiled again.

"It's still very small," she pointed out.

"Ah, but you are just beginning," Lytton said energetically. "Don't worry. Even Socrates began with one pupil."

Unable to bear the idea of Socrates or any other Greek so early in the morning, Sidney turned toward the hallway, hoping Lytton would follow. As he moved, the sound of a carriage could be heard approaching, and he paused with his brow creased. Could Miss Manville have other irons in the fire?

Clarissa's entrance moments later laid this argument to

an early grave. In no way, thought Sidney appreciatively, could this Beauty be mistaken for a gentleman even by the shortsighted. Tall, slender as a willow, she was perfectly composed in a cream-colored muslin while under its matching bonnet peeked a head of absurd curls. And she carried the most improbable bouquet of red roses. Sidney's eyes swept over her face again, his eyes narrowing in amusement. She also possessed a masterful little chin.

Emily, coming out of the schoolroom, gave Clarissa a quick smile of welcome.

"It is of no use for Owen to ask your name," she said to Sidney's profound relief, for he had no taste for another shouting match. "You have the great look of Carlton."

Clarissa shook her head and the curls, much to Sidney's delight, bounced.

"How he would shudder to hear you say that, Miss Manville. No man likes to be told he resembles a sister."

"It is a fate worse than death," Sidney agreed gravely.

Clarissa, far from perturbed, eyed his tall patrician figure with good humor as she acknowledged the hit: Sidney found himself smiling back. But what was such a prime article doing in the country? He had no further time for speculation since they were returning to the parlor with the two ladies deep in conversation.

"My gardener sent these along," Clarissa said, relinquishing her bouquet.

"But they are lovely, and just what the parlor needs," Emily declared as she searched for a vase.

"I'm glad to hear that," Clarissa said, sitting down in the armchair Sidney drew up for her. "For I have not been at Claring one day before Giles would engross me in the most exhausting discussion of roses and rhododendron beds."

"A fascinating discourse," Sidney murmured.

Clarissa gave him another of her frank looks. "You

might think so, sir," she confessed, "but I found it a dead bore."

The spark of interest rekindled in Sidney's eye, and he leaned forward.

"You say you are at Claring, Miss . . ."

He got no further.

"I am too shatterbrained!" Emily declared, taking herself instantly to task. "You have not been introduced, though I daresay you may have already met in London. Miss Clarissa Claringdon, Mr. Sidney Montcrieff, and Lord Lytton."

Clarissa shook their hands, thinking that Emily need not have censured herself so harshly. Although she lacked formal acquaintanceship with the Montcrieff pair, Clarissa had immediately recognized them on sight. But what was Trixie's staid friend doing with such a pair of swells?

"This is a great pleasure," she said. "For I have heard a great deal about you both."

This innocent remark sounded to Lytton like an ominous threat, and his face turned crimson.

"Pray do not let the tattle boxes influence your judgment of us," he said in strangled tones.

Sidney, however, remained calm. "Miss Claringdon is too shrewd a woman to listen to *on dits*," he declared.

Clarissa smiled. "Then it's not true, Lord Lytton, that you are considered one of the most eligible men of the ton?"

"Oh, that's true," Sidney declared, eyeing his cousin's discomfiture with relish. "Larry's always been the top of the class though he don't like to boast."

"And you, Mr. Montcrieff," Clarissa went on smoothly, "would be as great a prize except . . ."

"Except?" Sidney asked sympathetically.

"Except that you are the despair of hostesses, arriving

51

late, departing early, and finding yourself saddled with the reputation of a man easily bored."

Lytton slapped his cousin on the back. "Well struck, Miss Claringdon."

Miss Manville, who was arranging the flowers in a Chinese vase, ventured a question from across the room. "Will you not be bored in the country, Mr. Montcrieff?"

"I hope not," Sidney said with some sincerity. "I shall have Bengal Court to occupy me for considerable time. I daresay I shall contrive to stay amused." He turned back to Clarissa, loath to relinquish so excellent a sparring partner. "And you, Miss Claringdon? How long are you in the country?"

Clarissa hesitated a moment. Her quarrel with her father was her own private affair, and she would not bandy it about with gentlemen such as these.

"Perhaps a few weeks," she said quietly.

"But how is it you leave London at the height of Season?"

Clarissa tossed her head. "Too high by half, all this fuss, and for a czar!"

Sidney's lip quivered. "You have some quarrel against czars or merely their entertainments?" he asked as Lytton gravitated toward Miss Manville and her flowers.

"My quarrel is with neither," Clarissa said. "But I do draw the line at being uncomfortable."

"Uncomfortable?" Sidney stroked his chin with a forefinger, looking puzzled. "But how is your comfort called into question?"

"Nothing is more uncomfortable than standing up with clumsy men on the dance floor."

The laughter in Sidney's gray eyes reflected her own. "Yes, most disagreeable."

"I assure you, Mr. Montcrieff, I know of what I speak!"

"As do I!" Sidney exclaimed at once. "Gracelessness is

not a flaw reserved for my sex. I have danced with some ladies who could no more follow a lead than could shoe a horse!"

A quick trill of laughter escaped Clarissa. "I am delighted to hear it," she said, recovering quickly. "Rumor had it that you rarely stood up with any woman."

"That depends on how well she can dance," he said promptly.

Clarissa gazed up at him for a moment, wondering to herself how so noted a Corinthian came to be in the country and more especially in Emily's parlor.

"How long are you in the Cotswolds?" she asked.

"Since yesterday," Sidney explained. "Our carriage broke down on the way, and we were forced to seek shelter in the vicarage."

"Most unfortunate."

"Not in the least," he contradicted. His eyes darted over to Lytton and Emily and then returned to Clarissa's puzzled face. "Miss Manville was visiting the vicar's wife, and had that accident not occurred we would not have met her. And then I should not be sitting here chatting so amicably with you."

Clarissa accepted this salute with a gurgle of laughter.

"You doubt me?" he asked.

"Indeed not. I merely observe that your reputation as a flirt is on the mark."

"And I see your reputation is on the mark as well," he responded with perfect courtesy.

"Mine?" Clarissa's voice hovered on that syllable before her eyes met his. Then her quick laughter spilled forth again. Whatever she had expected of Miss Manville's parlor, it was not to trade sallies with someone like Sidney Montcrieff. She gazed at him now with some curiosity. Handsome without a doubt, by reputation toplofty, but he had shown no arrogance thus far.

"Yes," Sidney was saying now, polishing his quizzing glass. "We gentlemen hear as much of you ladies as you do of us. Only we are too well-bred to repeat the rumors."

"How vexing for you," Clarissa said. "But what have you heard of me, I wonder?"

Sidney's eyes searched her face indolently and lingered for a moment on the upturned nose. "My dear Miss Claringdon," he said calmly, "a gentleman never gossips."

"Nor does a lady," Clarissa agreed without a blink. "Now that we are comfortable on that score, you shall tell me the truth."

Smiling a little at this threat, Sidney relented. "All I have heard is to your credit. You have half the gentlemen of the ton as suitors and seem disinclined to accept any. This has given you the reputation of a woman of marked discrimination."

"Has it indeed?" Clarissa asked, quite amazed. "I had no notion of it."

"It is also a masterful tactic," Sidney said.

Clarissa's chin rose along with her color. "Tactic, Mr. Montcrieff, I assure you . . ."

"For it challenges your beaux," Sidney said without a pause. "Each pursues you more ardently, convinced that none but the best shall contrive to win you. Each by this time is fully determined to be the best."

"Are they really?" Clarissa asked. "But how kind of you to tell me, as I should never have thought of it myself. I did often wonder why some did not take my hints and seek out more obliging young women." She turned a thoughtful face toward Sidney. "You have done me a great service."

"It was wholly unintentional, ma'am," Sidney said shakily.

"You laugh, but you have set me straight on a point that

often perplexed me. . . ." Clarissa would have continued, but Emily across the room let out a sudden cry.

"You are hurt!" Lord Lytton exclaimed. Sidney and Clarissa exchanged glances and hurried to investigate Miss Manville's distress.

"It is just a scratch," Emily was protesting in vain. "Really, my lord, your handkerchief will get quite soiled."

"Too late," the earl replied. He wrapped the injured thumb in his linen and pressed it firmly between his strong fingers.

"I should have warned you about the thorns," Clarissa said.

"But it is not your fault," Emily said distractedly. "What would a rose be without thorns? It is my fault for being so stupid."

"There is an ointment I have heard of which is excellent for such scratches," Lytton said to his cousin. "Sidney, you must know the one I mean."

His cousin, however, was looking quite blank. "Unhappily, Larry," he said weakly, "I do not."

"I know our aunt must have some," Lytton insisted. "I shall fetch it for you straight away, Miss Manville."

"No," Emily said quickly and with mounting distress. "My thumb is quite better, and there is no need to vex yourself."

"But I insist."

At this point Sidney thought it wise to intervene. He was no medical expert, but Emily did not appear to have sustained a mortal wound. However, she was beginning to look pressed, and who wouldn't be pressed with Lytton badgering her out of patience. He fully intended to drop a word of advice in his cousin's ear in private. Miss Manville had all the look of a skittish woman when it came to romance.

As for Emily's injury, it was best handled by one of her

own sex, and Sidney had every confidence that Miss Claringdon fully qualified in this realm.

"We must be off, Larry," he said now, pulling his cousin ruthlessly away from yet another examination of Miss Manville's thumb. "Our aunt still awaits."

"Oh, yes, you must not tarry on my account," Emily said. "So kind of you to call."

"I shall call tomorrow and see how your thumb is," Lytton declared before Sidney could lead him off.

Minutes later, when the sound of the carriage had faded, Clarissa turned toward Emily on the couch.

"Does your finger still trouble you?" she asked.

Emily looked up, surprised. "Oh, no. Indeed not. I do not even think of it." She shook her head. "Forgive me for being such a pea goose. It is so lovely to meet you finally, and just seeing you brings Trixie to mind."

"But it is I who have been the pea goose," Clarissa declared, digging madly into her reticule and resurrecting Trixie's letter. She passed the missive over to Miss Manville explaining that the note was written in haste.

"Dearest Trixie," Emily said as she finished the letter. "Could you not have persuaded her to accompany you to Claring?"

"Carlton would have shot me. He is quite lost without her." Clarissa peered intently into Emily's face. "But how do you go on?"

"Slowly," Emily admitted, rubbing her thumb for a moment. "People are kind to me, never fear, but some think a woman my age cannot handle a school alone. As though I were some chit and not in my twenty-first year."

Clarissa hid her smile. "Twenty-one is not so very old."

"Perhaps not. But I have been teaching since I was fourteen," Emily said, laughing at Clarissa's surprise. "I helped my mother in the school she ran, so I have had

56

some experience. There's so much I yearn to do if only . . ."

"You lack funds?" Clarissa asked delicately.

"Funds are the least of it," Emily said, waving Trixie's letter in the air. "I need books. Not horrid old ones but new ones with all the latest theories."

"If only I had known," Clarissa chided herself, "I could have brought some with me."

The color in Emily's cheeks deepened. "Oh, Clarissa, I did not mean for you . . ."

"I know that, and I also know the value of education, though I don't have your book learning. And I shall be glad to offer my services to you."

Emily stared, a trifle confused by this offer. "Your services?" she asked dubiously.

Clarissa gave another merry laugh. "Yes, as a second in command."

"But you are only here a few weeks."

Clarissa shook her head. It would make things easier if Emily knew the truth. "I think I shall be here much longer, perhaps as long as several months."

"Several months!" Emily's eyebrows shot up.

"I am sent down by my father."

"Sent down," Emily started, grew thoughtful, then glanced at Clarissa with such meaning that Clarissa laughed again.

"It is not what you think," she assured Emily. "Though I did warn Papa that if he banished me people would think I were increasing. I assure you I am not."

"No, of course not," Emily said, blushing. "I beg pardon for even thinking of it."

"You see," Clarissa said, settling comfortably back in her chair, "it all started one night when Papa flew into a pet . . ."

Emily listened raptly until the tale was completed. Dismay was written on her gentle face. "But won't he reconsider, Clarissa?"

"Oh, I doubt that. He is so thick-skulled."

Miss Manville's shock at this cavalier attitude toward a parent was considerable, but Clarissa took no notice as she stretched a sandaled foot out on the parlor rug. "So I am quite willing to help you with your school. And I daresay it shall keep me from being bored to death."

"I welcome your help and you as well," Emily said, "for I am in desperate need of advice."

Clarissa's brow knitted at the unexpected note of passion in Emily's voice. "Advice on your school?"

"Oh no, on quite a different matter." Emily's hands flew up to her flushed cheeks. "I own I have been in such a state of utter confusion since yesterday."

Since yesterday? But what had happened yesterday? Revelation dawned almost at once. Of course! Emily had met the earl just yesterday!

"I have been in such a whirl," Emily confessed. "And then having him here today was the most amazing coincidence."

"Lord Lytton is a most amazing man," Clarissa agreed.

Emily stared at her. "But I am not talking of the earl!" she protested.

It was Clarissa's turn to look bewildered. "Then who?" she demanded.

"Sidney Montcrieff, of course!"

5

"You are in love with Sidney Montcrieff?" Clarissa asked, gaping at Emily like a dimwit.

Miss Manville turned scarlet, stammered, wrung her hands feverishly and sought refuge in her handkerchief. Contradictions spilled from her lips, making it difficult for Clarissa to discern much less comprehend the truth.

"It sounds strange, Clarissa, I know, but I have loved him forever!"

"Forever?" Clarissa exclaimed. "You just met him yesterday."

The mode of love, surely even in the wilds of the Cotswolds, would indicate a more leisurely attachment.

Passion brought color to Emily's cheeks. "He has been my idol for years!"

Idol? Years? How could this be? Clarissa sought counsel in the parlor drapes. The smell of intrigue as well as fresh roses filled the air. "Is he acquainted with your feelings?" she asked after a moment's silence.

"Oh, no!" Emily ejaculated. She paced restlessly, her blond braids swinging in rhythm to her stride. "How repulsed he would be by anything so vulgar. I am not so bold or so fast, I assure you. And yet—" Her face lit up. "Just seeing him in this room, being close to him—" She blushed prettily, lifting her eyes to Clarissa's. "A very good thing you were here and Lytton as well."

Clarissa mulled this over, wondering to herself what the earl's reaction to such a statement might be.

"Don't you think Sidney the handsomest man you've ever seen?" Emily asked.

"The handsomest?" Clarissa frowned, the better to consider the question. "He is handsome, though his face lacks the classic cast of someone like Brummel, the nose being a half-inch too long and his jaw perhaps too square. But he wears his clothes well and has considerable charm."

Miss Manville waved away these shortcomings. "I think he's more handsome now than even before."

"Before?" Clarissa asked, still trying to piece together the clues.

"When my mother used to tell me stories about him."

"Is that how you developed a tendre for him?"

"Partly," Emily admitted. "He was in the habit of visiting our school with his friend. Not this school but the one that Mother ran in Devonshire. His friend, Roderick, was Mother's cousin. I was only fifteen that first time I saw Sidney. I knew him to be the handsomest man I'd ever seen. But I think he has grown twice as handsome since then. And when I saw him yesterday at the vicarage I knew his identity in a trice, and yet I could only stand like a dolt, tongue-tied."

"Don't chide yourself," Clarissa said, comforting Emily while her own mind whirled. Trixie's friend was in the throes of infatuation and with Montcrieff of all people! "I don't think he thought you foolish at all."

"I hope not," Emily said, turning shining eyes toward Clarissa. "When I remember how I used to dream of him when I was younger . . ."

"Do you still?"

"No. That's why meeting him here has been so remarkable. And when his carriage called at my door today it seemed as though all my dreams had come true."

"You are attached to him?"

"I have loved him forever!"

"And Lord Lytton?" Clarissa inquired gently.

Miss Manville looked for a moment as though an insect had been found afloat in her soup. "You cannot compare the two gentlemen, Clarissa."

"An odious occupation," Clarissa agreed, dropping the question of Lytton for the time being. Miss Manville was clearly in no mood to investigate anyone's passions except her own. "How agreeable it must be to be finally acquainted with your hero," Clarissa said.

"Yes," Emily admitted shyly, "but I wish to be more than acquainted with him."

"Friendship . . ." Clarissa agreed.

"Stronger than friendship."

"Oh, dear," Clarissa murmured.

Emily's hearing was considerably more acute than her butler's.

"I know what you must think," she said, throwing herself onto the couch. "I sound so vulgar. But he is the man I have dreamed about for years. Can I just sit back and let him go without a lure?"

"No," Clarissa said, thinking that it would take more than a lure to land Sidney Montcrieff.

"Do you think my chances of marrying him are so absurd?" Emily asked soberly.

Clarissa took her time before answering. Emily was a pretty thing, intelligent too, and there was no earthly reason why she should not win a prize like Montcrieff.

"In marriage," she said gently, "there is always some absurdity. But you must bear in mind that Sidney is one of the largest prizes on the Marriage Mart, for all his boasting to the contrary, and if you only knew the number of caps that have been set at him . . ."

"I know," Emily said. "Which is why you must help me."

"Me?" Clarissa sat back, bereft of speech. The situation was taking a ludicrous turn. To observe from the side was one thing, to participate in the field of love something else.

"I don't know the first thing about marrying gentlemen of quality," she protested. "You forget I am sent down for that reason."

"But you can tell me about the London fashion and what to do and how to say things without appearing fast," Emily said. "Oh, Clarissa, it almost seems meant to have you here right when I need you most." She clasped her new friend's hand. "You must help me."

"Advice I have aplenty," Clarissa said with quick sympathy. But it would take more than advice to lead Sidney Montcrieff to an altar. The idea, however, intrigued her. She had wondered how to keep from being bored in the Cotswolds. Capturing Sidney Montcrieff would be diversion indeed. She glanced down. Emily's forlorn face clinched the matter.

"You are certain it is love?"

"Oh, yes!"

"Then I shall help you all I can," Clarissa promised, whereupon the campaigning began in earnest.

A different kind of battle was shaping up in Agatha Beale's drawing room. Sidney and Lytton had driven up to Bengal Court, which looked every bit as gloomy and drafty as they both recalled from childhood. The mummified monkey paws were just as Sidney had remembered. So too was his Aunt Agatha.

"You're very late, the pair of you," she declared, reducing him at once to the station of a schoolboy.

"An errant carriage wheel, Aunt Agatha," Sidney replied in his indolent way, smiling at her then greeting

Elizabeth. "We were obliged to seek shelter in the vicarage."

Agatha's steely gaze did not move from her nephew's face. "A pretty tale," she sniffed. "But I suspect an even prettier ladybird lurking somewhere with you."

Sidney's eyes danced. "No ladybird," he assured her.

"And you, Lytton?" Agatha barked at her younger nephew. "Have you nothing to say for yourself?"

"Just that Sidney is right, Aunt Agatha," Lytton replied. "You may ask the vicar if you like. By the bye, he says you've turned atheist. Is it true?"

"No, it isn't true," Agatha said, shaking her ebony cane on the rug. "But who can blame me with all these heathen gods and goddesses in the house?" She glared at them both for another moment. "For pity's sake, sit down and don't fidget. I don't bite."

Sidney, amused, sank down on the chair next to her.

"I don't know what Edward meant by leaving the estate to you."

"Nor do I," Sidney agreed. "But since the matter lies in his coffin in India, we have no recourse but to accept it."

Agatha sniffed again. "What do you know of running estates?"

"Every gentleman knows something of estates," Sidney said promptly. "Just as every lady knows something of a household."

"A pretty remark but dead wrong, Montcrieff," Agatha cackled. "I never cared for households."

"But you are a lady who set the mode and never followed it blindly," Sidney said blithely. "Pray, do set your mind at rest, Aunt. I know Edward left a mess for me, but I am prepared to put the matter right."

This remark, intended solely to ease her fears, merely

sparked a new show of temper. "Do you mean to dispose of me so handily?" Agatha asked in frigid tones.

Sidney picked up a brass monkey with a red tail and gazed over at his aunt. "Dispose of you?" he inquired faintly.

"If you read the will, you know that I come with the house," she said.

"Yes, indeed. Like a slave, do you mean?" Sidney murmured sweetly. Lytton found himself sorely afflicted by a ticklish cough. "My dear Aunt, you may remain in this house for as long as you wish while I am alive," Sidney said.

"Gracious pup!"

He smiled engagingly at her. "Not in the least. And I feel obligated to remind you that many of your friends in London still yearn for your visits."

"Such as Lady Twiddings," Lytton said at once. "I ran into her the other day in Green Park."

"Twiddings?" Agatha asked. "Are you sure, lad? I thought she had died."

"She had formed the same opinion of you," Lytton said with a laugh. "I was obliged to assure her that you continued to exist."

"Did you now? I just hope you also didn't invite her down to visit me. I've no mind to run a guest house for friends." She waved her cane toward the door. "You may all go. I am tired of the lot of you and want my bed. If you desire lunch, tell Tibbs."

"Is she always so twitty?" Sidney asked in the hallway with Elizabeth and Lytton.

Elizabeth shook her head. "In fact, cousin, she is quite happy to see you both."

"Is she?" Lytton declared. "I would not have known it."

"She feared that you might throw her out, Sidney."

Sidney threw back his head and laughed in astonishment. "Throw Aunt Agatha out? My dear Elizabeth, even if I were fool enough to make such a command, who would obey it?"

"I own I am relieved to hear it," Elizabeth said. "You are both fatigued, I'm sure, and shall want a wash and some lunch. Whatever Aunt Agatha may have threatened, we do not plan to starve you. And if there is anything else you need, just ask . . ."

Lytton perked up his ears at this last remark. "There is just one thing, Elizabeth," he said hesitantly. "Do you by any chance know of Dr. Radcliffe's Restorative Jelly?"

Elizabeth, who nightly rubbed the ointment on her chest to ward off the grippe, bestowed a look of approval on the earl. She had not hoped to find him such a sensible young man.

"But of course, cousin," she said. "I would not go anywhere without it." She led him off asking quietly, "Do you mean you have lost yours?"

6

Carlton Claringdon entered his London home one morning to find his wife frowning over a letter. His thoughts flew immediately to her family, never a deuced healthy lot.

"Bad news, love?" he asked gently.

At the sound of his voice Trixie looked up, smiling. "Oh, no, Carlton, nothing like that."

"But you frown," he pointed out.

"Clarissa has written," Trixie said, giving him the letter to scan. Carlton sat down next to her on the couch.

Dearest Trixie and Carlton,

I am at Claring and have met your wonderful Emily. We have great plans for her school. Carlton, I rely on you to send me some books. Emily says ours are woefully behind the times. I mean to help her in the classroom.

I miss you both and our parents as well. If you see Papa do tell him that I am enjoying my banishment.

Love,
Clarissa.

"Enjoying her banishment." Carlton could not keep a smile of admiration from appearing. "She doesn't sound eager to return to London, does she? And if Papa only knew she was planning to teach school!"

"Will you tell him, Carlton?" Trixie asked, smoothing a pleat on her dove-colored crepe.

"I don't know," Carlton said with a sigh. "Clarissa wouldn't like it by half."

"But she talks as though she will be at Claring for months!" Trixie said forlornly.

"There, there. . . ." Carlton put his arm around her. Was it just his imagination or had she become more pensive than usual. "Do you miss Clarissa so much?"

"Oh, Carlton, you cannot imagine," Trixie burst out. "How I wish she were here. She is such a comfort. Do you remember when I had that tooth pulled last year? Clarissa came with me and held my hand and almost glowered at the surgeon, and afterward she bought me ices and told me such amusing stories that I was obliged to beg her to stop since laughter made the pain even worse."

"Yes, Clarissa is a right one," Carlton said, squeezing his wife's hand. "And I know you miss her dearly; we all do. But you can always write to her at Claring. Unless"— here he gazed into her eyes—"you anticipate another toothache soon."

"No, not a toothache," Trixie said absently.

"You are ill," Carlton said, alarmed. "I knew you looked rather pale, Trixie. I had no idea, and I shall put you to bed immediately." He reached for the bellpull, but Trixie caught him by the sleeve and pulled him away.

"I am not ill, Carlton. At least not in the way you think."

"Then why all the talk of Clarissa?" he demanded, dipping into his snuffbox.

"Merely because I should like her close at hand when I am to be a mother and you a father," Trixie announced.

Upon hearing these words Clarton was surprised into inhaling his snuff a shade too vigorously. A sneezing fit assailed him, and he searched for his wife through tear-filled eyes.

"A baby . . ." he stammered, sneezing.

"Yes, a baby," Trixie laughed.

"A baby," he repeated. "Oh, Trixie!" He hugged her tightly as another sneeze rocked them both.

"You're pleased?" Trixie asked shyly.

"Pleased? Must you even ask? But how do you feel?"

She snuggled closer to him. "Dr. Eldon says he's never seen a healthier patient," she boasted.

"I'm overjoyed, and father and mother will be as well."

"And Clarissa, if she only knew."

The cloud descended on Trixie's face.

"Now, now . . ." Carlton said. He wiped his streaming eyes with a handkerchief. "The babe shall not be born for some months. Surely Clarissa and Papa will have patched up their quarrel by then."

"Do you really think so?"

"Yes," Carlton said, far from certain about anything in his volatile family. "The news will make Papa relent. He cannot mean for Clarissa to remain at Claring forever."

He pulled Trixie to her feet. "And to prove it, we shall go over and tell him the news."

The drive to St. James Square was accomplished in ten minutes. Sir Arthur and Lady Claringdon were just sitting down to a table of cold meats, but on hearing the news from Trixie all thought of food vanished. Sir Arthur rang for his footman to fetch not one pillow but two, each to be placed behind the back of the young mother-to-be while Lady Claringdon embraced Trixie, then Carlton, then Trixie again for good measure.

"A grandfather," Sir Arthur beamed and puffed up his cheeks. "This calls for champagne. A baby, just imagine, and an heir to the name as well."

"It might be a girl," Lady Claringdon said, casting the first stone into the clear waters.

"Don't speak nonsense," Sir Arthur said irritably. "It will be a boy and an heir."

"But girls have their uses too, Papa," Carlton said, accepting the champagne that Walter, the butler, poured.

Sir Arthur glowered at his son. "I suppose you refer to your sister?"

"Your father is upset because Clarissa has not written to him," Lady Claringdon revealed as she sipped her champagne.

"Ill-mannered brat! Spoiled chit!"

"Who spoiled her, sir?" Lady Claringdon asked, quizzing him.

Sir Arthur sought assistance from his son. "Is it too much for her to write a letter home to her parents?"

"Parents yes, gaolers no," Lady Claringdon interrupted.

"Gaolers!" Sir Arthur growled. "Have you heard from her, Carlton?"

Knowing the anxiety that lay behind his parents' distress, Carlton nodded. "She is quite well and has met Trixie's friend, Emily. It seems that Clarissa means to help Emily in the schoolroom."

"Schoolroom!" Sir Arthur spluttered in the midst of swallowing his champagne and turned a bright red.

"Does she indeed?" Lady Claringdon asked, taking the glass from her spouse. "Most curious. What do you make of it, Arthur?"

"There is nothing to make of it!" Sir Arthur answered, looking like a very wet thundercloud. "She brought this disgrace upon herself by disobeying my wishes."

"But think how disagreeable it must be for her," Trixie said. "To be in the country for weeks or months would exhaust me."

"The minute she is ready to write and ask to return, she may," Sir Arthur said graciously. Mother and son exchanged meaningful glances.

"I consider that to be highly unlikely, Papa," Carlton said. "Clarissa is as proud as a bantam. Reminds me of you in a way, don't you think?"

"No, I don't think," his father said acidly. "But I am tired of thinking of that silly chit and talking of her as well. Let's talk of some other things. What do you all think of the name William for this grandson of mine?"

"Oh, Arthur, not William!" Lady Claringdon declared. And the conversation switched to an animated discussion of names.

* * *

Three hours later Arthur Claringdon sat in White's reading room, the afternoon papers on his lap and his mind miles away. It had been Sir Arthur's custom to spend his afternoons settled at the club, enjoy a light meal and a hand of whist while debating the news from the Continent, but since reaching White's today, these simple entertainments had palled.

He settled himself into the leather chair and wondered where everyone had gone to. The fire in front of him blazed and crackled, sending up sparks. He wondered what his daughter was doing.

"What say, Arthur." A voice then a hearty handclap pulled him from his gloom. Lord Peter Whalmsey, his boyhood friend, gazed down at him, dropped the quizzing glass from one eye, then sat down in the armchair next to Sir Arthur.

"You know, Arthur," he said, peering closely at his friend. "I don't like your color."

"Oh, don't you?" Sir Arthur returned. "Next you'll be pushing potions at me like a quack."

"What have you been eating?"

"Ain't hungry."

"Losing at cards?"

"No."

"The gout still troubling you?"

"No. I've things on my mind." He glanced over at the silver-haired Whalmsey. "Felicitate me, Peter. I'm to be a grandfather."

"But how splendid." Whalmsey beamed his warm approval. "Congratulations. Although you don't look too happy over it."

"I am happy," Sir Arthur said testily. "It's just that I could be happier. And it's that chit's fault."

Since Arthur was happily married and had been so for nearly three decades and had never dabbled in the petticoat line, Lord Whalmsey knew to whom his friend referred. As befitted a longtime friend of the family—and Clarissa's own godfather—Sir Arthur had poured the whole tale of his trouble into his friend's ear.

"Your quarrel with Clarissa still ailing you?" he asked sympathetically.

"A father can come to grief over just such a daughter."

Lord Whalmsey ventured no reply, having enjoyed a comfortable bachelorhood all his life and having formed no opinions of daughters or sons.

"Cheer up, Arthur. I thought you sent her away to mind you."

"Yes, and precious good that has done me." Sir Arthur tossed the newspapers back onto the table. "Do you know she had the cheek to write to Carlton to ask him to send her schoolbooks?"

"Strange," Whalmsey said, puzzling over this news. "Pretty poor reading they used to be."

"She means to teach, Peter."

"No!" Whalmsey said, shocked.

"It's the truth."

"Well, well. Perhaps the country air is getting to her." Sir Arthur snorted.

"Let's have a drink," Lord Whalmsey said. "That will cheer you up."

"Nothing will cheer me up," Sir Arthur said gloomily, but he drank the claret his friend ordered and placed in front of him.

"How does Trixie go on?" Lord Whalmsey asked, his palate refreshed enough to return to his friend's dilemma.

"Trixie? Oh, quite well so far. Carlton is pleased too." He gazed at his friend sullenly. "But Trixie would like Clarissa to be near at hand when the babe arrives."

"Then what are you waiting for? Send for her at once."

"I can't," Sir Arthur grumbled. He put his claret down

71

hard on the table. "It's all very well for you without wife or daughter to suggest such a thing. You don't understand. If I back down now, I shall never hear the end to it. I'll never get a minute's peace. A man must show just who is the head of his family."

"Quite true," Lord Whalmsey acknowledged. Privately, however, he was of the opinion that no man could be married and still be the head of his family.

"Clarissa's only been gone a few days. She may come around."

"She had better!" Arthur said gloomily.

"Does she know of the babe?"

"Not yet. Trixie means to write to her."

"Well, there you see," Lord Whalmsey pointed out. "When she does hear the news, she'll return to London. She won't want to miss that, and she'll have the perfect excuse to return."

Sir Arthur's face brightened. This had not occurred to him before.

"You may be right," he said with some satisfaction. He drained his glass and refused the offer of another drink. "Nor a game of whist. I am deuced tired. Perhaps some other day."

"Family quarrels are always troubling to the digestion," Lord Whalmsey said.

"Hah."

Sir Arthur gazed across at the placid face of his friend. "You may find yourself tied to a pair of apron strings some day."

"Not I!" Whalmsey replied with the confidence of the lifetime bachelor.

Sir Arthur left the reading room, almost colliding with Joseph Cranley, who also made the afternoon papers a habit at White's. Whalmsey returned to his claret, trying at the same time to recall the newcomer's name. Familiar-looking chap, if a bit thick around the middle. He dug through his famous memory before he found the link.

"You're Montcrieff's cousin, aren't you?" he asked, snapping his fingers.

"Yes, my lord," Joseph said, pleased that someone of Whalmsey's stature would remember him, though irked that the connection as always had been made through Sidney. "Joseph Cranley."

"That's it, Cranley. For some odd reason I had a notion it might be Cranville. How does your cousin do these days?"

"He is out of town."

"Yes, I'd heard that," Lord Whalmsey said, recalling the rumors that had swept the ton following Lady Vye's canceled dinner party. "Does he mean to stay away long?"

"I don't know. We hardly move in the same circles."

"Pity for you," was Whalmsey's only reply.

Joseph meticulously picked up the papers and settled himself in a chair further away from the fire to read. Kentmere entered the room, looking as nervous as a kitten.

"Excuse me, Lord Whalmsey," he said, stopping in front of Whalmsey's chair. "I wonder if I might have a moment with you."

"You may have several moments," Whalmsey said indulgently. "Sit down, lad."

"It's my pair of grays, my lord," Kentmere said finally. "I remember that you admired them."

"So I have and so I shall continue to do so," Whalmsey replied kindly. "Why do you bring them up?"

"Are you interested in purchasing them?"

"In Dun territory, Philip?"

Kentmere colored. "No, my lord. At least," he said grimly, "not yet, nor will I go to Howard and Gibbs over

73

a matter so trifling. Selling my grays will cover my losses nicely. Do you wish a look at them?"

"By all means," Whalmsey replied. "Is ten thirty tomorrow morning too soon to try them out?"

"Not in the least," Kentmere said, relieved. A good chap, Whalmsey, not the type to get on his high ropes or read a lecture, and there was no danger of being cheated. Whalmsey's reputation for honesty was famous throughout the ton.

"I would have spoken to you sooner, my lord," Kentmere said now, "but you were engaged with Sir Arthur."

"Ah, yes, Claringdon," Whalmsey shook his head. "Poor Arthur."

"Is he in some difficulty?"

"The man is about to be a grandfather," Whalmsey explained.

"But that's splendid."

"So one should think. But Arthur is not happy, and you may blame his daughter for that!" So saying, Lord Whalmsey rose. "I shall see you tomorrow, Kentmere. Good day to you, Cranley."

Joseph hastily acknowledged the adieu before returning to his paper. But the lines of print jumped back and forth in a blur. His understanding was by no stretch of the imagination as large as either of his cousins, but he was no slow top! There could be only one reason in the world why a man of Sir Arthur's stature was not pleased at the prospect of a grandchild. But, as he told himself later, he would never have dreamed it of Miss Clarissa Claringdon!

7

Sidney's first few days at Bengal Court passed with devastating alacrity. The estates were in the appalling condition he had feared back in London, due in large measure to Akins, Edward's manager, who had shown no signs of judgment in allowing the estates to deteriorate so rapidly. Sidney's first order of business would have been to fire this miscreant, if only he could have been located. Unfortunately, Mr. Akins had taken full advantage of the six-month delay in the change of ownership to flee the territory with a goodly amount of estate funds in his pockets.

For several days Sidney himself took to the saddle, traversing the countryside, pausing to speak with the tenants, and reassuring them that the rents would not be increased until all felt recovered. He was also obliged to examine the inevitable flocks of sheep thrust his way for inspection, and soon, he thought wryly, he would be smelling like a sheepherder himself. As he made his rounds Sidney looked, listened, and kept his eyes peeled for a suitable replacement for Akins.

On the third day he found just the fellow: John Braun. Likable, sturdy, and industrious, and—what Sidney deemed most important—Braun stood on excellent terms with the rest of the villagers. He told the surprised Braun of the job offer, and a quick handshake closed the deal.

"And with Braun in charge I can rest easy," Sidney told his cousin that night over their port.

"Not the type to fleece you, I fancy?"

Sidney smiled ruefully. "No, by all accounts he's first-rate, and the vicar speaks highly of him."

"That's famous."

Sidney stretched. "It also means we can return to London sooner than I expected."

"Return . . ." the earl said. He broke off abruptly.

Sidney looked across the table, surprised. "What's the matter, Lytton? Don't you like London any more?"

"Certainly I do," the earl said impatiently. He wrinkled his nose and pointed a finger toward the ashtray. "I wish you would smoke that disgusting cigar, Sidney. It smells to the heavens . . ."

Sidney picked up the offending cigar. "What about London?" he asked quietly.

"You may return if you like. I'd liefer remain at Bengal Court for a little while."

Sidney surveyed the ash at the end of his cigar and said nothing. No doubt pretty little Miss Manville had something to do with the earl's reluctance to leave. A few minutes later Lytton himself left for his bedchamber pleading a mild fatigue.

Sidney finished up his cigar and watched the fire die down. His preoccupation with Bengal Court had not precluded him from observing Lytton's growing involvement with Emily. Had it been any other man of his acquaintance he would have thought no more of the matter; but this was Larry.

Sidney frowned and flicked off a speck of dust from his sleeve. Larry was more like a younger brother to him than a cousin, and he felt a responsibility. Lytton had inherited his father's easy spirits and generosity, the flaws accounting for most of the scrapes that Sidney had rescued him from in the past. But marriage would be the greatest scrape of all, and by Jupiter, there would be no escape from that!

And it would have to be marriage. Whatever his flaws, Lytton was not so idiotic as to offer *carte blanche* to someone like Miss Manville. Which led Sidney on to an even more perplexing problem. Just who the devil was Emily Manville?

Sidney poured himself another glass of port and considered the matter carefully. For all the flirtations the earl had engaged in previously, this would be his most serious affair to date. Sidney himself was acquainted with several in the ton who had been badly scorched by the fortune hunters. A man like Lytton was easy prey to them. True, Miss Manville did not give the appearance of a gold digger, but appearances in females—his thoughts flew unbidden to Lady Vye—could be deceiving.

Retired to his bedchamber, Sidney sat up thinking hard. He had no desire to put a crimp in Lytton's courtship, but he intended to acquaint himself with Miss Manville. The opportunity presented itself almost at once the following morning when Lytton announced his intention of calling on Emily. Sidney, much to the earl's surprise, invited himself along.

Emily was in the garden with Clarissa when Owen ushered the two gentlemen in. Clarissa, who had lain in wait for just such a moment, now had the opportunity to observe Emily's reaction to the presence of her paragon. Miss Manville herself appeared on the verge of a faint, stammering a dim-witted response to Lytton's friendly greeting, and looking as frightened as a hare when Sidney shook hands with her.

Clarissa stifled a groan, yearning to shake her charge by the shoulders. Though by no means unsympathetic to Emily's plight—had she not spent several mornings pointing out just what to say to a gentleman of Quality?—Clarissa could not help the feeling within that in love, every woman, even a bluestocking like Emily, turned into a henwit.

The men joined the ladies on the path. Lytton rather mysteriously found himself escorting Clarissa while Sidney accompanied Miss Manville ahead. Clarissa, who bore the responsibility for these adroit arrangements, paused now and then during the course of her walk with Lytton, calling his reluctant attention to the opening of one rose and then another. So long did she tarry that Sidney and Emily found themselves some distance ahead. Lytton had no great love of flowers to begin with, and he fidgeted like a fugitive. But he was not so impolite as to be rude to so great a friend of Miss Manville's. So he chafed, fretted, and found himself wondering what the deuce Sidney could be saying that would possibly interest Emily.

Sidney, having observed that the pair behind had fallen far back, lost no time in furthering his limited knowledge of Miss Manville. "How do you find yourself a schoolteacher?" he asked, as a bee whizzed noisily past his ear.

"My mother was one before me," Miss Manville explained.

"And her mother before her?" Sidney asked.

Emily shook her head. "No, my mother was forced to teach school after she married my father and was cut off by her family."

"The alliance was frowned upon?" Sidney asked sympathetically.

Miss Manville nodded. "It was a pity that Grandfather would not agree. They were so in love and forced to elope. What else could people in love do? Mama never regretted it, and I do think it was most romantic."

"Elopements generally are," Sidney said. "Am I to understand that she was disinherited?"

"Oh, yes. My grandfather was so proud, and my father had no family who would dare come to his assistance. And Mama's family was just as bad except for a cousin, Roderick Grant."

Sidney paused between two potted roses and stared blankly into Emily's eyes. "Roderick Grant was your mother's cousin?"

"Yes, sir."

"This school your mother ran wouldn't have been in Devonshire by any chance?"

"Yes, it was!" Emily beamed her approval.

"But I used to visit her now and then when I rode with Roderick," Sidney exclaimed in astonishment. "He was a good friend though several years my senior. I do beg your pardon, Miss Manville. I never made the connection with you."

Emily walked on, speaking quietly. "There is no need for apologies. It was all so long ago and who could blame you for forgetting."

"And poor Roderick dead at Salamanca."

"Yes." Emily blinked back tears of remembrance. "But he left some of his money to Mama, what little he had. For there were so many gambling debts, which quite shocked us both. And when Mama died, a little of her money passed on to me, and that is how I got this school."

She spoke with the delight of a child with a new toy.

"Do you mean to keep the school?" Sidney asked.

"It has been my wish up to now," Emily admitted. She glanced over her shoulder and spied Lytton and Clarissa still engrossed in the shrubbery.

"But has something happened to persuade you otherwise?" Sidney inquired.

"Being a woman, I sometimes think of marriage," Miss Manville replied sensibly.

"You would hardly be a female if you did not think of

it," Sidney declared with considerable relish. Emily laughed nervously, but she was sufficiently emboldened by his quiet sympathy to press her advantage.

"Do you think a good connection would be out of the question for me, sir? Considering my background, I mean . . ."

Sidney glanced down into the upturned face. A pretty thing. Perhaps quiet and a trifle shy. But these were attributes that many men fancied in wives. And whatever he may have thought about her before, if she were cousin to Roderick her lineage was good.

"Speaking for myself, Emily," he said kindly, "I would say you have a very good chance of a connection."

A radiant smile engulfed Emily's features. Sidney, prepared at best for a mild show of gratitude, was stunned by this largesse and wore a perfectly dumbfounded expression on his handsome face. What was the matter with the woman?

He was not the only one present in the garden to wonder. Clarissa and Lytton had both been avid witnesses to the marked glow on Miss Manville's countenance during the garden tour. With mounting impatience Clarissa sat through the rest of the visit, and only after the gentlemen had departed was she able to pounce on her friend.

"Oh, Clarissa," Emily said breathlessly. "It is the outside of enough. Better than I could have dreamed."

"What do you mean?" Clarissa demanded. "Speak!"

Emily laughed. "He questioned me at length about my family and background, thinking it odd I ran a school. When I mentioned Roderick, he remembered!"

"And that has cast you in alt?" Clarissa asked dubiously.

"No," Emily said, regaining her composure. "There's more."

"I should hope so," Clarissa said. "Do tell me . . ."

"He questioned me about Mama, about what things had led her to the school. And I asked if he thought my situation and Mama's before me made a good marriage impossible." She gave Clarissa an apologetic nod. "I thought you might think it fast of me . . ."

"Never mind that, what did he say?"

"He said, 'Speaking for myself, Emily, I would say you have a very good chance of a connection.' He called me Emily!"

"But that is splendid," Clarissa said. She was, however, conscious of a slight disappointment. "I would not have thought it so easy to lure Sidney Montcrieff into such a declaration and on this only your third meeting with him!"

"But it wasn't a declaration exactly."

"It was near enough," Clarissa said, waving away this trifle. "Don't fall into a pelter, Emily. He shall make an offer yet. We have only to bide our time. A man does not inquire about family attachments unless he is thinking seriously of marriage."

Sidney, on his way home to Bengal Court, was not thinking seriously of marriage or of Miss Manville. He was thinking that Lytton was turning into a nuisance.

" 'Is she not pretty? Is she not amiable?' " he mocked. "Yes, Larry. She is, and now I implore you not to go on about her any longer."

"But what did she say about me?"

"You were not discussed," Sidney said with crushing pretension.

"But you were talking to her for at least fifteen minutes!" Lytton exclaimed.

"You did not figure in the conversation," Sidney said, running his fingers through his hair in a way that would have struck his valet to the core. "I asked Emily some questions."

"Questions?"

"I'm sorry, Larry, but I did need to know her background . . ."

The earl froze. "And did you unearth anything of interest to you?"

"Yes," Sidney returned. "There's some scandal in her family."

"Scandal? I don't believe it."

"It happened before your time," Sidney explained, "and it's nothing so bad unless you happen to be an old woman, which you are not . . ."

"Thank you," Lytton murmured modestly. "But what happened?"

"Her mother eloped with her father, and both sides cut up stiff over it. If not for a cousin on her mother's side, who happened to be a friend of mine, she would be penniless."

"I don't care if she were," the earl said angrily. "I'd marry her anyway."

"Yes," Sidney said, bestowing a thoughtful gaze on his cousin. "I suppose you would."

His lordship frowned, but it was not in his nature to take umbrage at Sidney. "Do you think we should suit, Miss Manville and I?"

"Suit? Why shouldn't you?" Sidney inquired. "And why the devil are you looking at me in that calfish way?"

Lytton grinned. "It occurred to me, Sidney, that you are my nearest male relative. Would you speak to Emily for me?"

Incredulity warred with amusement on Sidney's face.

"What a whisker!" he exclaimed. "You have been using your tongue to great acclaim all your life. What is this fustian about my speaking for you? I remember the first syllables you ever uttered. Mama. It had my aunt in raptures."

"I wish you will stop roasting me."

"I beg pardon," Sidney said, patting his horse. "I had feared the presence of the country air had turned your head around."

Far from offended, Lytton merely asked, "Do you fancy that she thinks of marriage, Sidney?"

"Probably. In point of fact, yes, she does. Told me so herself."

The earl reined in. "With me?" he asked.

"Well, you are the only man within miles paying court on her," Sidney declared.

"She hasn't accepted me," Lytton said mournfully.

"Merely because you haven't asked her," Sidney pointed out with amusement. "And she may not accept you if you make a cake out of yourself. You have been trying to sit in her pocket, Larry. That won't do, not even here in the country. Emily's the skittish sort or I'll go bail. She's not used to your town bronze. In fact, that cravat alone is enough to scare her off. If I were you, I'd bide my time."

"Oh, I suppose you're right," the earl said ungraciously. They rode on in a silence broken by Lytton. "Sidney, what say we hold a dinner party at Bengal Court."

This statement, rather unprecedented in their long and pleasant relationship, caused Sidney to wonder if the earl had been in the sun too long. "What the devil do you want a party for?"

"I was thinking of Aunt Agatha and Cousin Elizabeth. Must be boring for them half the time all alone. Company might make a pleasant change."

"Company such as Miss Manville, I warrant?" Sidney asked, lifting an eyebrow.

Lytton had grace enough to laugh. "Diversion for everyone. We'll invite Clarissa as well. What do you say?"

"Leave the matter to Aunt Agatha," Sidney declared. "If she's willing to have company underfoot, I suppose I can't object."

The topic was duly broached to Lady Agatha soon after their return to Bengal Court. Although Agatha had made her reputation as a hermit, she had no real dislike of company, and as she listened to Lytton's suggestion of a dinner party with meticulous courtesy, a scheme of her own arose.

"No dinner party," she said imperiously.

The earl's face fell. "You mean you don't care for company?"

"I mean I don't care to have a dinner party. I'd rather a ball."

"A ball!" Sidney exclaimed, jarred by this reversal. Lytton's little party would have made for a passable evening, but he would be dashed if he would sit still for a ball that would rain havoc on Bengal Court.

"Yes, a ball," Lady Agatha said distinctly, taking a slice of ham from her footman.

"That's a famous idea," Lytton said, his lunch forgotten. "Much better than my poor notion of a party. We can use the ballroom and hire musicians and mustn't forget the flowers. The area does need to be polished up." The earl rubbed his hands. "But we shall contrive. The ball is the best idea, don't you think, Elizabeth?"

"It will make for a change," Elizabeth agreed across the table.

"Too much of a change!" Sidney declared, pushing away his plate and trying to nip this scheme in the bud. "A ball is out of the question. A dinner party for a few agreeable friends is one thing, but a ball where I shall be obliged to do the pretty to dozens I've never met is a penance I feel unwilling to shoulder."

"But think, Sidney . . ." his aunt commanded.

"Think of what, ma'am?" he asked acidly.

"Think of how the music and company shall cheer up a decrepit old woman like me."

One glance at her impudent face and Sidney erupted in laughter.

"Aunt Agatha, you are infamous and well you know it." He threw up his hands helplessly as he gazed around the table. "Very well. We shall have a ball, though how we shall manage or whom we should invite I have no idea."

8

No problem with guests arose except in Sidney's own imagination. In her thirty-odd years at Bengal Court Agatha had been invited to many teas and dinners and had a full array of acquaintances. But each of these friends was flabbergasted upon receiving a gold-edged invitation the following week.

The invitations were duly examined and their contents bandied about over numerous lunches and teas. Dressmakers were besieged with requests for fittings, and materials became in rather short supply. As one modiste complained bitterly to her seamstress, "Trust all the women in the county to be demanding silk at such a time and Norwich silk at that!"

While the ladies fretted over their toilette, the gentlemen professed a marked curiosity about the newest owner of Bengal Court. Since the last male occupant had been as near to an Indian as were possible and still remain an Englishman, it was the easiest thing to imagine Sidney an Indian too. No one, it occurred to the vicar who was much diverted by these opinions, had met Sidney yet, and so the rumors flew.

One story had Sidney as old and enfeebled as Lady Agatha, while a second that he had wasted his ready and stood on the gallows before the provident rescue by Edward's solicitor, and a third that he had of late returned from the Americas where he had had a hand in the spying there. The last of these tales found its way to the attentive ear of Miss Clarissa Claringdon, who fell into whoops of laughter and was as diverted as the vicar.

The days leading up to the ball were frantic at Bengal Court. Servants, newly hired and commissioned to help out, polished railings and dusted windows. Several of the more garish of Edward's Indian pieces were removed from the hallway and escorted to the attic. It was all very well—the earl pointed out—for the family to laugh at an Indian goddess with six or eight arms, but what must someone of Miss Manville's sensibility make of it?

The drapes of the ballroom discovered faded with the sun were replaced, and Cousin Edward's prize elephants were retired to the attic, where Sidney promised his aunt they would remain during his lifetime at the very least. Sidney, persuaded by the earl that his help was needed, gave his reluctant approval to all the plans laid out for him and even went so far as to oversee a menu that boasted not only a turtle soup but a full baron of beef.

"But I do draw the line at ordering cakes and tarts!" he told his cousin.

"There is just one other thing, Sidney," Lytton said, catching him just as he was about to step out.

Sidney lodged a mild protest. "There seems to always

be another thing, Larry. What, pray, is it this time? It cannot be more mummified monkey paws, can it? We took care of them yesterday."

"It's our relatives."

Sidney hunched his shoulder and glanced up and down the hallway. "Lytton, I implore you . . ."

"I don't mean Agatha and Elizabeth," Lytton said, grinning widely. "It's *those* relatives." He screwed up his nose and indicated the portraits on the wall.

"They do look like rabble, don't they," Sidney said, studying them through his quizzing glass.

"Rabble is much too mild, Sidney. They must go."

"No quarrel from me, Larry, but what about our aunt? It's bad enough that she had to part with that snake goddess of hers."

"She won't mind. She hates them too."

"How fortunate," Sidney murmured. He tapped his glass lightly. "But what will you put in place of the portraits? The walls shall look rather bare without them."

"Oriental rugs," Lytton explained, going into the library and opening a trunk. "I found them in the attic. Why Edward hid these beauties I'll never understand."

Inspecting them, Sidney found they passed muster. "Very well," he said. "Put them up quickly, and let us hear no more about dead relations."

Leaving Lytton to contend with the last details of the ball, Sidney drove himself over to the vicarage and, accompanied by Felix Boatwright, drove into Cheltenham. Felix, allowed the luxury of holding the reins himself, was beside himself with joy. Sidney sat languidly in the box, alert to every movement of the horses, who seemed a trifle nervous at the unfamiliar hand on the rein. Aside from a certain exuberance, and that would be tempered with time, Felix demonstrated notable skill for his years.

"You are certainly a better whip than I was at your age," Sidney said.

"Thank you, sir," Felix said.

"Now," Sidney asked as they stepped down, "what do you think of some cakes and ices?"

It was obvious from Felix's expression that cakes and ices would do very nicely. The two companions soon found a small café and sat down to enjoy the ices that would have done credit to Mr. Gunter himself. While Sidney nibbled and Felix gorged himself, they spotted Clarissa and Emily strolling down the street together. Felix, being a decade younger and more nimble of foot, ran out to greet them, leaving Sidney to trail in his wake.

"Felix says you have had quite an outing!" Clarissa smiled as he strolled up to greet them.

"We have. Should you like to share some tea with us?"

"We cannot," Clarissa said with a pang of genuine regret. She was, Sidney thought, looking remarkably youthful with a sable-trimmed pelisse and matching gown.

"We shall see you at the ball on Saturday, Miss Manville?" Sidney inquired.

Emily gave a shy nod.

"And you, Miss Claringdon?"

"I would not miss it for the world," Clarissa declared.

"Yes, but I'm not offering you the world," he pointed out affably, falling into step with her.

"No," she gurgled. "But you are offering me the chance to see you at your own party. Not many in London can claim such a feat."

"It's not my party alone," Sidney answered as Felix scampered ahead with Emily. "Lytton has a rather large hand in it. Perhaps too large. Do you know he overruled my request for a few waltzes at the party? Said it wouldn't wash."

Clarissa shook her head severely. "Now you are trying to shock me, sir!"

He studied the glint of amusement in her eye. "How so?"

"Even you who do not frequent its Assemblies must know that the waltz is not yet danced at Almack's."

"It shall be," Sidney said with such authority that a laugh sprang unbidden from Clarissa's throat.

"Are you a connoisseur of dance as well as horses?"

"Hardly," Sidney said, smiling down at her. "But even you must know that if the waltz is not danced at hallowed old Almack's, it is danced in many other circles. Vienna and St. Petersburg to name only two. Alexander is said to be quite fond of it, and if he dances it, as he must or he shall think all London so dowdy, then we shall follow. Confess, Clarissa, can it be you do not know how to dance the waltz?"

Clarissa chuckled. "I have known the waltz for the better part of a year, and half the other ladies of society must know it as well. But it is one thing to know the waltz and another to dance it at Almack's."

"That is just what Lytton said," Sidney announced. "I suppose we shall have to follow Alexander's lead. But when we next meet in London you shall see it is the rage and then will you favor me with a dance?"

"If the waltz is being danced in London, and you are there, I shall be glad to dance it with you," Clarissa promised.

The topic of the dance having been explored exhaustively, Sidney helped Clarissa and Emily into their carriage and returned to his own with Felix. He smiled indulgently at the boy's chatter, but his mind was still fixed on that lovely smile on Miss Claringdon's face.

At ten o'clock Saturday morning the staff of Bengal

Court was treated to a rare sight. Lord Lytton bounded up the marble stairs three at a time and flew into his cousin's room without the courtesy of a knock. Sidney was in the midst of applying the last of the dextrous turns to his muslin neckcloth under the watchful gaze of his valet, Clemmons, and gave no sign of even noticing the earl's entrance.

"Sidney . . ."

"Quiet, Larry. Have you no manners?"

"It's an emergency, Sidney. You really must come."

Sidney stared up at the ceiling, then dropped his jaw before he nodded in satisfaction at the mirror. "Where is it you wish me to go, Larry?" he inquired.

"To the kitchen."

"To the kitchen!" Sidney slipped his arms through the coat of blue superfine his valet was holding out, wondering if the earl had been dipping into the punch a little earlier.

"Why don't you tell me why you want me in the kitchen?" he was asking as they descended the stairs together.

The earl's tale was quick and precise. Mr. Tibbs, the chef retained at enormous cost on the staff of Bengal Court, had fallen into a quarrel with Lady Agatha over her suggestion of a roast lamb to be placed on the already overburdened menu. Unable to reach a compromise, Tibbs had quit.

"And without a cook we won't have a supper to sit down to unless you plan to cook, Sidney."

"You do think of the most peculiar things for me to do, Larry," Sidney protested mildly. "Has Tibbs left?"

"Not yet. I told him you'd want to see him before he could think of leaving. He's in the library."

A few minutes later Sidney faced Tibbs, who looked as intractable as any chef nursing a wounded pride.

"Now, Tibbs, what is all this talk about quitting?" Sidney asked.

"It's not talk, sir. The Lady Agatha fired me."

Sidney seated himself at the desk. "Tibbs, how long have you been with my aunt?"

"Ten years next December."

"Then you know her ways. I beg you to reconsider and return to your kitchens."

"But what about this?" Tibbs demanded, brandishing a menu. "She wants lamb, sir, and she won't listen when I say I have the nicest pheasant for tonight as well as a plum sauce, not to mention that side of beef . . ."

"I'm sure," Sidney said, dodging the proffered menu. "Is this what prompted the quarrel?"

"Yes, sir."

Sidney plucked the document from the chef's fingers and tore it in half. "Tibbs, I have at least a hundred dinner guests descending on me tonight. All I ask from you is that you refrain from poisoning us."

"Very good, sir," Tibbs said, breaking into a smile and returning to his kitchen whistling in a most unseemly way.

"Quite masterful, Sidney," Lytton said as he picked up Agatha's menu and tossed it into the fire.

"I thought so, yes."

"What will you say to Aunt Agatha?"

"Nothing," he replied gloomily. "Those in her black books are not allowed speech with her."

While Sidney was solving *l'affaire cuisine*, Clarissa sat in her garden seat, idly sniffing one of Giles's prize roses and engrossed in the continuing travails of Miss Emily Manville.

It had taken Clarissa only a day, if that long, to realize that under Emily's delightful air of intellectualism beat the soul of an impassioned romantic, and that for good or ill the target of those passions was Sidney Montcrieff.

Was she doing the right thing by Emily? Clarissa wondered as an insect landed on one of the petals in front of her. It was all very well for Emily to protest that she loved Sidney, but he was no ordinary man about town, and Emily, despite her book learning, was a very green girl.

Clarissa's doubts surfaced again moments later as she walked toward Claring House and found Emily just stepping down from her carriage. Emily saw her immediately and flung herself into Clarissa's arms, scattering rose petals all over the driveway.

"My dear child," Clarissa protested, meeting Mrs. Quill's sympathetic eye over Emily's head.

"Oh, Clarissa. . . ." Emily's voice was choked with emotion, and she drew away, revealing a tear-stained face.

"You have been crying today of all days! You must not, for your face will get quite blotched for the party. And what is that you have in your hands."

"My dress!" Emily said in accents of loathing.

"It will get quite crushed between us."

"I don't care," Miss Manville said rashly. "Oh, Clarissa, I vow I don't know what to do. I'm here to beg your help and advice, for I cannot wear it! I shall look horrid, I just know. And if I do not wear it, I shall not go at all."

Having deduced from this speech that the gown was in some measure responsible for Emily's hysteria, Clarissa took the offending garment on one arm and her friend on the other and brought them both into the house up the stairs to her bedchamber.

"Surely you must exaggerate," she said, closing the door. "This dress appears quite pretty to me."

"And so I thought when Mama purchased it for me," Emily said. "But you shall see for yourself. Only what am I to do?"

"Put it on," Clarissa said.

With her assistance Miss Manville donned the hated garment. "Look at me," she said unhappily.

Clarissa was already engaged in doing just that. Mentally she could only agree with Emily that the dress did not do justice to her figure, and moreover that it made her appear to possess none at all. And as for the color, that made her look positively sallow, green being a color few females could wear successfully, and almond green being hopelessly outmoded.

"You do see!" Emily howled and burst into a fresh supply of tears.

"Yes, but do stop your crying, my dear," Clarissa said, distracted by the wailing. "For I am trying to think."

"I shall not go to the party looking like a dowd," Emily said wretchedly. "You must know what a man of mode Montcrieff is and the mere thought that he will view me like this makes me want to sink. I look like a chimney!" She hunched her tiny shoulders. "I have made a decision, Clarissa. I shall not attend the party tonight."

Unfortunately, Miss Manville lacked the height to make such a threat good, and Clarissa, her brow still wrinkled in thought, looked up momentarily and begged her not to be a dunce.

"For you must attend. You have been looking forward to it since forever. How many trips Lytton has made to your house to advise you on the plans. To decline now would be an odious insult to all the Montcrieffs."

"I had not thought of that," Emily said, visibly shaken at the idea of insulting an entire clan. "I don't mean to offend anyone. But I cannot walk into the ballroom looking like this."

"No, we are agreed on that. But I don't think the problem insurmountable. You shall borrow one of my dresses. I daresay Polly can put the hem up quite easily."

"Oh, no, Clarissa . . ."

"It is no good your telling me what I cannot do," Clarissa warned. "I am not about to go to this ball alone." She flung open her wardrobe and allowed Emily to feast her eyes dizzily on the garments assembled there.

"It was so idiotish of me to bring so many here," Clarissa confided. "But I was in such a rage with Papa I did not bother to be sensible. So you shall take your choice." Seeing Emily's hesitation, Clarissa brought out two of the nicest.

"The blue satin will bring out your eyes," she said, laying the dress against Emily and frowning. "Or perhaps the yellow for your hair. On me both dresses look dismal, so do try them on."

With Clarissa's urging Miss Manville threw off her green dress and slipped on the sapphire blue gown. She gazed raptly at her reflection as Clarissa helped her with the row of tiny buttons cresting at the bodice.

The cut of the dress accentuated Emily's best features, the high curve of her body and the creamy whiteness of her skin. Sidney would have to be blind not to notice, Clarissa thought as she finished the buttons.

"What do you think?" Emily asked anxiously.

"I think you look lovely," Clarissa said. "But do try the yellow silk before we decide."

The yellow silk, although becoming, was a far second to the sapphire blue.

"I cannot think how to thank you," Emily said, hugging Clarissa tightly. "You have saved the day."

Clarissa shrugged away the praise.

"We shall return from Bengal Court rather late. Do you think you should like to stay here for the night? We can ride to and from the party together."

"I cannot imagine a more wonderful plan," Emily declared, and the two ladies went down to make the announcements to the household.

9

At six o'clock Sidney appeared in the great ballroom of Bengal Court wearing the knee breeches, silk stockings, frilled shirt, and black coat of the well-dressed gentleman. Indeed, he thought with some chagrin, he might be readying himself for Almack's instead of his own home. He stood for a moment, observing the musicians who had arrived and were now busy arranging their music, then he crossed the hall into the great dining room where Lytton was nimbly reversing the cards on several of the table settings.

"Skullduggery afoot, Lytton?" he asked.

"Dinner partners," the earl answered. "I do think Elizabeth will be more comfortable talking to the vicar, don't you?"

"Doubtless and that puts Miss Manville on your left, I observe."

"Yes, and Aunt Agatha is at the head of the table," Lytton pointed out. "Fitting, don't you think, since she is the hostess of the affair."

"Although you wouldn't know it by the treatment I receive."

A trenchant voice spoke beside the two men. It was their aunt standing as stiffly as her black silk, with Elizabeth next in an amber-colored gown.

"How are you, Aunt Agatha?" Sidney asked warily. "Quite rested after your long afternoon's sleep?"

"No." A muscle worked in her jaw. "What right do you have to contradict my orders to Tibbs?"

Braver men might have tried to put on a bold front, but Sidney capitulated at once.

"None whatsoever," he admitted, taking his aunt by the arm and leading her into the hall where they would await their guests. "But I had your well-being in mind and Elizabeth's."

"Mine?" Agatha thundered.

"Yes. It would have been so disagreeable for you or Elizabeth to cook the dinner for our guests tonight. Neither of you is especially familiar in the kitchen, I fancy. And so I prevailed on Tibbs to stay on."

Agatha hooted. "Nothing shy about you, is there?"

"I'm afraid not."

"Good," she barked. "I'm tired of namby-pambies and mealymouths myself." She walked into the ballroom, now glittering and shining, and thumped her cane. "This is supposed to be a ball. Where the devil are our guests?"

Lady Agatha had not long to wait. The guests soon arrived in droves with much clattering of carriage wheels and hellos that rang out in the evening air. The first of the arrivals were Lady Agatha's friends from Cheltenham, Lady Maria Cunningham accompanied by her husband and a woman whom she pronounced her niece. Sidney smiled, pressed the gnarled hand in his and sent up a silent prayer to be relieved from simpering nieces.

He was rescued by this last difficulty by the arrival of the Boatwrights, who shook hands all around and professed their delight with the changes at Bengal Court.

"Some of your Indian things are gone," the vicar said to Lady Agatha.

"Shiva."

The vicar, startled, was compelled to ask her to repeat the remark.

"My aunt refers to the statuette of Shiva," Sidney said, "the Indian name for the lady with the arms." He raised his own two helplessly.

"She's the goddess of war and fecundity," Agatha pronounced while Elizabeth blushed.

"My, my," the vicar said, smiling. Sidney let out his breath in a rush. Not the kind of man to cut up stiff over an old woman, thank heavens.

Other guests streamed in. Sidney, who recognized few of the faces in the crowd, shook hands with several of the gentlemen and reeled at the comments issuing forth from them. To wit that he didn't look Indian, that he was rather fit for a man of his years, and had he recovered yet from the arduous trip to the Americas.

"And if that's not havey-cavey, I wish to know what is!" Sidney complained to Lytton when these guests were out of earshot. The earl, who had heard some of the rumors himself and enlarged upon them at some length, was on the verge of explanation when he found his tongue again failing him. Sensing the presence of Miss Manville by the glazed expression on his cousin's face, Sidney turned. Clarissa and Emily were fast approaching, Clarissa in a rose crepe that looked delightful to Sidney's observant eye. Her hair was brushed back in some semblance of order, nevertheless Sidney still perceived a few intransigent curls peeking out. Masking a smile, he shook hands with her and Emily and introduced both to his aunt.

The earl, although he welcomed Clarissa cordially, had eyes only for Emily. As well he might, Clarissa thought with justifiable pride. Emily looked ravishing in a blue satin that fit her to perfection. About her neck was strewn the one heirloom of her possession: pearls. She had debated long and hard on whether to wear the jewels until

Clarissa, grown weary by her indecision, had finally begged her to don them and have no further discussion on the matter.

"You both look beautiful," Sidney said to them.

"Too beautiful by half," Lytton agreed.

Emily and Clarissa smiled and then passed into the grand ballroom where the lights were already shimmering and the musicians played. No sooner had they entered than their hands were immediately solicited for the sets forming.

Upon occasion Sidney had given dinner parties for his closest cronies back in London, but these had been bachelor affairs and in no way prepared him for the current round of doings. However, he found as the receiving line broke up and he mingled with his guests that his fears were without foundation. The event was progressing famously.

Whatever the upheaval in his kitchen, Tibbs had not let it stand in the way of his artistry and the supper of asparagus soup, followed by a large striped bass sprinkled lavishly with truffles, a roast pheasant—the dish that had caused the mutiny—then the lobster patties, and as a note of concession to Lady Agatha several lamb cutlets before the baron of beef, were sufficient to cause one guest to beg Agatha's leave to steal her chef. The guests ate and drank their fill and danced until they were fagged to death.

Clarissa on the dance floor was not fagged to death even though she had been obliged to stand up with several gentlemen, none of whom possessed a modicum of skill with their nether limbs. She took the opportunity to rest her pair by begging off the last of her admirers and seeking solace in a wing chair where Sidney found her unattended some minutes later.

"Don't tell me you are tired, Clarissa?" he teased. "You are not dancing."

Clarissa smiled into his brimming eyes. "Your duties as a host make it impossible for you to have observed that I did stand up for every dance but this one."

Sidney swept his gaze around the crowded room. "But I have observed you on the floor," he protested, thinking that the rose color became her beautifully. "You started the evening on the arm of the vicar, proceeded in due fashion to the squire—Ames is his name is it not?—endured the frightful follies of that Tulip Petersham, and then finished up in the arms of a disappointed military man."

Clarissa laughed at this too accurate account.

"I hope the music meets with your approval," he said, quizzing her lightly. "I'd rather a waltz myself but was told by my cousin and a woman known for her discrimination that it was not yet danced by polite society."

"Certainly I am enjoying the music," Clarissa replied, smiling. "Every woman is fond of music. It is one of those things on which there is universal agreement such as a sunny day or a ride in the park."

"Are you especially fond of riding in the park?"

"That depends on whom I am with," Clarissa answered at once. "To be forced into a carriage with one I dislike goes against the grain."

"I was not thinking of abduction," Sidney said wryly. "That would be too fatiguing but merely a drive. The hills are so lovely, I'm sure you agree, and Cousin Edward's horses are in shocking need of exercise. Neither Elizabeth nor Aunt Agatha ride. Would you and Miss Manville be interested in accompanying Lytton and me sometime?"

"But you never ride with females."

The words were out of her mouth without a moment's pause, and Sidney hunched his shaking shoulders.

"I beg your pardon," she said. "But it is quite true. I

have heard it said many times that you detested the presence of ladies on horseback any time and any place!"

"Now that is not so," Sidney said with great aplomb. "It was possible that I did make such a remark in my younger and more . . . freakish . . . days. But I have since mended my ways, and I quite assure you I find female companionship most welcome on or off a horse." His smile was gentle as he glanced down. "Can it be that you are afraid of horses, Clarissa? You needn't be. These are quite tame creatures, and as I said, in need of exercise."

Clarissa's eyebrows arched in feigned hauteur. "Mr. Montcrieff, I assure you I am considered a notable horsewoman."

Sidney grinned at her boast. "I am glad to hear it. Would Tuesday be too soon to take your measure?"

"Not in the least," Clarissa said promptly.

While they had been chatting, Sidney had kept one eye out for the rest of his guests. It fell now on Lady Maria surreptitiously working her way forward through the crowds and headed in a rather zigzag fashion for the very spot on which he stood. And that niece of hers was just a step behind her billowing skirts!

Sidney turned hastily toward Clarissa. "We have talked about dancing, Clarissa, but never attempted the feat together. Shall we?"

A bit surprised at this offer since he had hitherto stood up with no one, Clarissa acquiesced, and he led her out onto the floor just as Lady Maria, panting and flushed, turned the corner. Clarissa's lips shook in amusement at the dowager's frustration.

"Do you run away from all dowagers?" she asked lightly.

"No. Just those with grandnieces they would foist on me." He shuddered delicately. Her eyes were the most penetrating shade of gray. "I hope you do not think me uncivil."

"I see no reason to quarrel with your manners," Clarissa answered. "At least now I am given the opportunity of dancing with you. Not many can claim as much."

"Is my reputation so lamentable?" he asked as they moved effortlessly to the music, much to the admiration of several in the room including Lady Agatha herself.

"Lamentable?" Clarissa frowned. "No, sir. Merely that I have heard it said you ventured to Almack's more to eat than to dance!"

"Having sampled the teas and cakes there and found them staler than anything a scullery maid would throw out, I assure you, Clarissa, it was not refreshment I was after."

But if not refreshments and dancing, then what? Clarissa wondered. Flirtations? She knew his reputation as a notorious flirt, and more than one would claim he was rake as well as flirt, but she had long ago learned not to listen to *on dits*. And he had behaved toward her and Emily with not the slightest show of impropriety.

"You dance well, Clarissa."

"As do you, sir."

"And you are surprised?" he asked ironically. Her quick laughter bubbled up again. "That's a pretty gown you are wearing," he said, changing the subject.

"Since you are well known as a man of mode, sir, I am in raptures that you even noticed," she said demurely.

"I should always notice what you wore, Clarissa."

The words were simply spoken but with such sincerity that the color stained Clarissa's cheeks. She felt a certain giddiness in her head, and why that should be she had no notion. In silence she finished the dance.

"You have done me a great favor," Sidney said, watching for Lady Maria as he led Clarissa back to her chair. "And I mean to repay it someday."

"Why not tonight?"

He held his surprise in check. "If I can . . ."

"It's a simple favor, I promise, and not so unpleasant. Dance with Emily."

"With Emily!" Sidney said, astonished. "I should think Larry has been taking care of that." He looked quickly in the direction of Miss Manville and found the earl, as promised, a few feet away. "Is he being too noticeable in his attentions?" he asked Clarissa.

"Oh, nothing ill-mannered," Clarissa said, "but he has danced with her three times so far."

"And to stand up again with her would be bad ton," Sidney agreed. "So he chooses to stand by all night and glare at anyone else who might wish to dance with her. Such a jackanapes." Sidney shook his head. "You are correct, Clarissa. Emily fully deserves to be rescued."

He left her in the hands of Squire Ames and strolled over toward his cousin and Emily.

"You are not dancing, Miss Manville," he chided softly.

Emily, who had started at the sound of his voice, reddened and felt her tongue tie itself into knots again.

"No, but . . ."

"Lytton, you shan't mind if I dance with Emily, I hope?"

The earl grinned. "I do mind, Sidney, but I'll allow you one dance and one dance only."

Miss Manville, highly incensed at this high-handed attitude of Lytton's, followed Sidney out onto the dance floor, two spots of color burning on each cheek. As though, she fumed inwardly, the earl had some prior claim to her, which he did not!

But Emily could not remain angry long, especially when she was twirling giddily in the arms of Sidney Montcrieff. All her displeasure and fatigue flew away. Her heart pounded madly in her chest, and her breath came in ragged bursts. To be so close to him. She felt intoxicated and her head spun.

"Are you feeling quite the thing, Miss Manville?" Sidney asked, alarmed at Emily's drastic change in complexion.

"Oh, yes," she nodded weakly. "I am just a little out of breath."

"No wonder. The air is so close here. Some fresh air will revive us both." She followed him meekly out the doors of the ballroom and onto the empty terrace. The fresh air did the trick, and the healthy color returned to her face.

Sidney, standing close by and observing these signs of health, congratulated himself on preventing a collapse. It would never do for a lady to swoon on the dance floor, especially with him partnering her!

"I hope Lytton does not worry about you," he said now with an indulgent smile. "He has been so attentive to you tonight."

"Too attentive," Emily said grimly.

Her note of displeasure rang sharply in Sidney's ear. "Do you dislike it?"

Emily hunched a shoulder. "Not dislike . . ."

"Perhaps annoying?"

"Perhaps. Especially since I do not return his feelings."

This revelation caught Sidney off guard. "I am sorry to hear that," he confessed. Whatever his thoughts of the match between Emily and Lytton, he had never foreseen that she might not want his cousin.

"Your feelings are engaged?" he probed delicately.

Emily nodded. She took several more deep breaths and turned to watch the full moon riding in the sky. It glowed radiant and golden. Perhaps it was just such a moon that inspired Juliet and Romeo in Verona years ago.

Her eyes darted over to Sidney standing on the terrace next to her with a bemused expression on his handsome face. Whatever the cause, the moon or the glasses of champagne she had consumed earlier, Emily's shyness deserted her. The time had come for boldness. Even Clarissa would have to agree. She took a step, closing the distance between herself and her idol.

Sidney, who had been mulling over Emily's remarks about Lytton, sensed the movement and looked over with a bewildered frown. In the moonlight Miss Manville's eyes glittered like sparks from a fire. Involuntarily he stepped back. Could it be? Good Jupiter. The chit had the look of a woman in love . . . and she was looking at him!

"Sidney!" Emily declared, recklessly reaching out a hand toward him.

Instinctively Sidney caught the hand in his. What a coil this was. "Miss Manville. . . ." He choked for words but got no further.

"Unhand that woman!"

The earl stood on the terrace looking like an outraged hawk.

"Larry!" Sidney stiffened. "I can explain . . ."

"An explanation is entirely unnecessary," Lytton replied. He fixed a withering eye on his cousin then on Miss Manville, who had never seen him look anything but cheerful, then he turned on his heel and stalked away.

10

The earl pushed his way through the crowded ballroom and into the hallway. Sidney, fighting the crush of guests eager to talk to him, caught up with his cousin near the library and dragged him inside.

"For we must have a chat, Larry."

"A chat? What need is there for a chat?" the earl asked, squaring his jaw. "What is that Chinese expression of Prinny's? One picture is worth a thousand words."

"We aren't Chinese, and I don't have a thousand words," Sidney said rudely and sank into a chair. "And any picture you may have drawn about Miss Manville and myself is in the gravest error." He looked his cousin warily in the eye. "Let's not stand at cross-points with each other, Larry. Whatever you may think, I am not—I repeat—I am not dangling after Emily."

"Oh no?" the earl returned, looking as rigid as his collar points. "Then why did you dance with her?"

"Because Clarissa requested it."

"Clarissa?"

"Yes, blast it. You were showing such an untidy interest in Miss Manville that few of the other guests even dared ask her to stand up with them for fear that you'd bite their heads off. Clarissa didn't want to see Emily on the side all night so she asked me to dance with her, no doubt thinking

105

that others might follow. This is supposed to be a ball, remember?"

"I suppose Clarissa instructed you to lure Emily out of the ballroom as well?"

Sidney tugged at his cravat. "I didn't lure her anywhere."

"Oh no? Quite the contrary, I suppose Miss Manville lured you away."

It was on the tip of Sidney's tongue to acknowledge the truth in this rather wild suggestion of the earl's, but he banished it at once. Lytton had been dealt a rude blow and no telling what he might do if informed that Emily—for reasons that defied earthly interpretation—was wholly infatuated with one Sidney Montcrieff.

Sidney crossed his arms on his chest and met the earl's contemptuous gaze.

"I did not lure her," he said somewhat lamely. "I simply brought her to the terrace for some fresh air. All that dancing had made her feel faint."

The earl surveyed a pinch of his best snuff between thumb and forefinger.

"You must think I'm a coxcomb, Sidney," he said coldly. "Do you really expect me to swallow such twaddle? Miss Manville needed a bit of fresh air? So you, ever the gallant, take her outside where she can revive and you can pursue your seduction in private."

"Seduction!" Sidney yearned to throttle his cousin, but he felt duty bound to forgive the earl his excesses. He was lovesick.

"I'd be a fool if I attempted to make love to a woman on a terrace," he said. "Believe me, Larry, I have no interest in Emily, and as for seduction she's hardly my type."

"I daresay she's not good enough for you," Lytton

inquired, snapping the lid of his snuffbox shut. "There is a flaw you perceive in her?"

"Flaw? For pity's sake." Sidney glared at his relation. "First you rip up at me for daring to converse with Emily and accuse me of attempted seduction, which I might add I had no intention of doing, then when I profess no interest in the lady, you fly into the brambles, demanding to know her imperfections." He gave the globe on his desk a savage whirl.

"Acquit me, Sidney," the earl said, rising from his chair. "You need witness no further outbursts of temper. And as for Miss Manville, I, too, profess no interest in her."

Sidney stepped quickly in front of his cousin. "Larry . . ."

The earl stared at his cousin's outstretched hand.

"We must get back to our guests, Sidney. Someone will notice we are missing."

Among those who did notice the absent hosts was Clarissa herself. But it was well after midnight at Claring before the full story of the incident on the terrace was revealed to her.

"Oh, Emily," she cried out at once. "You cannot have been so stupid!"

Emily screwed up her face in mortification. "I was that stupid, Clarissa," she admitted. "And bold. I vow not even Caro Lamb could have acted so *fast*. . . ." She shuddered and drew the folds of her dressing gown closer for warmth. But oddly it was not Sidney's look of stupefaction that she remembered as much as the earl's shock and pain.

"I can never face either of them again," she said wretchedly.

Clarissa patted her friend on the back. "It was not the wisest move you could have made," she said calmly. "Perhaps it was the champagne. You should have thought! Some men in the ton might enjoy being pursued but not such a creature as Sidney Montcrieff."

"It's too late, Clarissa. I quite disgraced myself. I can never face him again."

Clarissa pulled free of her friend. "But you must. It is imperative that you stay on civil terms with him. Besides, aren't you still in love with him?"

Emily blew her nose into a handkerchief. "I'm not sure," she admitted.

Her infatuation had dimmed considerably after the evening's proceedings. Sidney on the terrace had not acted like a gallant Romeo in the least, tearing after Lytton to explain and leaving her alone.

"Sidney has invited us to ride with him and Lytton on Tuesday," Clarissa said. "We shall have that day to make amends."

"Amends? But how? What should I do?" Emily asked anxiously.

Clarissa's tone was strict. "You shall say nothing of the incident. Such follies are best forgotten. Even Caro Lamb was forgiven much until she threw that odious scene over Byron. And he was much to blame for leading her on. What you must do is continue to act as you have in the past." She smoothed her friend's hair. "Sidney and Lytton are too much the gentlemen to bring it up. In time they may forget."

Emily left for her own bedchamber, a trifle teary-eyed. Clarissa watched her go, then dimmed the candles. This was certainly not what she had in mind when she had pressed Sidney to dance with Emily!

An hour later she was still wide awake in her bed. Her head throbbed lightly, and speech was well nigh impossible. Too many jelly tarts? Or merely the excitement of the ball? Or was it poor Emily's foolishness? Clarissa kicked off her quilt. Why, pray, was she so agitated tonight of all nights?

In answer to this question the face of Sidney Montcrieff popped into view. A nice face with a shapely mouth and handsome brow and eyes that twinkled good-humoredly. Clarissa turned over in her bed and beat her pillow with a fist. Absurd to be thinking of Montcrieff at such a time. Why did she now? Unless . . . unless she were falling in love with him herself!

Clarissa sat bolt upright in bed. In love with Montcrieff? Outrageous! She had only glimpsed him four times, and surely no one but a fool could fall in love so quickly. She would be a nitwit or worse! And there was poor Emily to consider. Clarissa fell weakly back against the pillow.

I am not going to fall in love with Sidney, she repeated to herself. But the memory of their dance together flitted into her mind. Stupid, stupid creature. She was not so silly as to imagine that every man who danced with her must be in love with her. If that be the case, all her flirts in London would have to love her, and despite their forms of address she knew that none of them did.

Such a muddle! But wasn't that what love was rumored to be? Muddle and madness and absurdity? Clarissa closed her eyes and finally fell into a long and exhausted sleep.

The next morning she woke to find a letter from Trixie waiting for her on the hallway tray.

"I am to be an aunt!" Clarissa announced to Emily when she came down to breakfast. Miss Manville appeared tired and frazzled, obviously having spent a restless night herself.

"A baby?" Emily asked, clapping her hands.

"Yes!" Clarissa said. For a moment she was filled with a longing for London. "Only I am here and the child—do you know my father already calls it a boy—shall be in London."

"But you cannot mean to remain here then," Emily said, swallowing her chocolate with a gulp. "Your father cannot wish you to stay away at such a time. And Trixie asks for you repeatedly, or so it says here. It would be heartless for your father to refuse."

"So would my marrying a monkey," Clarissa replied, "and if I return, Father shall have me betrothed to one in a trice."

"Perhaps your quarrel will be over by the time the babe arrives," Emily said, unconsciously echoing Carlton Claringdon.

"I hope so," Clarissa said fervently. She was suddenly quite eager to be away from Claring and from the alarming presence of Sidney Montcrieff.

Emily departed, and Clarissa, after a brief stroll in the gardens and an hour exclaiming over Giles's prize roses, sat down at her writing desk. She spread Trixie's letter out in front of her, frowned, and dipped her quill into the ink. If only Trixie were here to advise her. Clarissa felt in dire need of an experienced hand to guide her through the perilous waters ahead.

"Dear Trixie," she began, applying pen and ink to the paper. "I seem to have gotten myself into the strangest of fixes . . ."

Clarissa was not the only lady in the county with the urge to write to London relations. Lady Elizabeth had for several years corresponded faithfully with several members of her family, among them Mary Cranley.

Elizabeth, a woman of moderate intelligence, was good-hearted, devoted to her family, and sorely addicted to her medicines. Previous to meeting at Bengal Court she had always thought Sidney a frippery fellow, but now as she picked up a sharpened quill, she confided to Mary that he was not such a blackguard.

110

He had been charm enough to Agatha, had attracted the goodwill of the vicar himself, and had even consented to hold a ball at Bengal Court. Here Elizabeth embarked on a long description of the festivities the night before. Her pen hovered judiciously between the pheasant and the lobster patties, coming to a rest only because Lytton entered her sitting room.

"Have you seen Sidney, Elizabeth?" he asked.

"He's in the breakfast room," Elizabeth answered, wondering why the earl should look no how so early in the morning. "Are you feeling all right, Lytton?" Perhaps he was in need of a tonic.

"I am quite well," Lytton assured her. "Or shall be as soon as I reach London."

"Do you mean to return so quickly?" Elizabeth squeaked in surprise.

"There is nothing to keep me here any longer," Lytton said under his breath. He left the room while Elizabeth speculated on what might have passed between him and Sidney.

The temperature down in the breakfast room was several degrees cooler than it had been in Elizabeth's sitting room. This was due partly to the earl's icy announcement that he would be returning to London, and Sidney's equally icy announcement that the departure could be delayed until they had returned some of the invitations that they had already accepted.

"What invitations might those be?" Lytton asked irritably.

"The vicar's for one," Sidney said. "He has invited us over for tea this afternoon and our aunt has already agreed." The earl shot a quick look over at Agatha, placidly chewing on some toast.

"And we are riding with Miss Claringdon and Miss

Manville later in the week. You suggested the outing to me!"

"Oh, very well," Lytton said ungraciously. "But I have precious little interest in teas or horseback rides."

Lady Agatha, her temperament rendered difficult by too many lobster patties indulged in the previous night, waited until the earl had withdrawn before demanding to know from her remaining nephew why they were on the outs.

Sidney sighed. "What makes you think I am on the outs with Lytton?"

"I'm not blind yet!" Agatha declared as she pushed away the pots of jams. "What happened?"

"Nothing."

"I can stand a great deal, Sidney," Agatha said, "but I have no liking for civil wars in my family."

"There is no war," Sidney answered. "Merely a border clash."

"I just hope you are right."

But as the day progressed, Sidney feared that he might be in error. True, he did not regard the quarrel as substantial, but the earl certainly did. Lytton went to considerable pains to avoid meeting him in the halls and when forced to accompany the family to the tea at the vicarage, spent the better part of the hour playing with Felix. Not even the presence of Emily there with Clarissa could coax him into an appearance of goodwill.

Hitherto, Miss Manville had never failed to win a smile or a pleasant greeting from the earl, but on this occasion she felt a distinct snub.

"As though she had the scarlet fever," Sidney complained under his breath to Clarissa as they stood near the piano.

"One cannot blame him for being a trifle out of sorts,

on account. . . ." She paused, hesitating to speak so bluntly on so delicate a matter.

Sidney came to her rescue. "On account of what happened at the ball?" he asked.

"Yes," she said, glad to have the air cleared.

"I don't care if he is a trifle out of sorts. But if he continues to act the ugly, perhaps it would be better for him to get back to London. Otherwise the family will get the reputation of being more odiously starched up than we are."

Clarissa laughed, and Sidney was once again treated to the sight of her curls bouncing under a charming confection of white taffeta. With some difficulty he pulled himself away from his enjoyment and attended to the topic of Lytton.

"So he is thinking of returning to London."

"So far it is merely talk," Sidney explained. "You must not worry about him."

Clarissa smoothed her hands together. "I am not worried, exactly. It's just that one does hate to see one's friends in a quarrel. I know we have not known each other long, but I dislike seeing you two at odds."

"Kind of you," Sidney said, touched. "But let me assure you the matter is temporary. I don't like having him on the high ropes either."

"He is very young and so in love."

"It is his being in love, Clarissa, that has prevented me from taking advantage of his follies. Had he not been so in love, I would have wrung his neck like a chicken by now!"

Clarissa looked up, startled at the vehemence in Sidney's voice, then she caught the twinkle in his eye and laughed. He smiled down at her, thinking that he had rarely enjoyed a female's conversation more. Unfortunately for Sidney, Lady Agatha shared this same opinion of

Miss Claringdon, and the rest of the afternoon was given to Agatha questioning her on the latest *on dits* in London. He would have to bide his time, Sidney told himself impatiently as he watched her converse comfortably with his aunt.

11

Due to her foresight in being born a mere two years after her brother Carlton, Clarissa had been schooled at an early age in the ways of a saddle. However, she woke on a brilliant Tuesday morning with a definite case of the jitters. In no way could Carlton—excellent rider though he was—hold a candle to Sidney Montcrieff, and while Clarissa felt she might have forestood Sidney's scrutiny safely by herself, the event seemed complicated by Lytton and Emily both mooning about and suffering the pangs of unrequited love.

A difficult morning ahead, Clarissa thought as she stood in an autumn-colored riding suit with lace cravat. Mr. Quill loaded the picnic lunch in hampers and divided them equally between Lytton's mount and Sidney's. She mounted the bay that Sidney himself had selected for her, and after another moment to ascertain whether Miss Manville was comfortable on her chestnut, the four riders started down the path.

Clarissa's bay was gentle but spirited, and she rode easily, sure enough of herself to allow the horse its head.

A light wind blew against her cheeks, and she felt her spirits rise. It was glorious to be outdoors on such a day. The sun shone brilliantly, and only a few clouds dotted the sky.

It was evident to Clarissa after only a few minutes into the ride that the earl was determined to turn Emily a cold shoulder. The few attempts Miss Manville had ventured about the weather and the morning outing had been met with words of one syllable tersely emitted from a clenched jaw. After those attempts, Emily—and who could blame her!—had fallen into an awkward silence. Clarissa veered left on the pathway, determined to pray for the best.

The path they were riding on led into one of the loveliest regions of Claring. For the next mile or two Clarissa relaxed as the others in her group—even the taciturn earl—murmured surprise and praise. The Claring grounds were as beautiful as those sculpted for the Royal Dukes and had been designed by Capability Brown himself. Not only did the estate boast gardens of the finest order, but there were lakes as well: four in number. The lakes had been, and still were, Clarissa's favorite spot on the grounds. She gazed now at the long-necked swans floating haughtily by on the water.

"Very handsome, Clarissa," Sidney said as he drew his horse near.

"There's more."

On learning that stone bridges were popular in Japan, Sir Arthur had ordered several constructed at Claring. Although much too narrow to support horses, the bridges were wide enough to support a pair of strollers, and Trixie and Carlton had been especially fond of such walks during their courtship.

"It's all lovely," Sidney murmured as they headed toward the meadows and the rolling hills. He cocked his head at Clarissa. "If your father had the foresight to think

115

of all this, he must be quite a fellow. I have not had the pleasure of meeting him, though I have seen him I think at White's with that boon friend of his . . ."

"Lord Whalmsey," Clarissa said with a laugh. "They are bosom bows and have been since their youth. In fact, Lord Whalmsey is my godfather."

The ride continued with Clarissa keeping up a brisk pace and turning now and then to direct a look of inquiry at Emily. Emily shook her head sadly and stared moodily at Sidney Montcrieff. It would have been difficult for Clarissa to fault Emily for showing an interest in Montcrieff. Most ladies of the ton had been at one time or another fascinated by him, particularly those females with marriageable daughters under their matronly wings.

This May morning Sidney looked even more fascinating than usual in a burgundy-colored riding outfit that had the unmistakable stamp of Weston. Clarissa glimpsed a well-muscled forearm through the cut of the cloth. No wonder Emily was thoroughly smitten.

Clarissa had known dandies who looked the part of horsemen to perfection and yet fell short in the saddle. Lord Pedlow, for instance, had been heard to question aloud which side of the beast one was supposed to mount. But she was not surprised to observe Sidney had an excellent seat and would not put her to the blush.

Sidney, for his part, was coming to much the same favorable conclusion about Clarissa during their first hour. Not one of the types to turn missish, quaking at the merest feel of an animal. But then he doubted whether she would turn missish at anything. He thoroughly approved, too, of her no-nonsense manner with the bay, stroking it calmly until it had adjusted to her.

The exercise had brought spots of color to her face, and her hair was blown loose from the fetching hat she wore, trailing after her in the wind. The effect to Sidney was darling.

"You ride well," he said, complimenting her.

Clarissa smiled into his sparkling eyes. "And you are surprised, confess?"

"Not at all, Miss Claringdon," he protested. "You warned me at the outset that you were an expert horse-woman. And a gentleman always believes a lady's word."

Clarissa looked away quickly. Could he be carrying on a flirtation with her under Emily's nose? And if so, she would put an end to it at once. Smiling still, she touched her heels lightly to the flanks of the bay, and it sprang forward obediently into a canter. She would keep distance between herself and Sidney. Alas, this proved impossible. Sidney, though disinclined to boast, was one of the top sawyers in the saddle, and he soon closed the gap.

Emily watched these maneuvers with a jaundiced eye. That Sidney preferred Clarissa to her would have been obvious even to a henwit, which she hoped she was not! Curiously she felt no overt despair over this situation. Since that night on the terrace her feelings for Sidney had suffered a rude buffeting. She glanced at the earl now, observing again his icy courtesy and rigid spine. Her heart sank. What would it take for Lytton to treat her like a friend again? She shook her head, refusing to speculate on the matter.

A half hour later Clarissa came to a stop. Sidney, who had been keeping an easy pace with her, reined in as well.

"Shall we stop here?" he asked.

She nodded. "The meadow is so lovely I thought we could picnic. There is a stream further up ahead where the horses can drink."

"Then it seems the very place to rest," Sidney remarked. He dismounted and held up his hand to assist her. Her skin tingled lightly at his touch.

Five minutes later the hampers were open. The horses were contentedly upstream drinking their fill. Mr. Quill's excellent lunch was inspected, approved of, and eaten with relish. Lytton lovesick or not suffered no symptomatic loss of appetite, devouring a half dozen chicken drumsticks and a goodly number of berry muffins.

"This is a lovely spot," Sidney said to Clarissa as he gnawed on a drumstick.

"Yes," Clarissa acknowledged. "The stream is filled with fish. Carlton is fond of the sport."

"And you?"

"Alas, I am no angler, sir."

"But you have a way with horses," he pointed out. "Do you hunt as well?"

"No." Clarissa screwed her face up and laughed. "It's cowardly to own to such a weakness, but I fall into a pelter over the fox, if you can believe such a thing. My father was quite disgraced." She reached into the hamper and pulled out four apples.

"I have not forgotten the horses. They did most of the work and must be rewarded. Will your groom object?"

"Not in the least," Sidney answered. "I would join you, but I am determined to beat Larry to the last chicken leg."

Laughing, Clarissa wandered over toward the horses. The animals needed no coaxing to gently nibble at the apples in her palms. Sidney sat up watching her. She was one of the most unique women he had ever come across. Not just in the ordinary style of the Beauties he had met before. Something different about this one. Unconsciously he searched for a reason behind this difference. Her intelligence was first-rate, to be sure, but he had known other keen-witted women before. There was her good humor and her undeniable beauty as well as her honesty. He chewed on the chicken leg and felt a pang. Thanks to Mr. Braun, Bengal Court was in perfect order, and there was

118

no further need to linger in Cheltenham. Sidney wiped his hands on a handkerchief. Then why was he so reluctant to go?

Good God, he thought to himself suddenly, *can I be falling in love?* He stared at a blade of grass for enlightenment. The very thought of love made his knees quake. Surely he could not be so afflicted! Love and marriage had no part in his life. Very bothersome he'd find it to have a wife in his home at all hours of the day, and yet when he pictured Clarissa in his home and himself tied to her apron strings—did she even wear an apron?—the picture did not dismay. He closed his eyes to the sun, musing over the possibilities in front of him. From the distance he heard his name called. Lytton, blast him, was the culprit. He opened one eye.

"Sidney! Clarissa!" the earl was shouting. "It's Emily! I think she's ill!"

Emily had been feeling ill for most of the morning. She had left for Claring without partaking of a single bite of nourishment, protesting that she was too excited to even think of eating. Her giddiness did not subside when she was mounted on her horse, since she was a poor horsewoman and clung to the reins with unmitigated terror.

Nor had the picnic lunch brought any relief to her distress, the rays of the sun combining with the food consumed to make her feel distinctly unwell. Now fully conscious of the earl on one side of her shouting her name, she collapsed on the grass. Lytton caught her slender form against his chest, and he grew frightened at the sight of her flushed cheeks.

"Sidney! Clarissa!"

Clarissa dashed up from the stream and took in Emily's condition at once. "Too much sun," she deduced. "Lord Lytton, if you would bring her into the shade."

The earl complied with Clarissa's order, asking, "Can she die of such a thing?"

"No, certainly not," Clarissa soothed.

"What shall we do?" Sidney asked, his voice having an immediate calming effect on Clarissa.

"Water," she said, grateful for his matter-of-factness. "Cold compresses. It is lucky that we are so close to the stream. If you would wet these handkerchiefs," Clarissa said, passing over her cloth and Emily's. She untied Emily's bonnet and fanned her face. Emily's lids fluttered weakly.

"Clarissa?"

"I am here, my dear," Clarissa answered. "We shall have you right very soon."

"I am such a nuisance."

"Don't scold yourself," Clarissa said, laying a hand on her friend's forehead and growing dismayed at the heat that registered. Sidney, meeting her eyes, held out the damp cloths, and she applied them quickly to Emily's face.

"Should one of us ride back to Claring House and fetch a carriage?" he asked, quietly observing her skill.

"No, I think we'd best remove her on horseback."

"But she is in no condition to ride," the earl declared hotly. The crisis had brought about a full collapse to his feigned indifference to Miss Manville.

"If Emily rode with one of you holding her," Clarissa said, "I think she can reach Claring. We would be able to get her to the house sooner."

"I shall take her up with me," Lytton said at once.

"Good. Now I think the cloths can be wet again, and then perhaps she can be coaxed into drinking a little of the remaining lemonade."

Although the lemonade cooled Emily's parched throat, her stomach felt queasy, and she lurched alarmingly when

Lytton helped her to her feet. Frightened and repentant, he swung her up into his arms, astonished to find that she weighed next to nothing. With Sidney's help he held her on the saddle.

"We shall get you home quickly, my dear," he murmured into Emily's ear.

Clarissa and Sidney mounted quickly. Sidney took a moment to reassure her. "She shall be all right."

Clarissa's eyes dimmed, but her voice was strong and clear. "Yes, I think so. If only she were indoors."

"She shall be soon," he promised, touching her lightly on the hands.

For three members of the party the journey to Claring house seemed to take an eternity. As for the fourth, she was in and out of consciousness, waking now and then to find herself pressed deeply into the bosom of the earl, who attempted to shield her from the jolts.

"You shall be fine," he muttered. "You shall be fine, my love."

Emily, unused to being so addressed, closed her eyes to the scorching sun and nestled deeper into the folds of Lytton's coat.

Not a moment too soon the entourage reached Claring House. Mrs. Quill looked at her mistress in alarm. "Miss Clarissa?"

"Emily has had too much sun," Clarissa said, sliding off her horse quickly. "Lord Lytton, if you would carry her into the morning room." She led the way into the house and toward the room still shaded from the afternoon sun. Lytton carefully relinquished his precious burden on the sofa.

"We shall need some cool water," Clarissa ordered as Mrs. Quill bustled about.

"Yes, miss. Right away."

"Will she be all right, Clarissa?" Lytton asked.

"I believe so," Clarissa answered. "Would you or Sidney fetch that fan from my reticule? That should help to set her right."

Within the half hour the cool room, the fan dutifully plied by the energetic earl, and the presence of her friends combined to make Emily recovered enough to begin a stream of heartfelt apologies.

"For I have spoiled our picnic," she said distractedly. "Too stupid not to have eaten breakfast."

"No one thinks you did it on purpose," Clarissa answered. "And we can always go on another picnic."

"I must get up," Emily protested. "I am not such a weak kitten." So saying, she tried to rise but was gently pushed back by Clarissa.

"You shall remain here for the night."

"I shall be too much trouble, Clarissa. Anyone would think you were running an *inn!*"

"Better an inn than a hospital," Clarissa insisted. She felt Emily's forehead. Much cooler, thank heaven.

"But Mrs. Boatwright is expecting me for dinner," Emily said suddenly, recalling this previous engagement. "I must tell her."

"I shall send John with a message."

"There shall be no need for John," Lytton said promptly. "I shall be happy to tell Mrs. Boatwright myself and carry your careful apologies."

"That's kind of you, my lord," Emily said shyly.

"Larry," he replied, gazing deeply into her eyes.

Sidney, seeing that the cold shoulder had melted from the sunstroke, spoke up quietly. "I think Miss Manville could do with some rest."

"Yes, so do I," Clarissa agreed. She withdrew with Sidney to the hall while Lytton showed no sign of hearing them.

"Will you send for a doctor?" Sidney asked.

"I don't think so. I am quite sure that she is all right."

"A relief to everyone. You acted nobly," he said, shuddering to think how other women of his acquaintance would have acted in the crisis. Certainly it would have been vapors or hysteria for Lady Vye. He turned, hearing the earl's footsteps. "Ah, Lytton. Have you sufficient wit to ride to the vicar?"

Lytton turned dreamy eyes to his cousin. "What vicar?"

Clarissa laughed with some relief while Sidney sighed and took hold of his cousin by the arm. "Mr. Boatwright, cousin. You were to relay Miss Manville's regrets. You cannot have forgotten so quickly!"

"Oh, no. I shall go there immediately."

Clarissa, smiling at this exchange, shook hands with the two men and gave them her thanks. "For if you were not with me, I would not have known how to bring her back," she said.

Sidney held her hand and pressed it strongly. "Too modest, Clarissa, and too kind to speak of us. If anyone of us were the hero of this piece of drama, it's you." He kissed her hand lightly. Once again Clarissa felt a slight shock pass through her body, causing a dizzy sensation in her head. For a few minutes after the men had departed she remained in the hallway.

Then, shaking her head and adjuring herself not to behave like a mooncalf, she went back to the morning room. Emily lay on the couch wearing a smile identical to that last seen on the earl's face.

"Is your head better?" Clarissa inquired gently.

Emily's head swung round at the sound of her friend's voice. "Oh, yes, Clarissa," she said, bestowing a radiant smile on her. "I can't think what I would have done without you." She paused and clasped her friend's hand. "Clarissa, do you not think him the most heroic of men?"

123

"Sidney? To be sure. We have established that long ago."

"No." Emily shook her head impatiently. "I am not talking about Sidney but of his cousin. Larry."

"Larry, is it to be?" Clarissa asked, smiling. "But how is it you are on such good terms with the earl when you are in love with Sidney?"

"But I'm not . . . I mean . . ." Emily said, looking startled then guilty, until she noticed the amusement in Clarissa's eyes. "You are roasting me. I own I deserve it. Have you ever known a more volatile creature?"

"I daresay love afflicts some that way."

"But to think I could imagine myself in love with Sidney Montcrieff. It was the merest of schoolgirl crushes, I do assure you. Today when the earl caught me up in his arms and held me as we rode here . . ."

Clarissa patted her hand. "Yes," she agreed. "Most romantic."

"Not only romantic, Clarissa, but kind and thoughtful. Not that Sidney was not kindness itself, but when I look at Larry, it vexes me to think I never noticed him much before."

"I take it your tendre for Sidney is at an end?"

"Oh, yes. In fact I can't think how anyone could notice him when Lytton is close by."

Clarissa might have enlightened her on that score but she chose to hold her tongue. "Do you think you should like to stay here or shall we go upstairs to your room?"

"I shall stay here," Emily said, "if you don't mind."

"Not in the least. I shall just change and have a little rest myself."

Clarissa mounted the stairs and entered her bedroom. After changing her riding habit, she picked up a hairbrush, but instead of brushing her hair she began to wonder idly what Sidney was up to.

12

Lady Maria Cunningham was, in the immortal words of the Earl of Lytton, an even bigger tartar than his grandaunt, and when her invitation to a dinner party arrived at Bengal Court a mere week after Sidney's own party, both Montcrieff cousins tried to cry off from the engagement.

"There is still much work to be done about the estates," Sidney explained to his aunt, whose skeptical gaze succeeded once again in making him feel like a scruffy schoolboy with smudgy fingers.

"Don't be absurd," Agatha replied with just the right touch of asperity in her voice. "You have been riding that poor gray of yours to death. Besides, you have hired that man, Braun, haven't you? You can't really like sheep that much or can you? And it shan't be so bad," she cackled. "I have it on very good authority that Miss Manville and Miss Claringdon have been invited to the party too."

This information caused a reversal in the opinions of both Lord Lytton and Sidney, and the latter cast a thoughtful, measuring look at his aunt holding court in her favorite Windsor chair.

"How do you know that?" he asked curiously.

"Because," Lady Agatha replied tartly, "I told Maria that if she did wish to have you present—and she does because she has a ridiculous notion about you and that bran-faced niece of hers. And you needn't poker up, sir, because I have a mind that such a match would be fatal for the two of you, so you may rest assured that I for one won't be pinching at you to marry the girl. . . ." Having momentarily lost her train of thought, she stamped her cane on the rug and demanded grumpily to know what she had been attempting to say.

"It had something to do with Miss Claringdon's and Miss Manville's presence at Lady Maria's party," Lytton supplied helpfully with a grin.

"So it was," Lady Agatha nodded in satisfaction. "I told Lady Maria that if she wanted you both there at her party, which will undoubtedly be the dullest one in Christendom, for she has never had the knack of giving parties, not being the type to possess any sense of surprise such as Lady Sefton, who I vow once persuaded a highwayman to grace her occasion and the stir that caused, I am sure I needn't tell you. As I was saying, I told Lady Maria that she had best invite those two ladies. She didn't like it above half, of course. But I insisted."

It was the prospect of seeing Clarissa again that induced Sidney to attend Lady Maria's party, for despite his devotion to his aunt, he did not wish to suffer alone through an evening of tedium.

The house in which Lady Maria had decided to take up residence was a grand building in the center of Cheltenham and was ablaze in lights and color as the Montcrieff party arrived. It had, Lady Agatha confided as their carriage pulled to a stop in front of it, been rented out to a Royal Duke several years ago, but Lady Maria, appearing oblivious to this fact, apologized for the cramped rooms, leading Lady Agatha to demand if she thought her guests were elephants instead of people.

Elizabeth, who was standing next to Lytton and Sidney,

126

gave a sigh of distress. "It shall be a difficult night," she predicted.

Sidney pressed her hand reassuringly. "I wouldn't worry about our aunt."

Had Sidney been of a more nervous disposition, he would have undoubtedly bolted straight away as his hostess, replete in a shimmering apple blossom sarsnet, a glittering row of diamonds about her throat, and a turban that seemed on the verge of losing the feathers that adorned it, greeted him with outstretched arms.

"My dear Mr. Montcrieff," she said, clinging to his hand. "It is too kind of you to grace this silly party—"

"The pleasure is mine, Lady Maria," he said adroitly as he attempted to snatch his hand out of Lady Maria's iron grip, sending his aunt a supplicating look.

"Where is that silly niece of yours, Maria?" Lady Agatha asked, taking command of the situation.

Lady Maria's smile froze on her face, thus allowing Sidney to slip his hand out of her grasp. With icy courtesy Lady Maria informed her old friend that her niece, like the good girl she had been brought up to be, was busy mingling with their other guests, and that she knew dear Agatha to be jesting by calling her silly.

"For I am certain she is no such thing," she continued with some emotion. "I am not saying that she is a bluestocking, mind you. But she is no featherbrain. She takes after my side of the family."

"I had noticed that," Agatha agreed sweetly. However, Lady Maria was not deceived by the tone, and the mask of civility slipped momentarily from her face. A second later she had composed herself and, after throwing another dagger look at her old friend, turned to address herself once more to Sidney, whose attention had been wandering away from her.

"Diaphne will be playing the harp for us later this

evening," she informed him. "She is quite an accomplished harpist."

"Another trait from your side of the family?" Sidney inquired.

"Well, no," Lady Maria acknowledged since all her relations were known to be tone deaf. "That comes from her father's side of the family. She has talent on both branches of her family tree."

Lady Maria was forestalled from an excursion up her family tree by Lady Agatha who, fearing that her friend would summon the unlucky Diaphne over to have her teeth examined by Sidney, pronounced herself thirsty. With some relief her nephews sped off to the refreshment room to procure her and Elizabeth glasses of lemonade.

She took advantage of their absence to take her friend immediately to task over these attempts to attach Sidney to her niece.

"It is all to no avail," she warned, paying no heed to the coughs and sighs of distress issuing from Elizabeth. "It's not that she ain't pretty because I daresay she is passably good-looking and might do better if someone would do something about her freckles. And she would do better undoubtedly if you didn't insist on throwing her at Sidney. You ought to be fixing her with a young man more in tune to her age."

"It seems to me," Lady Maria answered with a sniff, "that your nephew acts in a more than civil way toward Diaphne. Perhaps you are not privy to his nearest and dearest wishes."

"Lord, Maria, do you want him to act the ugly toward her?" Agatha demanded, throwing up her hands in disgust. She soon abandoned all attempt at civility and warned her friend in what Elizabeth later characterized as the bluntest speech she had ever heard not to push the child into a disastrous marriage, and then stalked away, intercepting both of her nephews with the lemonade.

"What did you do with the body?" Sidney inquired, reading the glint that flashed from his aunt's eyes.

Agatha laughed shortly. "No body, not yet at any rate. But I shall never cease to marvel that Maria lived to such a ripe age without having been strangled."

Lady Agatha had most of the evening to ponder this question. Her nephews, after seeing her and Elizabeth comfortably settled with a group of old friends in one corner of the room, discovered that Emily and Clarissa were being greeted by their hostess in the entrance hall and moved across to greet them.

Lady Maria was still bristling over her war of words with Lady Agatha and stiffened when she saw them approach. She could not have been blamed for inwardly ruing the day she had succumbed to Agatha's demands and included Miss Claringdon in the festivities. One had only to compare Clarissa's tall figure, garbed this evening in a delicate blue water silk, and her ease and friendly manners with that of Diaphne, who was lamentably hidden in a dress of ruffles and bows and who had a tendency to squeak whenever a stranger addressed her.

Clarissa had been astonished at receiving Lady Maria's invitation, but naively assuming the invitation a cordial one, she greeted her hostess now with such a sunny smile that Lady Maria could not harbor any ill wishes against her for long.

Emily, looking radiant in the yellow satin gown Clarissa had given her, passed immediately into the earl's impatient hands, and Clarissa found herself with Sidney at her side as they entered the long drawing room. It was amazing to her that of all the men she had known back in London, he alone seemed perfectly at ease in evening dress.

"I see that Emily has recovered sufficiently from her bout with the sun," Sidney said as he led her toward a vacant chair.

"Oh, yes," Clarissa nodded. "She is fully recovered, to my great relief."

"But perhaps not enough to risk another turn on a horse?" Sidney asked as a high-bosomed matron plopped herself on the seat before he had a chance to install Clarissa.

"I fear Emily is not a notable horsewoman," Clarissa agreed. "But she does have other talents."

Sidney lifted an eyebrow. "It seems this evening that the room is filled with talented ladies," he complained and, seeing her look of puzzlement explained, added, "Lady Maria's niece."

Clarissa bit back a gurgle of laughter. "Lady Maria does seem rather taken with you," she acknowledged. "And you needn't bother about a chair since I'd rather stand."

"Well, I'm glad of that," Sidney said since the chairs were all occupied. He smiled down at Clarissa. "Do you know that if Lady Maria were twenty years younger and looked at me with that peculiar glint in her eye I would take to the hills?"

This sparked another gurgle of laughter from Clarissa that so enchanted Sidney that he was unaware that one of Lady Maria's footmen was standing in front of him with a request from his mistress. Alerted by his companion to the servant's presence, he excused himself and strolled back to Lady Maria, who greeted him with another lavish display of affection and informed him that he had been singled out with the honor of escorting her niece in to dinner. Since escape was impossible, he proffered his arm to Diaphne, hoping that the opportunity to speak further with Clarissa would avail itself later in the evening.

Lady Maria, obviously subscribing to the belief that the

way to a man's heart was through his stomach, a theory attested to by the girth of her own spouse, had given her chef free rein. Lobster patties and quail eggs were only two of the delicacies that her guests sampled during the course of the dinner. It was Sidney's lot to be seated between his hostess and her niece and was now and then interrupted from his dinner by the flow of chatter from his hostess. However, Lady Maria needed only a nod or two of encouragement during a conversation, and his role in the dialogue was modest. For his other partner, she was too tonguetied to venture more than a word or two his way.

While the gentlemen lingered over their port, the ladies withdrew to the blue drawing room, where Clarissa and the other ladies were forced to listen to Diaphne at the harp. The young lady played well and her voice was pleasant, but none of this could drown out the sounds of altercation from one corner of the room where Lady Maria and Lady Agatha were having at each other.

Elizabeth, growing more and more distressed, murmured, "Oh, dear. Oh, dear."

Emily nudged Clarissa with an elbow and inquired what was going on.

Clarissa shrugged. "I think Lady Agatha is giving Lady Maria some advice."

Lady Agatha was, of course, doing more than advising. She was scorchingly reminding her friend that meddling had never been one of her strong suits and that she ought to stop while the stopping was good. To which Lady Maria, wholly forgetting her other guests, responded that she would do what she wanted to.

"And I suppose you want to make a curst cake of yourself," Agatha said, now dropping her voice to a whisper, thus frustrating the listening majority in the room.

"A cake," Maria squeaked. "Who are you calling a cake?"

"You," Agatha returned bluntly. "Maria, Sidney's not interested in your niece."

"Perhaps he will be when he learns she will inherit my fortune."

Agatha stopped, and her jaw snapped shut. "If you think you can bamboozle me into believing that! And if you think a fortune will entice Sidney, you're wrong there. My nephew is no fortune hunter. But I suppose if you spread that story around, the fortune hunters will be here . . ."

How long the advice and the harp playing would have lasted was left up in the air, for the men soon returned. Lady Maria brusquely abandoned her tug of wills with Lady Agatha, applauded her niece's talent at the instrument, and led her guests into the ballroom where an orchestra had been hired for dancing.

The crowd surged toward the door, carrying Clarissa and Emily along with them. They had just reached their chairs when Emily was whisked away by the devoted Lytton, and Clarissa found herself with Sidney demanding her hand for the first dance.

"Demand is it, sir?" she asked with some surprise.

"Yes," he answered with a smile on his lips. "I have done enough for one night, I believe. I've done the pretty to my aunt's great friend, endured what passes for conversation at dinner, and now I should be allowed to please myself. Can you deny me that, Miss Claringdon?"

"After such a statement how could any woman deny you," Clarissa answered and followed him into the set now forming.

After five Seasons in London Clarissa had danced with hundreds of gentlemen but rarely had she felt such instant harmony with a partner. She searched for some clue behind this occurrence but could find nothing that would allude to his skill on a dance floor. If anything, his height would have warned of awkwardness, but for a tall gentleman he was light on his feet.

The same could not be said for her second partner that evening, a nephew of the vicar and his wife who was staying at the vicarage for a week. Young Boatwright was not the worst partner Clarissa had ever been paired with but he was close to it. It was almost enough to make a woman foreswear dancing altogether.

Fortunately, since she did enjoy dancing, she was not forced to abandon it entirely as the Earl of Lytton proved to be an able partner. He had been sent, he confided with a grin, by his cousin to rescue her. Lytton was followed in turn by Sidney again, who caused a certain sensation in the dowager circles as he singled out Miss Claringdon for the second dance within the first hour.

"I am obliged to you for sending Lytton to rescue me," she said during the set.

"What else could I do?" Sidney asked, laughing. "In his eagerness to apply for your hand, young Boatwright came close to ruining one of my best pairs of shoes and only your quick-wittedness in leading him out prevented me from a thundering scold from my valet."

Clarissa laughed. "I had no idea you placed shoes at such a priority, sir."

He smiled. "It's obvious you are not acquainted with Mr. Hoby the bootmaker."

"But I am. My brother and father go to him."

"As do I," Sidney explained. "And it is Hoby's belief that shoes make the distance between triumph and defeat on the battlefield. The quelling of Napoleon in large part was due, according to Hoby, to the superiority of English boots over French."

Clarissa, who had heard other theories espoused for the routing of Napoleon but never boots, promptly declared that theory as good as any offered by a politician.

Leaving aside the thorny problems of politics and boots, Sidney inquired if the brief scare with Emily on the day of the picnic had changed Clarissa's interest in riding.

"Not at all," Clarissa answered quickly. "It would take more than a bout with the sun to cure me of it."

"I'm glad to hear it," Sidney said with a smile, "for we had only begun to gather each other's measure as riders when the unfortunate incident with Miss Manville occurred. Would you chance another ride?"

"Surely, whenever you wish."

"Tomorrow," he said promptly.

She was just agreeing to it and setting the hour when he would call at Claring when the dance came to an end. He surprised her then by asking for the next dance as well. Clarissa looked up in some doubt. Convention even in Cheltenham indicated that a woman should not stand up with the same gentleman more than three times in an evening, and what of two dances one after the other?

"It is kind of you to ask," she said now as he awaited her reply, "but don't you think you should dance with Diaphne? I know how insistent her aunt has been, but she cannot be blamed for that."

"My dear Miss Claringdon, I fully realize that Diaphne is not to be blamed for her unfortunate aunt, but neither should I be called upon to bear that burden. Besides, the last time I had occasion to follow your advice with regard to my choice in partners, it led to the most improbable of scenes, if you do recall."

Unable to resist a laugh at that, Clarissa accepted. But she was aware that the tongues would be wagging in the room. And wag they did until Lady Agatha adjured them all to stop acting like geese, saying that she, for one, fully approved of her nephew standing up for the third time with as charming a lady as Miss Clarissa Claringdon.

134

13

In all the years Polly had worked for Clarissa she had never known her mistress to behave like a flibbertigibbet. But now as she watched her make a shambles out of what had been a perfectly good wardrobe, hastily donning one riding habit after another, she was rapidly revising this opinion.

"Good heavens, Miss Clarissa," she scolded as a burgundy habit was flung down on the bed in favor of an azure blue outfit. "Are you all about in your head?"

"No," Clarissa said with a laugh, "but I don't seem to be able to make up my mind today." She turned as she buttoned up the last of the silver buttons on the blue outfit and stared at her reflection in the mirror. "What do you think looks best on me, Polly?"

Polly, coolly picking up the discarded garments, answered tartly that she had yet to see her mistress look bad in any of the garments in her wardrobe, but she did think the scarlet red riding outfit the most alluring.

"But I can't wear that, Polly," Clarissa said, rejecting this advice. "He'll think me a hussy."

"Miss Clarissa!" Polly said, much shocked. "I don't think Mr. Montcrieff will think any such thing."

"I hope not," Clarissa said fervently. "Oh, what am I to wear? He's coming at eleven." A new fear struck her. "What time is it now?"

"I believe it was approaching the ten o'clock hour when I mounted the stairs, Miss Clarissa," Polly answered.

Acute distress etched itself on Clarissa's face. "It can't be. That leaves me with just an hour to decide among these horrid outfits." So saying, she tore off the blue riding habit.

The urgency of the situation dictated a quick decision and, ruthlessly thrusting aside the scarlet habit that Polly favored, she settled on her burgundy habit with the plumed, fawn-colored hat. She sat down in front of her mirror with her hairbrush, attempting to bring order to her hair.

This attempt, however, was only a partial success, as she struggled with the brush. She thought vainly of changing her lot in life with those females blessed with perfectly straight and manageable hair who were wont to yearn after curls.

Despite these problems, when Sidney finally arrived at Claring, Clarissa was able to greet him with perfect composure.

"I have Sinbad for you today," he said as they stepped out of the house.

"Sinbad?" She looked astonished.

"The name of the horse," he chuckled. "You are not to worry. My groom tells me that she had been named at birth before they discovered that he was a she. It was too late then to repair the damage." He led her toward the mare, predicting that Clarissa would find her a good ride.

The morning was sunny with just a few clouds above, and neither rider had any qualms in allowing the horses their heads. Clarissa relaxed in the saddle, the activity of the ride having done much to disperse her bout of butterflies. Besides, she told herself, this was too beautiful a day to spend being nervous, and she darted a quick look at her companion.

As though he had read her mind, Sidney turned and, with a quizzical expression on his face, demanded to know what she was thinking.

"For you have such an expression on your face," he said, "I am sure I must be in your black books. But I assure you I have no idea what crime I have committed."

She chuckled. "You have committed no crime to my knowledge, unless you feel compelled now to confess to some wrongdoing."

He smiled easily across at her. "That would be intriguing. Now what should I confess to? Murder? That would be most foul as our good Mr. Shakespeare was wont to say. Theft? Surely nothing so paltry would tempt me. I know!" He snapped his fingers. "I'd be a highwayman."

He looked so pleased with himself that Clarissa gave another laugh.

"That would be the perfect crime," he said. "I'd have new victims every day. Money, jewels, fresh air. Exactly the sort of thing that would appeal to me. And don't forget those females swooning at the sight of me."

"Such an activity certainly has its appeal," Clarissa agreed drily. "But you are forgetting the Runners. They shall be after you."

"That is a quelling thought. But in my lifetime I have never met a Runner who could be found when one most had need of him, so perhaps that difficulty needn't arise. And now that I have confessed to my secret ambition, it is your turn. Come now," he said as she shot him a questioning look. "You must harbor some secret. Not murder I should think."

"No," she agreed. "But I have always thought the life of a spy would be exciting."

"And so it would," he agreed. "A good choice. Cloak and dagger stuff. But a dangerous career. Are you certain you have the talent for dissembling that the position would require?"

Clarissa affected a pretentious air. "My dear Mr. Montcrieff, you may not be aware of it but I have reached a high level of expertise in amateur theatricals."

"Have you indeed," he said, much diverted. "I'm intrigued to hear it, and I am glad we have agreed on our respective careers for this morning—a highwayman and a spy out for a mere summer ride."

Laughing, Clarissa followed him up one of the lanes in the Claring estate. She had ridden on it herself many times with her brother. Eventually they found themselves at one of the finest trout streams in the kingdom. They paused to watch the fish jump.

"Do you ever fish with your brother, Miss Claringdon?" he inquired.

"When I was a girl I did."

"Not of late?"

She shook her head, explaining, "Worms."

The smile rekindled on his face. "But surely such a noted spy as you, Miss Claringdon, would not be afraid of worms."

"Espionage is one thing," Clarissa answered, "worms another."

This succeeded again in making Sidney laugh. Dismounting together, they walked over the stream on the stepping stones. Once or twice because of the slickness of the stones Clarissa nearly slipped, and Sidney held out his hand for her to grasp. She was almost sorry when the stream had been crossed and then recrossed and she was forced to let go of his hand.

They were still wandering companionably about the edge of the stream when she noticed him casting a worried eye up at the sky. Puzzled, she looked up as well and was startled to find dark and billowing clouds where once there had been none.

"A storm is brewing," he informed Clarissa. "I suggest we head back."

Quickly they returned to the horses, but Sinbad, sensing the imminent danger, bolted before Clarissa had a chance to mount her. Sidney knew the horse would undoubtedly find its way back to Bengal Court. He helped Clarissa into the saddle of his own horse and swung himself up behind her. Together they headed back toward Claring.

Despite their haste, it was not possible to outrun Mother Nature and scarcely a hundred yards had been traversed before the first ominous drops fell.

"It shall get wetter before long," Sidney said in her ear with his arms clasped tightly around her waist.

Clarissa nodded to show she had heard, but she felt no fear, not with him close at hand.

Sidney's prognostication proved correct, for when they were halfway to Claring the storm broke. The skies opened, dropping a deluge of rain onto the two figures huddled together. Lightning flickered dangerously across the afternoon sky, and even the faithful mount whinnied in an effort to escape the storm.

The wind blew off Clarissa's riding hat, and the water by this time had made a soggy mess of her habit and hair, but to Sidney, holding her close and conscious of her heart beating intently against his, she looked perfect. Any other woman, he was fully convinced, would be in hysteria by now. But, he reminded himself again, she was no ordinary woman.

Pressed closely together they rode, both acutely conscious of the other. Sidney was soaked to the skin, and Clarissa was in as great a difficulty. But the storm was so dangerous that she had no occasion to worry about her modesty.

Sidney, well aware of her in his arms, controlled his urge to bring her even closer to him. This was not the moment, he told himself sternly, to make a declaration to a lady. Forcing his mind and attention back to the task ahead, he saw in the distance the welcome sight of Claring House.

"The worst seems over," he said, his breath causing her to react slightly against him.

"I didn't notice," she whispered back.

In this case it was Sidney who was partly right. The storm did seem to lessen as they flung the reins down into the waiting hands of John, the groom, and the others gathered there. But no sooner had Clarissa crossed the threshold with Sidney than the rain began to beat in earnest.

During the next hour, while Clarissa dried off in her bedchamber, Sidney did likewise in one of the other rooms. Wet clothing had by this time been stripped off, and each was allowed the luxury of a fire. Clarissa, however, had the advantage of a dry wardrobe awaiting her, while Sidney, wrapped in bed linens in the vain hope that somehow his own clothing would dry by the fire, was forced to don the only available garments that fit him—those of Carlton Claringdon. This he did with some reluctance, casting a nervous glance at his figure in the mirror.

Carlton, thank heaven, was no dandy, preferring moderate collar points, and the coat he had left behind was still in mode and passed muster nicely. The only fault that Sidney could find was that it was a trifle snug about the chest, but this he knew could not be helped.

Feeling suitably attired once again, he left the room and went down the stairs in search of a brandy, which he found in the parlor along with his hostess, who had exchanged her soaked habit for a pale muslin frock.

"I hope your brother doesn't mind that I am borrowing his clothes," Sidney said, taking the brandy she offered him.

"Not at all," Clarissa responded. "If anything, I am sure that Carlton, knowing your standards of fashion, will be pleased that you found something worthy of his to wear."

"It was either this or the bedsheet," he revealed, swallowing the brandy and enjoying the blush that suffused her face.

"The storm is still roaring outside," she said, feeling a little confused as he continued to look at her so endearingly.

"And it shall continue to roar," Sidney predicted. "Summer storms are the worst of the lot. I'm afraid I shall have to intrude on your hospitality."

"It is no intrusion," Clarissa quickly contradicted. "One cannot mean to venture out in such a storm. Once you have finished your brandy we shall have a little lunch. Quill has prepared a cream of asparagus soup that he vows shall warm you fully."

The ride coupled with the storm he had just weathered had left Sidney with a roaring appetite, and he quickly dispensed of two bowls of Quill's famous soup, as well as several choice slices of mutton.

Despite the thunder and lightning which occasionally flashed at the window, an air of contentment surrounded Sidney as he lunched. This he put unerringly to Clarissa's presence. He had never known another woman in whose company he delighted so much, whose simple manners were always pleasing and never pretentious. It was not her powers of conversation that held him spellbound during their meal, since inevitably at times silence would fall. But it was a companionable and restful silence, not one of those awkward moments which occasionally characterized relationships with females.

When they had finished with the meal, he consented to be coaxed into a game of chess and found to his surprise that she was a formidable opponent. She had an advantage over him since he was unable to devote his attention to his chessmen when her lovely face lay directly across from him at the chessboard. After five moves he confessed himself hopelessly mated and good-naturedly acknowledged the win.

"Shall you like another game?" she inquired.

He shook his head. "It would do me no good. I find myself hopelessly distracted by my opponent."

To Clarissa's relief the storm had begun to abate somewhat during the chess game, and after another ten minutes Sidney was able to venture home still clad in Carlton's clothing, which he promised to return when next they met. Clarissa was relieved to see him go since she had found his remarks this day flirtatious and his presence somewhat disconcerting. But at the same time she was conscious of a vague disappointment when he had gone.

"But why should I be disappointed?" she asked herself crossly as she wandered into the library. The storm was at an end, the road was muddy to be sure but certainly passable, and no doubt Mr. Montcrieff had pressing business at Bengal Court.

May was passing rapidly into June. In London the month was heralded by the arrival of their Majesties Frederick of Prussia and Alexander of Russia. These two along with others in their glittering entourage, including that great General Bucher, were greeted with festivities, fireworks, and parades such as London had rarely seen.

One man hardly noticed.

Sir Arthur Claringdon had no great liking of kings or

generals. Indeed, some might accuse him of harboring revolutionary tendencies. His town residence had once echoed with the exuberances of his daughter, but now everything rang hollow. Clarissa had kept her vow of silence and had refrained from communicating with him during her stay at Claring, which, as he declared to his wife one evening, was all he could hope to expect of such a spoiled chit.

"You could write to her," Lady Claringdon pointed out, her patience bearing the brunt of these daily complaints.

"Me, write to her? Bosh!"

"You miss her so much."

An idea kindled in Sir Arthur's brain. "Why don't you write to her, Constance?" he suggested.

Lady Claringdon directed a quelling look at her spouse and uttered a single word of reply: "Fiddlesticks!"

"Now see here, Constance . . ."

"You are the one who quarreled with her, Arthur," Lady Claringdon answered. "Even if I did write to her and requested her return, she would not. She has your temperament."

"Well, I wish she didn't," Sir Arthur said, paying no heed to this left-handed compliment. "And I can't write and ask her to come back."

"Then order her home."

Sir Arthur tugged at his mustache. "That won't wash either," he lamented. "She'll just take it into her silly head to disobey me further and remain where she is. We'll have to wait for her to come to her senses."

"That's what you said a fortnight ago," Lady Claringdon said to her husband's considerable annoyance.

14

In Cheltenham the days drifted by—idyllic, warm, and lazy. The weather, which had turned sultry by degrees, gave the promise of the summer ahead. The hills were sweet with the scent of grass, and baby lambs frolicked nearby. Lord Lytton, despite a profound aversion to sheep, showed no haste in quitting the countryside. He took part in almost daily excursions to Miss Manville's, where together they enjoyed cozy talks in the garden, brief drives into the hills, and lively debates on the latest educational theories.

Sidney Montcrieff, to everyone's surprise including his aunt's, showed no interest in returning to London to share in the festivities for the Allied Sovereigns. He was quite willing to linger at Bengal Court with the earl. Clarissa, had she thought much about the matter, would have supposed that his concern for Lytton's well-being lay at the bottom of Sidney's continuing presence, but she was wrong. Sidney dallied at Bengal Court only because she remained at Claring, and he was loath to see their friendship dwindle.

Had she been at all eager to return to town or had fixed the date herself for a departure to London, he would have lost little time making for his Hill Street residence, leaving Lytton to do as he pleased. And yet, curiously, Clarissa seemed fixed on the country. The few questions he had

144

posed about her return to London were met with the briefest of replies, civil of course, but stopping any further inquiries. It was puzzling, but since no law dictated a woman could not be enamored of the country, and he had no pressing obligations in town, the Cotswolds it would be.

One morning in June Lord Lytton rose early, refused any offer of sustenance, and rode off to see Miss Manville. Sidney correctly interpreted these eccentricities as related by Elizabeth as either too much port the night before or the inevitable; Lytton meant to pop the question. A few hours later his cousin returned looking as jubilant as any prospective bridegroom.

"Sidney!" he exclaimed as he caught sight of his cousin in the billiard room. "The most wonderful thing has occurred."

Sidney calmly sank a ball. "You have made Emily an offer, and she has accepted you."

Lytton stopped with his hand on a cue stick. "Yes, but how the devil did you know?"

"These things have a way of being obvious, coz."

"If you mean I've acted like a cudgeon since I've met her, you're probably right."

Sidney laughed and led the earl over to a tray of champagne. "To you, Lytton," he said, handing a glass to his cousin, "and to your lady."

They sipped the champagne. Sidney grimaced and shook his head. "Cousin Edward had his uses, but as a judge of champagne he was woefully lax." A shudder shook him. "I shall have to open a better bottle for you back in London." He led his cousin over to a chair. "Now then, when shall you be married?"

"I don't know. I have left the matter up to Emily."

"I should like to give you the wedding."

"Give me the wedding?" Lytton asked, agog.

"Yes," Sidney replied calmly. "Emily doesn't have any family, none that count, I mean. And Roderick was her mother's cousin and my friend . . ."

"You must be all about in your head, Sidney," Lytton said. "I have money of my own and while I may not rival Golden Ball I can see to my own wedding expenses."

"Very well," Sidney demurred. "But I shall throw a party for you in London. You cannot refuse me that honor. It shall be a very small party—just our friends and perhaps some of Emily's." He tried another sip of the champagne. "Does Emily have any friends in London?"

"I consider that unlikely," Lytton answered. "She did meet Clarissa's sister-in-law here. Quite probably Trixie and Clarissa are the only friends she has."

"We'll invite them both," Sidney said. Clarissa could not mean to remain in the country forever. He turned his mind back to Lytton's impending nuptials. "Have you told Aunt Agatha or Elizabeth?"

"Not yet," the earl answered. "But I shall at once."

In her drawing room Lady Agatha remained as closed as a clam as she listened to her grandnephew's plan to marry an impoverished schoolmistress.

"I know it's a surprise," the earl said warily after a few moments of august silence.

Agatha swiveled her head. "Not in the least. It's about time, that's what I say!" She gave a sharp nod. "All that dangling after opera ladies. A miracle your mother didn't live to see it."

"But I don't dangle after opera ladies," Lytton said, looking aggrieved.

"You have confused Lytton with myself," Sidney spoke, raising one finger to acknowledge blame and directing it toward his own breast. "I am the one with the regrettable tendencies toward opera ladies, and happily my mother, too, did not live to see it."

Elizabeth, a bit confused by this discussion of opera ladies, Sidney, and mothers long dead, fluttered her congratulations to the earl and began to pen a postscript in her mind to the latest epistle to Cousin Mary.

"Plan to be married in London?" Agatha asked, her eyes very bright.

"Yes," Lytton acknowledged. "We hope you can attend."

"I just may."

This quiet announcement brought an unquiet shriek from Elizabeth's corner. "London? Aunt Agatha, you mean to go to London?"

"There's no need to get into a stutter about it," Agatha replied, gazing with relish at the three open mouths in the room. "Look like three monkeys, you do. There ought to be some people I know still breathing besides Lady Twiddings. I'll never see them when I'm dead, will I?"

"Quite true," Sidney agreed, laughing. "You mean to reside in London?"

"I have a house, don't I?"

Sidney's eyes danced. "Indeed you do, Aunt Agatha." He held his aunt's gaze for a moment. "You are full of surprises."

"And you, Sidney," she returned, "are still full of dawdling excuses."

"But not for long," he promised. "Not for long."

"Your bridesmaid? How I should love to be!" Clarissa declared as a smile engulfed Miss Manville's face. "And yet, I cannot." She paced among the potted roses with her hands clasped lightly behind her back. It was wholly impossible to return to London while her father still hovered impatiently in the wings.

Emily's face betrayed her dismay. "Oh, Clarissa, why not, pray?"

"It is this wretched quarrel with my father," Clarissa said, turning quickly. "I know it is uncivil to speak about a parent, but he is the most stubborn man in the world."

"Perhaps he has forgotten the quarrel," Emily said optimistically.

Optimism did not run in the Claringdon family. Clarissa delivered a mild scoff. "On the contrary, my mother writes and says Father delivers a daily tirade against me."

"That means he misses you," Emily pointed out quickly.

Clarissa shrugged. "Even so, I know I could not set foot under his roof without finding myself betrothed."

"Perhaps if you wrote and explained about my wedding, that would induce him to relent," Emily said.

Clarissa shook her head defiantly. "Emily, that would make him only more livid. He is tired of my being the bridesmaid and never the bride, and as for writing to him, that would be the worst thing in the world. He would round up all his old cronies and have a bridegroom or two or three waiting for me on my arrival."

Emily giggled involuntarily. "I know I am being selfish, Clarissa, but if you are not present at my wedding, it shan't be the same."

"And I do wish to be there with you and Lytton," Clarissa declared. "But there's Papa. . . ." She broke off, thinking hard. "Unless . . ."

"Unless?" Emily asked, quick to catch the change in Clarissa's voice.

"Unless we do not tell Papa I am in London."

"Not tell him!" Emily sent a quick puzzled glance to her friend on the garden stool.

"I cannot stay in London," Clarissa said as the plan in her mind took shape, "but that does not mean I can't travel to London for your wedding and some of the festivities. Papa need not ever know. I shall stay at Trixie's."

"At Trixie's!" Emily squealed.

Clarissa shushed her quickly. "Yes, Trixie shall hide me under her roof. We must depend on her. She is the kindest creature and we have no other recourse."

Emily digested this point. "And Carlton?"

"We shall pledge him to secrecy," Clarissa said at once, having no doubt that her brother would come to her assistance. "I shall remain long enough for your wedding and then come straight back. My parents don't know you, and since you plan a modest ceremony, when they do learn, it shan't matter. I shall be back at Claring!"

This last remark brought a frown to Clarissa's face. The notion of being in the country without Emily for close comfort or Lytton or Sidney, who must certainly remain behind in London, was a chilling thought.

"What do you think, Emily?" she asked.

Miss Manville had no taste for intrigue, but her desire for Clarissa's presence was sufficient to throw caution to the wind.

"I think it is the best idea I have heard. Now I shall have you in my wedding party, and Lytton means to have Sidney."

Clarissa tickled her nose with a flower petal. "Do you mean to say you shall have Sidney in your wedding plans, after all?"

"But not as a groom," Miss Manville asserted and fell into a pretty blush at her friend's teasing. "It is the silliest thing to remember how I used to moon over him. If he walked through your door and made me an offer this moment, why I should just thank him but decline politely."

"But think what a blow it would be to his pride," Clarissa said as another laugh erupted. "I daresay no woman has had the opportunity to turn him down. You must be in love with Lytton."

"Can you doubt it?" Emily asked with such passion that Clarissa could scarcely recognize the woman who once had eyes only for Sidney.

"You did feel so strongly for Sidney in the beginning," she explained gently.

"Girlish fantasies," Emily said, pronouncing a severe sentence on herself. "I was dazzled by him, and who wouldn't be. Such a swell! And so handsome! But it took only a little time for that to wear off. My sight is fully restored and all I see is Lytton. But do you know," she turned a troubled face toward Clarissa, "if I had not had that touch of sun, I might never have noticed the earl."

Her note of censure was too much for Clarissa's gravity. "Quite true . . ." she stammered, then fell into a whoop of laughter.

Emily joined her, and the two ladies sat wiping their streaming eyes and debating the dubious pleasures of sun-stroke. At this fortuitous moment Sidney himself entered the garden, checking his progress when he saw them both.

"Tears?" he asked gently.

"Tears of happiness," Clarissa corrected, rising to greet him. "Emily has just told me the good news."

"Lytton has done the same," Sidney said, kissing Emily lightly on the cheek. "I am overjoyed to have you in the family, my dear. And speaking of the Lord Lytton, he is cooling his noble heels outside. He thought you might fancy a drive with him . . ."

Emily jumped up at once. "Clarissa, do you mind awfully?"

"Go along," Clarissa said indulgently. Emily sped off. Laughing a little, Clarissa picked up her straw basket of roses which Sidney immediately took possession of. They crossed the threshold into Claring House together.

"Would you care for some refreshment, sir?" she inquired. "Quill has made some excellent apricot tarts if you would like to sample them."

Sidney, with what Mr. Tibbs would have regarded as a disgraceful lack of loyalty, expressed great interest in the apricot tarts, and over several of these choice bits the two friends sat discussing Lytton's and Emily's engagement.

"How does your aunt react to the news?" Clarissa asked.

"Famously." A rueful grin spread across Sidney's features. "She has made plans to return to London for the ceremony."

Clarissa was so startled she spilled her tea. "But she is known to be such a recluse."

"She has tired of the role," Sidney revealed. "And I own I am heartily glad of it. She is much too young to have spent so many years as a hermit. She means to return to London while some of her friends remain alive."

With a laugh Clarissa pushed away the remains of her tart.

"I can just hear her say such a thing! But can she pick up the strings of her old life so readily? I should hate for her to meet with a snub."

"No one would dare snub Aunt Agatha," Sidney replied, refusing the offer of another tart. "Any one of her cronies would love to see her."

"Shall she stay with you in London?"

Sidney shook his head firmly. "I like my aunt, but my gallantry falls short of entertaining her for all hours of the day. She fully intends to lead the life of a social gadfly. She shall take up residence in her old house which she never sold."

He picked up his teacup and balanced it gingerly on one knee. He was a curst addlebrain or worse! He had not ridden over to Claring on a scorching day to speak of

Agatha but to broach the idea of another wedding: Clarissa's own to him!

Clarissa was the woman of his dreams. He felt more certain of this each time he saw her, and he had fully decided to make her an offer. But each time he had ridden over to Claring he had turned back shaking like a schoolboy. And now that he was finally with her in private he was behaving like a dolt.

He shot a quick, penetrating glance at his beloved on the day couch. She was looking perfectly composed, as always, in a yellow cambric and totally engrossed in her tea. How the devil did a man take the plunge?

Clarissa's eyes met his over their teacups. The speech Sidney had been laboriously preparing since his departure from Bengal Court turned to ashes in his mouth.

"More tea?" she asked gently, wondering why he should look as green as a frog.

"No. Yes. I suppose." He pushed the cup across the side table.

Taking this for an affirmative, albeit a strange one, Clarissa quickly filled his cup. Sidney screwed up the last vestiges of his courage.

"Clarissa . . . would you do me the great honor . . ."

Her eyes, luminous and clear, were turned his way. Impossible to get the words out! His voice faded into silence.

"Do you the honor of what?" Clarissa asked, bewildered.

"Do me the honor of playing the piano," he blurted out.

Clarissa's look of astonishment increased, and he quickly recovered some semblance of address. "I have heard you were quite accomplished on the instrument."

Clarissa's laugh rang out. "Whoever told you that was trying to roast you," she declared. "I am the despair of

152

several music masters, but I shall play if you wish it." She gazed uncertainly at him.

"By all means, yes!" Sidney said, rising to follow her into the adjoining room where the pianoforte waited. Clarissa seated herself at the instrument while he sank thankfully into a small Trafalgar chair next to a black lacquered Chinese screen thick with owls, determined to rethink his plan of attack.

Clarissa commenced a sonata. The notes wafted over the two of them alone in the room: beautiful and haunting. But no more beautiful than the pianist, Sidney thought, watching her. The music faded. There was a moment of silence, then he cleared his throat.

"You do your music master no discredit."

"Thank you." She moved to the couch, her eyes studying his face surreptitiously. "Is anything the matter, Sidney?"

He started. "No. Not in the least. I was wondering . . ."

"Yes?" she prompted.

"If you liked to travel."

"Travel?" Clarissa echoed, wondering if Sidney could be queer in his attic. "I once went to Paris," she said. "That was before Napoleon's time, and I was just a child. I regret to say I don't recall much of it. Italy, I am told, is quite beautiful."

"What do you think of it as a honeymoon site?" Sidney asked, seizing this road back to the topic of matrimony.

"Honeymoon?" Clarissa frowned, then gave a happy nod of comprehension. "Do you mean that Lytton is taking Emily to Italy?" She clapped her hands. "How wonderful that will be."

Sidney groaned. "I am not speaking of Lytton and Emily," he said thickly. Clarissa stared at him, bewilderment writ on her face.

"Were you not?" she asked, puzzled. "But you did say honeymoon, sir."

"Yes." Sidney jumped to his feet, unable to sit still and nearly colliding with the owls. "I wish you would listen to me, Clarissa . . ."

"But I have been listening," she returned, stung. "It is you who has been less than lucid, sir. What is it you wish to say?"

Here loomed the perfect opening. Clarissa's eyes were expectant, her demeanor attentive. Sidney opened his mouth, then snapped it shut. No use. It was impossible to come to the point. Botheration! He thrust his hands into the folds of his coat, and his fingers tightened on a small box. Pulling it out, he thrust it at Clarissa, who flinched at his movement.

"Open it," he demanded.

Clarissa obeyed his order, thinking that Sidney had eaten perhaps one too many apricot tarts. The diamond ring in the box sparkled flawlessly as the brilliant sunshine streamed through the windows.

"Oh," she breathed. "It's exquisite. This is Emily's ring, I warrant?"

"No, no, no!" Sidney shouted, goaded beyond human endurance. "My dear Clarissa, can you not think of any other couple besides those two boring lovebirds for just a fraction of a moment?"

"But who else is there to think of?" Clarissa asked blankly.

"Us!"

"Us!" she squeaked.

"You and I," Sidney said, looking at the owls for help and finding none. He threw himself down on the couch again and sat with his head in his hands. This was not the way to propose to a lady and well he knew it! But he'd be dashed if he would start again!

154

"The ring is my mother's," he said. "An heirloom. Oh, the devil. Who cares a rush about heirlooms at such a time. Clarissa, I know I am making a cake of it all, but I've never proposed to a woman before." He gazed into her brimming eyes. "If you knew what I have been struggling to say for more than a se'enight! But why should I bother with words?" He pulled her into his arms and crushed his mouth to hers.

Clarissa felt her breath driven away by the force of the kiss, and her head whirled madly. Could this be happening to her?

"I love you," Sidney said recklessly.

"You love me," she murmured into his shoulder.

"Yes." He held her off from him and shook her gently. "Speak. Do you love me?"

"Oh, Sidney," she said, flinging her arms around his neck. "You are too absurd." And she lifted her face to him.

Faced with such a dazzling sight, Sidney surrendered at once to the desire dwelling deep within him and bent his head, his lips meeting Clarissa's in a long and lingering exchange. Clarissa, who had had her hand and cheek sometimes kissed by the more daring of her beaux, was swept away on the tide of emotion she now experienced. A stirring deep within her bade, nay commanded, that she return his embrace with as much passion as she possessed.

When one kiss ended, a new one took its place, and Clarissa at times struggled for breath. Freeing her at last, Sidney gazed ardently into her eyes, murmuring her name. Feeling that she never wished to be parted from him, she dug deeper into his coat of Bath superfine.

15

The staffs of Claring and Bengal Court twittered happily with the news of the coming alliance, Mrs. Quill stating that she should have seen it coming the first time she laid eyes on Mr. Montcrieff, and Polly shedding copious tears that Clarissa was obliged to dry. Both Lytton and Emily were quick in their congratulations to the new pair of lovers, Lytton giving his cousin what passed for a wink and a clap on the shoulder at a job well done.

Lady Agatha, when presented with her nephew's news, remarked drily that the rank of bachelors appeared to be thinning rapidly in her family and then paid a morning call on the prospective bride.

"So you are set on marrying my nephew, are you?" she asked, making no attempt to beat around the bush.

"It's not I who am set on matrimony but Sidney," Clarissa protested.

"Hmmph," Agatha answered, appearing satisfied with what she had discerned from Clarissa's face. "You have the look of a female who would not marry unless it were her own idea," she said accurately enough. "So it stands to reason you must want to marry that nephew of mine as much as he wants to marry you."

"Of course I do," Clarissa said with a smile, "and I hope, ma'am, that we have your approval."

"I have nothing to say about it," Agatha barked. "Not

156

like it was in the old days when the young ones danced to the tune their parents played. Not that I miss it so much." She shook her head grimly. "Some terrible marriages were arranged by families that should have had more sense. No, this is Sidney's doing and yours and glad I am of it. You'll suit," she said with a nod of her head.

"Thank you," Clarissa said and passed her guest a plate of apricot tarts.

"Your cook is an expert pastry maker," Agatha said after she had demolished the tart. "Poor Tibbs shall be fit to cut his throat when I tell him that," she said in some satisfaction. "You have lovely roses too, I see."

"Would you like a stroll in the garden, ma'am?" Clarissa offered, and since Agatha had a real love of flowers she consented to be escorted about the garden, coming away with what she characterized as a much too large bouquet of roses which Giles insisted on cutting for her.

"They shall just wither otherwise," Clarissa pointed out. "And Giles is always after me to give them away."

"It's civil of you," Agatha said gruffly. "Had a feeling in my bones you were the right one for Sidney, not like that whey-faced niece of Maria's. And she lost no time in leaving Cheltenham after that party of hers. Anybody but a fool could see he was taken with you.

"Still," she went on, warming to her topic, "he's a Montcrieff, and as such he's prone to having his way, and when he is on his high ropes, do look out. But as taken with you as he is, I doubt you'll see that side of him. But if you do, mind that I warned you first."

Clarissa, smiling, assured her that she would be prepared.

"No female goes into marriage prepared to cope with a Montcrieff," Agatha answered and thereupon launched into a full litany of advice on the proper management of a husband, which Clarissa listened to with full appreciation and much amusement.

"I just hope she hasn't succeeded in scaring you off," Sidney grumbled the following afternoon as they walked about the Cheltenham Parade Grounds, thick with other couples enjoying a promenade in the warm sunshine.

"Don't be silly," Clarissa teased. "As though I could be scared off by anything now." She shook a finger at him. "I am holding you to your promise, sir."

"And glad I am of that," Sidney said, clasping her hand tightly in his. "But what did you and Aunt Agatha have to talk about?"

"Oh, this and that," Clarissa said vaguely. Seeing her beloved's skeptical look, she laughed. "Much of it had to do with how to manage a husband properly."

"Now that I must learn more about," Sidney said, sliding his arm about her waist as they continued on the path.

"But I cannot tell you so," Clarissa teased. "For to do so would betray your aunt's confidence. But from what little I gleaned, she was totally in favor of banishing a husband to the stables where he could lose himself among the horses and cattle and not bother either her or her servants. I confess to some curiosity about her own husband. What was he like?"

"According to what little I know," Sidney answered promptly, "he was mustachioed and thoroughly cowed."

The air rippled with both their laughter, and he wrapped his strong arms about her as they came to a more secluded area of the grounds.

"You will not treat me so badly, I hope?" he inquired.

"Never," she promised, leaning over to kiss him on the lips. "I am just so happy, Sidney."

"I, too," he acknowledged as he dropped a kiss on her forehead. "Now then," he resumed the walk, "have you thought of when you would like to remove to London? I don't mean to press you, but there are a hundred things we must see to. The announcement in the *Gazette* for a start, and then I must pay my respects to your father. I hope he will not think it forward of me that I spoke to you before coming to see him. I hope he will make no obstacle to our marriage."

"Papa an obstacle?" Clarissa trilled with laughter. She had as yet not written to her parents, preferring to impart the news in person and anticipating the expression of stupefaction on her darling father's face.

"Papa," she assured Sidney, "is quite eager to marry me off."

This statement so pleased Sidney that he linked his arms about her waist again and, wholly oblivious to the scandalized glances of two elderly dowagers who had chosen this afternoon for a walk of their own, commenced kissing Clarissa fully again. And what was worse, these good ladies confided to each other later in shocked accents, the young lady seemed to be relishing every moment of it!

Later that same afternoon Clarissa rode to the vicarage to inform Mrs. Boatwright of the happy tidings. The vicar's wife turned pink with joy and hugged her at once.

"Surprised? No, not a bit," she declared after catching her breath and fetching a pitcher of her favorite lemonade. "I did tell Charles that Sidney seemed quite taken with you!"

"But how is it you never breathed a word of that to me?" Clarissa protested. "It would have saved me many a sleepless night."

Mrs. Boatwright, in the act of pouring the lemonade, muffled her laughter. "If ever I saw a man in love it was Sidney Montcrieff. And the earl."

"Oh, yes," Clarissa agreed, taking the glass. "We must not forget Lytton."

"Just fancy," Mrs. Boatwright said as she sat down with Clarissa before a plate of biscuits, "you and Emily have attached two of the leading lights of society."

"So we have, haven't we?" Clarissa said, much struck by this point. She giggled. "I daresay we might start a parade of London damsels into the country. Instead of Brighton, it shall be Cheltenham for those unwed!"

Mrs. Boatwright threw back her head and laughed. "When shall the wedding be?" she inquired.

Clarissa shrugged. "We only know when Lytton's shall be, and he changes that daily. Emily has set the date for the fourteenth of July. Sidney and I shall probably wed a little time after. I shall leave it to Papa to make that decision."

"I have heard rumors that Lady Agatha will return to London also," Mrs. Boatwright said.

Clarissa nodded. "Sidney is delighted. He was always against her prolonged isolation here. Now Elizabeth can return to her own family with a secure mind. If ever Lady Agatha wishes to return to Bengal Court, she need only say the word. We have made that quite plain."

"How long will she stay in London?"

"I don't know," Clarissa admitted. "But judging by the orders she has given to her staff, I should think quite a long time."

"I hope her long absence does not cause problems back in London."

"I cannot see why it should," Clarissa said innocently.

Agatha's impending return to the London circle was already causing problems and headaches for one member of her family: Mr. Joseph Cranley. For two decades Joseph had resided in comfort in his aunt's town residence and had grown so thoroughly accustomed to it that he was hard pressed to remember that it did not belong to him.

Just because Agatha wished to use it again, he told himself, was no reason to oust him! Damn inconvenient that would be. By all rights his aunt ought to have been grateful to him. Hadn't he kept the house up to snuff and made repairs whenever necessary?

These modest repairs in his mind grew to considerable dimension as he thought forlornly of the trials of finding another suitable residence. But in London in June there were no suitable lodgings, especially with the czar in town.

When the first news of Agatha's return had filtered to him from snatches of Elizabeth's letters to Mary, his first instinct had been to ignore it. Old ladies in their sixties were prone to flights of fancy and, as he put it to his wife, Agatha was nearly queer in the attic the last time he had laid eyes on her and there was no telling what she was like now. But as the epistles from his cousin mounted, Joseph began to fear for the roof over his head.

"It's not just a dashed whim of hers," he said one evening in his wife's drawing room.

"No," Mary agreed, knotting a fringe and grateful that her husband was finally heeding her warning. "But what are we to do?"

"I don't know," he said impatiently. "But it can't be that difficult. She doesn't mean to throw us out, surely."

Mary, however, was less certain of his aunt's goodwill and felt that being thrown out was well within the specter of possibility.

"The house is hers."

"But there's plenty of room for us," Joseph exclaimed.

Mary abandoned her fringe. "What if she installs someone else in our place?"

"Replaced?" Joseph croaked. "By whom?"

"Lytton or Sidney."

Joseph turned this tidbit over carefully in his mind before rejecting it.

"They have houses of their own in town. And who would want to live in an old house like this. . . ." He rubbed his hands together. "Somehow, Mary, we must contrive to be as gracious as possible to Aunt Agatha."

"I am always gracious," Mary said coldly. She came from family that prided themselves on their manners.

But Joseph was off on a tangent. "We must make certain she has every comfort. That way she will have no reason to throw us out." He snapped his fingers. "I shall go to Bengal Court myself and bring her back to London."

Mary had heard outrageous ideas during her marriage to Mr. Cranley, but none like the one now unfolding.

"Why must you travel to the country?" she demanded. "We already know Agatha is coming to London."

"I shall help her pack."

"She will think you foxed," Mary said unhelpfully. "Lytton and Sidney are already present to help her pack."

"That's what worries me," Joseph answered, draining his sherry.

"Must you go?" Mary entreated. Sidney and Lytton might be Joseph's relations, but she did not like him associating with so dissolute a pair.

"I must," Joseph declared.

Any further misgivings he may have entertained were dashed for good the following day when Elizabeth's latest epistle arrived.

"Sidney is getting married!" Mary announced, coming into her husband's bookroom and waving the letter like a flag.

"Married!" Joseph barked as his mind flew involuntarily to the opera ladies he had seen on his cousin's arm. "Not to some ballerina, I hope?" Sidney might be a loose screw but he was his cousin!

"Oh, no," Mary replied happily. "It is to Clarissa Claringdon, just imagine."

"Did you say Claringdon?"

Mary glanced up from her perusal of the letter and perceived her husband's change of color.

"Joseph? What's wrong?"

For reply Mr. Cranley reached out a palsied hand and wrenched the missive away from his wife. His eyes scanned a full page of blithering nonsense before he found the timely reference to Clarissa.

" 'Sidney has made Clarissa Claringdon an offer and she has accepted. We are all pleased,' " he read aloud. Pleased, were they? Fools. They wouldn't be pleased for long, not if they knew what he did about her.

"Good gracious, Joseph." Mary clucked her tongue and retrieved the letter he had deposited on his desk laden with bills. "What quarrel do you have with Clarissa Claringdon?"

For just a moment Joseph was sorely tempted to share the truth with Mary, but his sense of propriety was keen. A husband's duty was to shield his wife from the unpleasant realities of life. It would not be proper to tell her of Miss Claringdon's fall from grace.

"I consider her quite exceptional," Mary continued. "And rather unlike Sidney to offer for her. One has only to think of his high flyers to give thanks . . ."

"I know all that," Joseph said impatiently. "But I must warn you, Mary, the betrothal is secret and must remain so. Sidney wouldn't like you to speak of it to your friends, nor would I."

"I shall say nothing," Mary responded haughtily, exiting the room in the style reminiscent of Mr. Kemble. Her husband, however, was too preoccupied to appreciate these talents. His mind buzzed. The letter from Elizabeth had clinched the matter. Now he must go to Bengal Court. Saving Sidney from a fatal marriage would win him not only Sidney's gratitude but Aunt Agatha's as well. And surely a life-long residence in her town house was not too little a boon to ask for.

Late the following afternoon an antiquated travel chariot wove its way up the drive to Bengal Court, causing the young Earl of Lytton pause in his afternoon stroll on the grounds. He waited, one hand on his quizzing glass, while the vehicle discharged its sole occupant, who looked fatigued, hungry, and in a foul mood from having been jousted all over creation.

The passenger's mood did not improve when he caught sight of the earl, and Lytton was treated to a rather indignant thrust of a double chin.

"By heaven, it's Joseph," Lytton said, moving forward to greet Mr. Cranley. "And whatever are you wearing?"

Joseph, who had attired himself rather handsomely, he thought, in a new cravat of vivid violet with a matching coat of purple superfine as well as a curly-brimmed beaver two sizes too small, responded acidly that the garments were considered clothing, and he did not want to hear another word about them from his younger relative.

"Nor would I if I wore them," Lytton said with a shudder. "But if I were you, Joseph, I'd go to Weston soon and part with some of your precious blunt. At least you wouldn't look like a man milliner."

"I am not the blade of fashion you profess to be, Lawrence."

"Yes, I know," Lytton said, flicking away a spot of ash with a fingertip. "But you are my cousin, and I have my reputation to think of." He took Joseph up the stairs and into the house. "But I haven't asked what you are doing here."

"I am here to help Aunt Agatha."

"Help Aunt Agatha do what?" Lytton asked politely.

"Help her return to London," Joseph explained.

Lytton, no fool, saw through this ruse at once. "Afraid she'll kick you out?" he asked.

"Certainly not," Joseph blustered. "I know how to handle old ladies."

"So you have said many times," Lytton drawled. "She is upstairs in her rooms. Do you wish to see her first or would you prefer a smidgeon to eat?"

Mr. Cranley wavered nobly in the face of food, having abstained from lunch on the road in the knowledge that delicacies from his cousin's kitchen no doubt awaited, and he saw no reason to fill a strange landlord's coffers. Rather lightheaded from this unfamiliar lack of nourishment, he nonetheless managed with dignity to reply that in such matters his aunt must always come first. Fully conscious of Lytton's grin, he mounted the stairs successfully and without any noticeable loss of breath.

Turning down the hall, he found his aunt at last in her rooms busy supervising her maids in the packing of what appeared to be an ominously large wardrobe. A few servants glanced apprehensively at him as he loomed in the doorway, but Agatha noticed nothing, and finally Joseph was obliged to clear his throat.

"Yes, what is it?" Agatha snapped and turned.

Joseph, who had had his ear bent by Mary on the importance of acting the role of a devoted nephew, was ready on this cue. He flung wide his arms and advanced into the room with the intention of clasping his aunt, who was looking rather Egyptian in a gold turban, warmly to his breast. But no sooner had he stepped forward than his feet were entangled in a pile of linen, and he sprawled the ten feet across the room to land in an untidy heap at Agatha's feet.

"Good heavens, it's Joseph!" Agatha exclaimed, emulating the earl as Joseph battled a quilt. "What are you doing here?" she demanded as she snatched up the quilt and uncovered him. "You haven't brought Mary with you, I should hope?"

Joseph, although glad to be rid of the quilt, was taken aback by this meager welcome. "Mary remains in London."

"Well, good for her," Agatha said, throwing down the bedding. "Sorry to be uncivil, Joseph, but you picked a wrong time to visit. I'm removing to London."

"So I had heard," Joseph said, finding his feet at last and bestowing an ingratiating smile on his aunt. "I thought you might need some assistance."

"Assistance in what?" Agatha asked, wholly at sea.

"To make arrangements for your London stay."

Agatha drew herself up to her full five feet. "That is unnecessary since I seem to recall a perfectly good house of my own. So it seems, Joseph, you have spent the better part of a day on a fool's errand."

"At least let me assure you that Mary and I are delighted to have you visit," he said, trying to salvage something of the meeting.

"I'm coming to stay," Agatha corrected. "Do you plan any unpleasantness on this issue?"

Joseph met his aunt's gaze fleetingly. "Mary and I are, of course, overjoyed . . ."

"Gammon," Agatha interposed with a nod of her turbaned head. "Now go away, do. You're making me as nervous as a hen, and I have much too much to do."

Feeling that the interview had not gone as well as he had anticipated, Joseph descended the stairs to find Lytton still at the bottom grinning from ear to ear.

"How now, Joseph?" the earl asked, laughing. "Can it be you have lost your touch with old ladies?"

Joseph, unable to think of a suitable rejoinder, was reduced to an acid glare and a furious splutter. The earl clapped him on the back.

"A little nourishment will change your testy mood."

Joseph shook off his cousin's hand. "It is not only on Aunt Agatha's account that I am here," he said.

"Oh, no?" his lordship murmured. "Not another set-to with Mary?"

"Certainly not," Joseph blustered.

"I am relieved to hear that," Lytton said, nodding happily. "We have never had a bill of divorcement in our family." He adjusted his cousin's cravat to a semblance of order. "But what other matter would bring you tearing down to the country?"

"That's Sidney's concern," Joseph said, wrenching free from the earl's hand. "And by the bye, where is he? I haven't seen him since my arrival."

"Since none of us knew you were arriving, you can hardly scold him for being a negligent host," Lytton pointed out. "I think he's at Clarissa's."

Joseph snorted. "Ah, yes, his ladybird."

Lytton's smile froze. He laid one hand on the polished bannister. "If you wish to keep your head attached to that body of yours, Joseph, you shall remember your place and never say such a thing again."

"Ain't your house, Lytton."

Temper flared in Lytton's eyes. "No," he agreed. "It's Sidney's house, and it's his lady you've just insulted. Don't worry, I shan't tell him about it. I don't carry tales, but you shall keep a civil tongue in that empty head of yours."

Joseph seethed inwardly. Empty-headed, was he? They would soon learn just who the fool of the family was!

16

It was well past four o'clock when Sidney strolled into his house with a smile on his lips. Lytton, who had been lying in wait for an hour, came out of the billiard room shushing him quickly.

·"What the devil?"

"In the library," Lytton said, pulling his cousin along with him down the hall. The earl swung open the door, and the two men gazed at the singularly unlovely sight of Mr. Joseph Cranley adorning the couch.

Joseph had seen fit to fortify himself with a snack as he waited for Sidney, a snack that had consisted of several roasted chickens, a ham, two cheese pies, and a small basket of his favorite strawberries. This lavish meal he had consumed had forced him to retire to the library couch with a handkerchief spread over his pendulous cheeks and a volume of Aristotle propped on his chest. Aristotle now lay forgotten as his snores wafted up through the linen toward the ceiling.

"Good Jupiter," Sidney ejaculated. "That's Joseph!"

"In the flesh."

"A bit too much flesh," Sidney said, wrinkling his nose. "And all of it on my couch. What is he doing here?"

"Claims he wants to help our aunt pack for her trip home."

"What a clacker!" Sidney snorted. "Does he mean to stay long?"

"I haven't asked," the earl said, admitting his ignorance.

"Well, I certainly shall," Sidney said. "He may intrude on my hospitality, but there are limits to my endurance." Two quick steps brought him to Joseph's side. One slender hand took possession of Mr. Cranley's handkerchief while the other he brought tight over the top of his cousin's mouth. Joseph, caught in mid-doze, came awake on the instant, his arms flailing wildly like a grounded pelican.

Lytton held his sides weakly with laughter.

"Ah, Joseph. You are awake," Sidney said, removing the handkerchief and folding it neatly.

"Sidney, blast you! You nearly killed me!" Joseph said.

"If I had wanted to kill you," Sidney said smoothly, presenting Mr. Cranley with his handkerchief, "I could have done it long ago, and I would certainly not choose suffocation." He paused. "Swords, perhaps."

Joseph rose from the sofa in a huff. "That's a fine greeting. I cannot rest after a shattering journey without being prey to another of your wretched hoaxes."

Sidney bore this speech with notable fortitude. "What are you doing here?" he asked.

"Here to help Aunt Agatha."

"Civil of you," Sidney said, picking up his Aristotle and blowing off a layer of dust. Frowning a little, he reshelved it in his rosewood case. "Lytton has probably informed you that our aunt stands in little need of assistance from anyone."

"I have another reason for being here," Joseph said. "A private matter." He sniffed at the earl sitting quietly in a curricle chair.

Lytton intercepted the look and roared, "Don't tell me you're strapped, Joseph. I shan't believe it."

A muscle in Sidney's cheek twitched.

"I ain't strapped," Joseph said, blushing furiously. "But go ahead and laugh, the pair of you. Practically killed me now, didn't you? I have half a mind not to tell you the news and let you be surprised like all the rest, except I do happen to prize my reputation and, though we sometimes wish we weren't related, we are for good or ill."

"Mostly ill," the earl murmured.

Sidney, who had been forced several times in the past to listen to this homily on family relations, saw no need to hear it again. He sat down at his desk. "If it's not money, Joseph, what do you want?"

"It's about your wedding," Joseph said, deciding to take the bull by the horns.

Surprise but no great alarm registered on Sidney's face. "My wedding? How the deuce do you hear so much? Oh, I suppose Mary and Elizabeth correspond, do they not? You must know that Larry is getting married, too." He saw Joseph's frown. "But why the gloom? Is not this what you have been preaching to us for considerable years? The joys of the marriage bond?"

Joseph drew his shoulders back. "Sidney, I must warn you. You are about to contract a fatal marriage."

Sidney's face turned ashen. Joseph, well aware that he was treading on very thin ice indeed, felt his heart pounding wildly in his breast.

"A fatal marriage?" Sidney repeated, placing both hands on the desk in front of him. "You forget yourself, Joseph . . ."

The earl was not inclined to mince words. "Let me throw him out, Sidney."

"I have not traveled all the way from London just to indulge in some freakish whim," Joseph said hastily. "I came to help you. Remember that in six months' time."

170

"And what, pray, shall occur in six months' time?" Sidney asked politely.

Joseph shot the earl another impatient look. "That's best discussed in private, Sidney."

Sidney searched Joseph's face with a modicum of curiosity. Whatever his faults, and he had many, Joseph was no troublemaker. A purse-pincher yes, and a bag pudding, but not the type to ride into the country to do mischief. So why did he rave on?

"Leave us, Larry," he said quietly.

"Sidney!"

"I know it's fustian, but please."

With poor grace the earl rose. "Very well. But I shall be just outside the door if you need any help in throwing Joseph out." The door closed firmly on his heels.

"I see he is as hotheaded as ever," Joseph said when he was finally alone with Sidney.

"Perhaps," Sidney acknowledged. "But we are not here to discuss the temperature of Larry's head, are we?" He strolled to a side table and poured himself a glass of sherry, contemplating the swirling liquid in the crystal for a moment. "I wonder if you've gone queer in the old attic, Joseph. You may be my cousin and my elder by some years, but I do not have to discuss my choice of bride with you."

Joseph mopped his forehead with a handkerchief. "Does it seem likely that I would want to?" he asked bitterly.

"No," Sidney admitted. "It's deuced out of character. Why do you go on about it?"

"Because I don't want our family to be the laughing stock of the ton," Joseph said. "The matter is quite urgent. You cannot marry Clarissa Claringdon."

"So you say," Sidney replied with a dangerous slant of his brows. "But she seems eminently suited for the match.

171

She is beautiful, and her lineage is of the finest quality, so I beg you to tell me in as few words as possible why I should not wed her."

"Because she is expecting a child!" Joseph blurted out.

Unprepared for such slander, Sidney froze with his glass halfway to his mouth. The sherry never reached its destination. With a flick of his wrist, he dashed the contents full into Joseph's face. Mr. Cranley fell back in a wild splutter. A muscled forearm reached out, and five long fingers clutched Joseph's throat, doing irreparable damage to his new neckcloth.

"Infamous mawworm. I shall make you sorry you uttered such a lie."

Joseph dangled from the end of Sidney's hand like a fish.

"It's the truth," he gurgled, trying to free himself from the iron grip. "Do you think I enjoy saying such ugly things and to you of all people? I may be a mawworm but I'm not crazy!"

"I should hope not," Sidney said, shaking him hard. The activity cleared some of the fog from his own brain. "I don't know what you stand to gain by such a thing, but if it's a jest, I assure you it is not funny."

"It's no jest," Joseph croaked. "It's the truth."

This was the wrong thing to say to a man like Sidney. His fingers tightened again. "Take it back, Joseph. Every word."

"I can't," Joseph protested. "Don't. Oh, by heaven you are going to kill me!" he wailed.

"Tell me you are lying," Sidney said.

"But I can't," Joseph moaned as the fingers dug deeper into his flesh. "I just thought you should like to know since I could scarcely believe it myself when I overheard her father's friend."

"What friend?"

"Whalmsey."

Sidney fixed an eye on his cousin's bulbous nose.

"Lord Peter Whalmsey?"

"Yes."

Abruptly Sidney released his hold. Joseph lurched back onto the sofa, nearly overturning a chair in the process. Sidney poured himself a fresh glass of sherry and downed it quickly. His mind was in a spin.

"Whalmsey told you that Clarissa is expecting a child?" Sidney asked, picking up the threads of the inquisition with his blood boiling.

Joseph, choking, nodded.

"Speak, damn you!"

"Whalmsey said that Claringdon was going to be a grandfather," Joseph stammered in his haste to comply with his cousin's order. "And he didn't like it one bit. Said his daughter was the reason. She'd been sent down to the country."

"Where was all this said?"

"In White's reading room," Joseph explained. "And I wasn't the only one there." Pudgy fingers sought the damage to his neckcloth. "Kentmere was there too. That's how it all came to pass. He asked Whalmsey why Claringdon should look so down in the mouth about things. That's when Whalmsey told him that Claringdon was about to be a grandfather and blamed his daughter."

"Whalmsey said this with his own tongue?" Sidney demanded.

"Yes," Joseph said, growing in confidence. "Whatever you think of me, Sidney, you know that Whalmsey never lies."

Sidney maintained a creditable calm, but Joseph's last remark had struck him to the core. He might have brushed aside Joseph's allegations as *on dits,* but there was

Lord Whalmsey. His reputation throughout the ton was incorruptible. And he was a great friend to Claringdon.

Sidney sank into a chair. Could it be true? Any part of it? Clarissa? Was this the reason behind her long absence from London? If she were expecting a child, he mused, the family would never countenance her staying in the town. Girls in those situations were swiftly removed . . . and where else but to the country. Sidney gnashed his teeth.

"She doesn't show," he said in a low voice.

"She wouldn't," Joseph replied. "It's early days yet. Mary and I had three. I know of such things."

Sidney bit his tongue. He devoutly wished that Joseph did not know so much. But Clarissa could not possibly be with child. That was absurd. And yet why was she at Claring? And why had she turned cold each time he had questioned her about returning to London earlier?

A fresh tide of doubts overwhelmed him in the chair. Joseph would never dare say such things without support. And support he had in Peter Whalmsey. If Clarissa were with child it was only natural that Whalmsey, Claringdon's old crony, would know of it. And, Sidney remembered suddenly, Whalmsey was Clarissa's godfather!

The minutes passed in agitated silence. Joseph, correctly deducing that any further remark might bring on a fresh attack, refrained from speech. Sidney sat as silent as a ghost in his chair with fingertips pressed together. He had loved her, imagined her to be the woman he had sought for so long, and she had turned out to be nothing but a hoyden! All trace of affection was rapidly disappearing as he sank lower in the chair. He had been tricked, by God. Neatly roped into the proposal and had almost made the trip to the altar with her, and she had probably been laughing at him at every turn, unable to believe her luck.

What pretense would she have used when the babe

arrived early? Not that it was so difficult. Midwives and doctors were easily bribed.

"Who else besides you, Kentmere, and Whalmsey know of this?" Sidney asked, turning to Joseph.

"Her family, I presume," Joseph answered. "I told no one, Sidney. Not even Mary."

"Good," Sidney said. "The news shall stop here, is that understood?"

Joseph's face approached the color of his tattered cravat. "You can't mean to still marry her!"

"I am not such a fool," Sidney said, unclenching his jaw. "Although she did mistake me for one. A fatal marriage, did you call it, Joseph? And by heaven it would have been. All London would have been in stitches at my spectacle. I stand in your debt."

Joseph, unaccustomed to such a situation, murmured nervously that he was glad to be of help.

"Are you in need of funds these days?"

"No, although I have been spending freely to get the house ready for our aunt."

"The sum involved?"

"Five hundred pounds."

Sidney took this without a blink. "You shall have the cheque when I return to London."

"Obliged to you, Sidney."

"The favor comes with a price, Joseph," Sidney said. "You shall not say a word about Clarissa's condition to anyone, is that understood?"

"You are still protecting her!" Joseph protested.

"I am protecting myself, man. I don't fancy being laughed out of the ton. And if I hear any whisper that you told anyone of Clarissa, I shall throttle you for certain when next we meet."

Perspiration beaded anew on Mr. Cranley's forehead.

Somehow the vivid picture of himself as a Rescuer that he had painted back in London was going askew.

"No need to worry there, Sidney."

"Good."

"And what about Miss Claringdon?" Joseph asked curiously.

Sidney's face blackened into a scowl. "I shall take care of Miss Claringdon myself!" He flung open the library door and stormed out.

Lytton, surprised at this exit, hailed him but he was already gone. A bit put out, the earl turned toward Joseph. "Where is Sidney off to?"

Joseph remained silent.

"What did you tell him?" Lytton demanded, taking in Mr. Cranley's disheveled appearance.

"I can't tell you," Joseph said, preparing to mount the stairs.

"Oh no?" Lytton asked, stretching out one hand.

"It's no use, Larry," Joseph replied. "I can't. I have his word that if I speak a word of it he'll kill me. And I fear he means it!"

Sidney rode toward Claring in a towering rage. Of all the deceits he had been prey to in his life, this one topped the list. Not even Lady Vye would stoop to playing such a detestable trick on him. He pressed his mount forward in his haste to be finished with Miss Clarissa Claringdon. Just the name was sufficient to bring the bile boiling to his throat.

So she would try and lure him into marriage, would she, he thought as he rode hard on the path. And he had no one to blame but himself. He had been dazzled and taken in by her innocence and charm. In women he should have known that added up to a trap. And he should have seen through the guise at once. But now his eyes were open, and

176

Miss Claringdon was about to receive a dose of her own very odious medicine.

In the faltering sunlight the shadows lay wide and open at Claring. Sidney dismounted quickly, throwing the reins to Henry and scarcely aware of the groom's cheerful greeting. Mrs. Quill's welcoming smile, too, faded at the door as he stood in front of her.

"Is Clarissa at home, Mrs. Quill?" he asked coldly.

"Yes, sir. She is in the drawing room. I can announce you if you wish."

Sidney shook his head grimly. "It shall be a surprise." His eye fell on the housekeeper's worried countenance. Was she party to the trick too, he wondered. "See that no one disturbs us, Mrs. Quill."

"Yes, sir."

Stripping off his York tan gloves, Sidney entered the house. He loathed scenes, but was fully prepared to hand Clarissa one she fully deserved. His cheeks still burned as he thought of the hoax. No woman played him for a fool and lived to laugh about it. A set-down was much too easy. Miss Claringdon was so fond of tricks, was she? She would encounter one from him that would guarantee no word of this disgraceful episode would ever reach the ears of the ton.

For a moment he hovered at the entrance to the drawing room. The figure on the couch looked so absurdly youthful in a pink muslin that he felt his resolution dissolve into the marrow of his bones.

Careful, man, he told himself. *She has played you for a nitwit.*

"Sidney?" Clarissa rose gracefully and came forward, smiling at seeing him again after an absence of only an hour. A knife twisted in the lower regions of Sidney's heart. He planted a kiss coolly on her hand for what he hoped would be the very last time. The Montcrieff diamond adorning her finger glittered every bit as her false smile.

"You are preoccupied?" he asked.

"Just in reading a letter I have written to my parents. You may think it forward of me, but I had to write and share the news. I know they shall be overjoyed."

"Overjoyed would be putting it mildly," Sidney said, his lip curling.

Clarissa, finding it difficult to follow this lead, put her letter aside and drew him toward the couch. "Can you stay for dinner, sir?"

"Unfortunately no. I have a guest at Bengal Court. My cousin Joseph."

"Ah, yes, you have mentioned him," Clarissa said, wondering why Sidney should stare at her so. "I hope he has not brought you bad news."

"Oh, no," Sidney contradicted. "It is just that I have an unpleasant task ahead to perform."

"What can it be?" Clarissa asked. "Has Lytton decided that his wedding must be put off and ours as well?"'

"No," he denied. "Lytton is unacquainted with any of this."

"Then it has nothing to do with our wedding?" she asked, relieved.

Sidney allowed himself a polite smile. "*Au contraire,* Clarissa. It has everything to do with it."

For a moment she stared at him in bewilderment, wondering if he had windmills in his head. He gazed raptly into her eyes, feeling no hint of discomposure in those gray orbs. Composed as usual. That was the discriminating Miss Claringdon. He would see just how long her pretense lasted.

"I wish to withdraw my offer of marriage," he said coldly.

"Withdraw?" Clarissa cried out as all color drained

178

from her face. Was this a jest? Involuntarily she clutched the ribbon dangling from the bodice of her gown. Was she all about in her head?

"You wish to cry off?" she echoed.

He nodded. "Yes."

The sharpest pain Clarissa had ever known shot through her body. "But I don't understand. Why? How could you just enter and say such a thing. . . ." Abruptly she halted her catechism, her cheeks burning.

"You are perplexed," Sidney said. "I shall be delighted to offer an explanation."

Stricken, she continued to gaze at him as he stretched his legs out in front of the couch. "You see," he confided, "I carried a jest too far."

"A jest?!" Clarissa recoiled as though scalded.

"Yes! Lytton was so full of glee on becoming engaged to Miss Manville that I meant to show it could be done by any gentleman possessed of sufficient wit. I could not resist the challenge you presented being so near at hand. If I attached Miss Clarissa Claringdon, the discriminating darling of the ton, well. . . ." He smiled and spread his arms wide apologetically. "I am sorry that you took me so seriously."

Pain and humiliation mounted in Clarissa's breast. "A hoax." Her tone was low and contemptuous.

Sidney paused a moment to admire her acting ability. The woman was a veritable wonder, playing the part of the high and injured to perfection.

"It started out as a jest," he continued, "to amuse myself alone. But lately my conscience has been bothering me . . ."

"Your conscience!" she said witheringly.

He smiled across at her. "I do possess one, Clarissa. I thought it best to stop the venture before it became impos-

179

sible to extricate myself. I have no intention of marrying anyone. And I certainly do not love you."

Clarissa had borne each syllable like an arrow to her heart, but this last statement wounded her so inexplicably that she let out a sudden cry and leaped to her feet, the room a blur, blinking hard and forbidding herself to shed one tear in front of so disgusting a creature.

"Pray do not be distressed," Sidney said, pursuing her across the room. "You and I are the only ones who need know the truth of this dreadful hoax. Engagements are often broken in the ton, and I think we can agree we are lucky."

"Lucky!" Her head snapped back in scorn.

"No formal announcement has appeared in the *Gazette.* You shall tell everyone you begged off. I insist on that point. Since only a few in our own houses are acquainted with the engagement, no great harm shall come to your reputation from me."

"No great harm," Clarissa repeated with icy courtesy. He had tricked her and toyed with her and now saw fit to fling his hoax in her teeth. "Pray do not do me any more favors, Mr. Montcrieff. You seem to have all the answers. Indeed, yours was a first-rate scheme, and I wonder that I could have been so goosish not to see it from the first. I congratulate you. You played the part of a lover to perfection. I just hope that Lytton is not engaged in similar sport with Emily."

"No," Sidney said, watching her carefully. "Lytton is in earnest."

She glanced down at her hands, angry to find them shaking, and pulled off the diamond ring from her finger.

"This belongs to you. Take it and go, before I forget myself and my manners."

Sidney pocketed the ring. "Do not think to spare me at

such a time, Clarissa. If you wish to say anything, now is the time."

She lifted her chin a fraction of an inch. "I wish to say nothing to an odious trickster like you!"

"Yes, that would be the feeling of anyone played for a fool, would it not?"

Stricken, she turned away, one hand pressed to her mouth. His adieu went unacknowledged, as did Mrs. Quill's call to dinner. Clarissa stared down at the letter to her parents so happily penned an hour earlier. All the pain she had felt with Sidney flew up. She snatched the missive and tore it into a hundred pieces with frenzied fingers, then toppled forward on the couch, crying as though her heart were broken.

17

The following morning a travel chaise departed the Claring grounds headed toward the road to London. Inside the vehicle Polly examined the wan face across from her in mute sympathy. No need to ask what kind of night her mistress had passed. The dark eyes, heavy-lidded and red-rimmed, said it all.

Polly, though by no means fully cognizant of all the details of the previous afternoon, had had her ear filled with Mrs. Quill's earnest interpretations and had even seen fit to formulate a few of her own. Ten minutes into the ride she ventured a shy query.

"Do you not think we should call at Miss Manville's?"

Clarissa gave her head a weary shake. "I have left a note for Emily with Mrs. Quill, and one for Mrs. Boatwright as well."

Polly tried another tack. "Then should we stop at Bengal Court and wish Mr. Montcrieff a good-bye?"

Clarissa's eyes, tired as they were from lack of sleep, flashed fire. "No, Polly," came the acid reply. "I'd much rather wish him to Jericho!"

"Miss Clarissa!"

Clarissa directed a quelling look at her abigail. "I do not wish to hear another word about Mr. Montcrieff," she said ominously.

Squelched, Polly lapsed into an uncomfortable silence, wondering to herself just what had passed between the happy couple.

Clarissa, her head turned toward the window, was in no mood to enlighten Polly on that matter nor anyone else. Sidney Montcrieff was a closed book as far as she was concerned, a book moreover, which she had no intention of ever opening again.

He had treated her like a veritable trollop with his disgusting hoax, and she was a goosecap for even imagining she might be in love with him. It was a pity, she thought, looking so grim that Polly grew frightened, that she could not reveal Montcrieff's true nature to the ton without betraying her own foolishness as well.

The miles rolled on in blessed silence. Although Clarissa had earned a respite from Polly's conversation, she could not still another voice.

I do not love you, Clarissa.

Nor I, you. Nor I, you, she whispered to the stone gray cottages faded into the distance.

At four o'clock the carriage rambled up St. James Square and came to a stop. Clarissa, travel-stained and weary, descended. A second later the door opened, and Walter's usually wooden face broke out in a smile.

"Why, it's Miss Clarissa!"

"Yes, Walter," Clarissa said, her eyes misting at the familiar sight of the butler. "Are my parents at home?"

"Yes, miss," he said, closing the door. "I shall fetch them immediately."

Walter had scarcely time to trouble himself with this task. Lady Claringdon was just descending from an afternoon's rest and had witnessed her daughter's timely entrance. One glance at the figure waiting and she screeched with such joy that her spouse came running from his office with a sheaf of bills clutched in his fist.

"Constance!" His mustache bobbed up and down when he caught sight of Clarissa. "By Jove, you!"

"Yes, Papa," Clarissa said in a small voice. "Your prodigal has returned."

Two hours later Sir Arthur was busy congratulating himself on doing the deed when Walter ushered in Carlton and Trixie to his drawing room. Carlton, surveying his father's air of unusual amiability, immediately discerned the reason behind the dinner invitation so hastily extended.

"Clarissa has returned, I warrant?" he asked as he greeted Sir Arthur.

Sir Arthur, on the verge himself of issuing a happy announcement on this very point, found his speech ruthlessly stripped from him by his very own flesh and blood.

"Yes, blast it!" he said, looking as red as the russet drapes on either side of the room.

Trixie, though no stranger to the Claringdon circle, shrank back against her husband's arm, her face alternating between delight and alarm.

"Has there been some new quarrel, sir?"

"No, no." Sir Arthur patted her on the hand and favored her with a smile. "It's just that Carlton would have to spoil my surprise."

"I'm sorry, Father," Carlton grinned. "You were so full of it, and what other reason could be behind such an urgent request for dinner?"

"Is Clarissa all right?" Trixie asked anxiously.

"Yes," Sir Arthur assured her. "And," he added with relish, "she's as obedient as a pup."

"That doesn't sound like our Clarissa," Carlton said, seating Trixie on a red satin chair.

"If you mean," Sir Arthur offered in measured tones, "that she is no longer as willful and headstrong as she used to be, then I can only thank God for that." He helped himself to some of his snuff and thrust the box at Carlton. "Take a pinch of this, please. I can't tell if I dislike it or not."

Carlton dutifully sampled the mixture, pronouncing it a shade too wet to suit his own tastes.

"But what were you saying about Clarissa, Papa?"

Sir Arthur banged his snuffbox shut. "I was saying that had I known the country would be so beneficial to her temperament I would have dispatched her there years ago. She'd be married by now, and"—he shook his finger at his son—"I should have done the same with you."

"But Father," Carlton said, hiding a smile, "then I might have married some perfectly dreadful woman instead of Trixie. And Trixie would not soon to bear you a grandson. So it's much better, don't you think, that you did not banish me to Claring!"

"Yes, very true," Sir Arthur said, following this circular reasoning with difficulty.

Carlton, who was on the verge of asking his father the details of his sister's return, was prevented from doing so by the advent of Lady Claringdon and Clarissa herself, who came into the room a vision in green sarsnet.

"Trixie! Carlton!" she cried out.

"Oh, Clarissa," Trixie exclaimed, running to her. "How could you have stayed away so long?"

Clarissa laughed and turned to her brother, congratulating him on the babe. "You look quite exuberant, the two of you."

"Afraid I can't say the same about you," Carlton answered, looking at her more closely than she would have wished. "The country seems to have had an ill effect on you. You're much too pale."

"That is the mode of all true penitents, Carlton," Clarissa explained lightly and drew away from his too penetrating gaze.

"Perhaps so, but don't do such a thing again," Carlton scolded. "Papa was in such a tizzy."

Sir Arthur was unaccustomed to having his behavior described in such terms and lodged a vociferous protest. "I was not!"

"Carlton is correct," Lady Claringdon declared, casting her weight with her son. "Your father was on the verge of penning a note to you himself, Clarissa, when you arrived today."

Clarissa's amused eyes searched for her father. "Capitulation, Papa?" she asked sweetly.

"Nothing of the sort," Sir Arthur scowled. "But all the same, don't go dashing off again."

Sir Arthur was spared from further roasting by Walter's entrance, announcing dinner. Clarissa, debating with Trixie the names selected for her soon-to-be nephew or niece, took her place at the table and bent an attentive ear to the tales of the London scene she had missed, including the czar's arrival and his finding Pulteney's Hotel more to his taste than Carlton House.

"Which had the Regent in a state, as you may well imagine," Trixie said.

Clarissa laughed. It was good to be home, and yet something was missing. Sternly she adjured herself not to be foolish and yearn after what was lost. A closed book, she reminded herself as she accepted another helping of duckling.

The evening passed quickly. Trixie and Carlton departed, and Clarissa retired to her bedchamber. Sir Arthur, now that his daughter had returned, was in an expansive mood and in his own sitting room confided to his wife his intention of having a little talk with Clarissa soon.

"For she must now be showing some inclination toward marriage—"

"Arthur," Lady Claringdon beseeched. "The child has not yet spent one night under our roof. Can you not postpone your serious talk until another occasion?"

Sir Arthur shot her a quick look. "Why should I?"

Lady Claringdon fell silent a moment. "There is something different about Clarissa. Yes, I know I sound like a shatterbrain, but I feel she is quite changed."

"Perhaps," Sir Arthur agreed. "But if so, it's all for the best."

"I am not so certain," Lady Claringdon answered. "Might you not delay this serious talk of yours for just a few days? I have the strongest suspicion that whenever you and Clarissa speak to each other you fall into another vile quarrel."

Sir Arthur was by no means mollified by this assessment of his form of address and answered coldly that he would do as he saw fit.

"Yes, of course you will," Lady Claringdon said soothingly.

A few minutes later in her own dressing room Lady Claringdon paused. By nature she was a devoted mother and had allowed her children to grow up without much fuss or botheration. However, Clarissa's situation now seemed to beg for motherly intervention. She donned a red brocade gown and swept down the hall to her daughter's room, halting briefly at the threshold when she spied a wan-looking Clarissa seated on the side of the bed. What in heaven had happened back at Claring?

"What a dinner," Lady Claringdon said, breezily entering and kissing Clarissa. "I vow that Pierre has outdone himself. I have eaten much too much. But you, I noticed, did not appear too hungry."

"I am too tired to be hungry, Mama," Clarissa answered.

Lady Claringdon clasped her by the waist. "Clarissa, are you feeling at all the thing?"

"Why, of course, Mama. I am just a trifle tired from the journey."

Lady Claringdon gave her a speculative look. "I suppose the country was very wearying?"

"Oh, no," Clarissa said, drawing away. "I had many diversions. There were the Quills, Giles, and John. And you should see the gardens now."

"It sounds like a rather dull visit if you ask me," Lady Claringdon said frankly.

Clarissa gave a rueful laugh. "The country is far from exciting. I'm sorry that I'm not in the mood for a chat tonight, Mama. But a good night's sleep shall undoubtedly put me to rights."

Lady Claringdon tactfully withdrew, but her curiosity was far from satisfied. This blue mood of her daughter's was serious indeed. Something was wrong with Clarissa, and she was determined to find the answer. The next morning after Sir Arthur had driven off with Clarissa on a round of errands, she summoned Polly to her sitting room.

"Polly," she said, casting aside her needlepoint when the abigail appeared, "what happened in the Cotswolds?"

"You mean to Miss Clarissa?"

"Yes, of course," Lady Claringdon said impatiently. "It's quite obvious that she is not at all herself. And I don't know whether to call for a doctor or to quack her myself!"

"It's a different kind of sickness, my lady," Polly said earnestly.

"Will you tell me before I burst?"

Without hesitation and with considerable relief, Polly poured out the tale she had carried with her from Claring. Lady Claringdon listened in amazed silence until the abigail abruptly halted.

"Sidney Montcrieff offered for Clarissa."

"Yes," Polly said, bobbing her head. "And everyone was so happy! There could be no doubt of Sir Arthur's approval since he was so anxious to see her settled, and Miss Clarissa herself was in alt."

"Was she indeed," Lady Claringdon said, mulling over this tidy bit of news. What she knew of Montcrieff was sparing but of good repute. She shifted her weight in her satin chair. "What happened to sour them on each other?" she demanded.

Polly wrung her hands. "I don't know. Mrs. Quill mentioned that Mr. Montcrieff had called the day before yesterday and left in a huff. Miss Clarissa was found sobbing and declaring that she had changed her mind. There wasn't going to be a marriage, after all. Then she ordered me to pack a few things, and the next morning we came right back to London."

Lady Claringdon straightened a matching pair of T'ang horses.

"You are certain that Clarissa turned him down."

Polly nodded. "Oh, yes, my lady. For certain."

"But why did she do such a thing?" Lady Claringdon murmured to herself. "I am not acquainted with Montcrieff myself, but Lady Peoples speaks highly of him."

"Oh, he is the nicest sort, my lady," Polly said quickly. "Or he was until all this happened. He seemed to be so taken with Miss Clarissa and she with him."

Lady Claringdon gazed thoughtfully into the abigail's soft brown eyes. "You think Clarissa may have loved him?" she asked, arching an eyebrow.

"It does look that way, my lady."

Lady Claringdon chewed on a lip. "Thank you, Polly. You have been most helpful."

Polly withdrew, and Lady Claringdon picked up her tambour frame. But after a few wayward stitches she pushed it aside impatiently. This was not the time to be thinking of stitches, not while her daughter languished with a broken heart!

While Lady Claringdon was deep in her brown study, her daughter and husband were enjoying their outing in Green Park. Clarissa's reappearance in London had not gone unnoticed, and acquaintances and suitors alike drew up alongside the phaeton to hail her.

"I feel like a damn coachman!" Sir Arthur grumbled. Despite his words, he could not help a flush of pride in his daughter so poised and beautiful in the seat next to him.

After Clarissa had passed a full half hour exclaiming over the changes in Green Park and the number of cows that seemed to be populating it, he turned the carriage up toward Bruton Street, where she descended to reacquaint Madame Fanchon with her return to London and to make an appointment for a fitting in the coming week. It was only a matter of time, Sir Arthur thought, as he fingered some of the bolts of cloth in the shop, before Clarissa would be ordering her wedding dress from Fanchon's.

In a very leisurely fashion the carriage progressed on to Hookam's lending library. Father and daughter entered together, and after an exhaustive search of the shelves,

Clarissa settled on Miss Austen's latest. She was carrying the book out of the store when Mr. Hedges entered, swinging a gilded cane. The collision of book and cane was immediate, and both objects flew out into the street.

Mr. Hedges, finding himself the object of scrutiny by a pair of gray eyes, turned as red as the hair on his head.

"I am most dreadfully sorry, Miss Claringdon," he said, scurrying after the book and dodging the path of several coachmen who hurled insults at him.

"You remember Mr. Hedges, Clarissa," Sir Arthur asked as Hedges dusted off the book with his handkerchief. He looked, she thought ruefully, even more simian-like than ever.

"Indeed yes," she said, acknowledging his greeting. "How are you?"

"Quite fine." He held out the book to her and dropped it again into the street.

And he was as clumsy as ever.

"You have been away, Miss Claringdon," Hedges said when Sir Arthur had taken control of the book.

"On a visit to Claring," Sir Arthur interposed. "Shall we see you at Lady Sefton's ball tomorrow, Hedges?"

"Oh, yes," the eager voice quaked. "Shall you be there, Miss Claringdon?" he asked shyly.

Clarissa drew the folds of her sable-trimmed pelisse closer and said she thought not.

Sir Arthur appeared vexed. "You must come, Clarissa," he cajoled. "Your mother and I are attending, and Lady Sefton shall have our heads if you are not there too."

Hedges bobbed his head in agreement. "Oh, yes. And will you save one of your dances for me, Miss Claringdon?"

"Yes," Sir Arthur said, taking reckless hold of his daughter's future. "And perhaps, more than one. Now you must excuse us. We are off on some errands." He handed Clarissa up into the waiting phaeton while Hedges made a valiant try for his cane still in the middle of the road.

"I do wish you would let me accept my own dances, Papa," Clarissa said when they were under way again.

"You would have said no," Sir Arthur snorted.

"Most assuredly," Clarissa answered. "You saw him yourself. He is as clumsy as ever, and when we dance he tramples on my feet."

"He's nervous and that makes him clumsy," Sir Arthur said.

"And that makes me nervous," she declared. "I do wish you would stop pushing him at me in this vulgar fashion."

"Vulgar!" Sir Arthur winced. Much good the country seemed to have done for her disposition! "Never mind Hedges," he said, pushing on. "Charles will be at the ball and Colonel Crowne; he has been asking after you since he came back from France."

"I'll be glad to see Charles," Clarissa said, opening her ivory fan. "But I do wish you will stop foisting me into the arms of the military. And I wish you will not do *that.*"

"Do what?" Sir Arthur asked, aggrieved.

"Pull your mustache," she answered. He dropped his hand. "That always means you are making up your mind to say something to me. And it is always, always unpleasant."

"Indeed it is not," Sir Arthur said, annoyed. "You must be the only woman in the ton who considers marriage an unpleasant topic for conversation. And I have not changed my mind, Clarissa. I intend to see you married at the end of Season!"

Clarissa snapped her fan shut. "I am well aware of that, Papa. Pray do not fall into a swoon, but I am quite prepared to be married!"

18

After an excellent luncheon, which had included her favorite smelts and curried eggs, Clarissa retired to her rooms to read the mangled work of Miss Austen. Sir Arthur, beaming beatifically, lost not a moment in acquainting his wife with their daughter's change of heart.

Lady Claringdon's reaction defied words. "I don't believe it!" she declared, pushing away a plate of smelts.

Sir Arthur, unaccustomed to having his veracity questioned, looked accusingly at her from across the table. "It's the truth," he protested with his mustache aquiver. "Although I can't blame you for being surprised. I broached the topic to her this morning as we rode home, and I was not ham-handed at all," he said, reaching for a peach and a paring knife.

"And she agreed?" Lady Claringdon asked, watching her husband's struggle with the peach.

"Yes!" Sir Arthur said. "She said she was no longer opposed to the idea of marriage, and that I might choose whomever I thought suitable."

These words did nothing to allay the growing fears within Lady Claringdon's breast. She fixed her fine gray eyes on her spouse. In no way did her genuine affection for him blind her to his powers of judgment.

"And have you selected some paragon?" she asked uneasily.

"Not yet, but I soon shall," Sir Arthur said. He saw her concern. "Now, now, Constance. No need to look that way. I shall not betroth her to a villain, I promise. All I ask is for her to marry someone who will treat her kindly and not act in a havey-cavey manner."

Lady Claringdon accepted a peach slice from her husband's knife along with this offering. "But will she have no say in the matter?" she inquired, chewing. "Even *I* had some say, and you know how *my* parents were."

"Lord, she don't want a say!" Sir Arthur exclaimed. "Told me so herself. I'm to draw up a list of the eligibles and let her have my choice. And bless me if I don't do just that." He finished the peach and wiped his hands on a napkin, thinking hard. "I'll put Hedges down; I know he's clumsy, but we must consider his fortune. And Pedlow, an Adonis, and never mind that mother of his. Then there's Wentworth, a gambler but so are we all." He mused on in this fashion for several minutes. "I daresay we shall see them all at the Sefton Ball."

"Is there room on your list for one addition?" Lady Claringdon asked.

Sir Arthur looked up in surprise. "Is there someone you favor, my dear? I wonder you did not tell me long ago."

"I do not favor him, exactly," Lady Claringdon said mildly. Seeing the quizzical look growing on her husband's face, she hastened to add, "I have heard good things about him. Sidney Montcrieff is his name."

Sir Arthur knitted his brows. "Montcrieff? I have heard the name, but I don't know the fellow. And how is it you know him, Constance?"

Lady Claringdon began a hasty search through the dregs of her memory for some reasonable offering.

"He is cousin to one of Trixie's friends," she said finally. "I believe him to be a gentleman, and if you are considering the likes of Hedges, who shall put me to the blush, then I beg you to consider **Montcrieff** as well."

"Oh, very well," Sir Arthur said with some grace. "But I've never met the chap. And who's to say he's interested in Clarissa?"

"We shall see," Lady Claringdon murmured.

"Will he be at the Sefton Ball?" Sir Arthur quizzed, tempted by another peach.

"Who can tell, sir. Who can tell."

Twenty-four hours after Clarissa had left Claring, a solitary rider set out from the nearby estate of Bengal Court along the southern route to London. Sidney's haste in leaving Gloucestershire found no favor with his aunt, who subjected him to a torrent of questions none of which he appeared to hear or wished to answer. He even came close to cuffs with the earl concerning his broken engagement to Clarissa, the earl finding it all but impossible to believe that such an idyllic romance could come to such a brutal end.

At midnight Sidney arrived at Hill Street where Bender greeted him without any show of surprise. To his relief his butler did not ask any questions about Lytton or Bengal Court. Just thinking of the latter brought her to mind again, and he had had quite enough of that.

The following morning he set out promptly for Grosvenor Square, intending to pass a few hours with Lady Vye again. Unfortunately he was halted in this plan by Lady Vye's butler, who ruefully shook his head when he saw who was at the door.

"She can't still be on her high ropes," Sidney complained.

"I'm sorry, sir, but Lady Vye is not within."

"Then I'll wait," he said with the ease of long acquaintance.

The butler shook his head again. "T'would do you no good. Lady Vye has departed for Vienna."

"Vienna?" Sidney was surprised and showed it. "What the devil does she want to do in Vienna of all places?"

"She's planning to live there, sir," the butler answered, "with her new husband."

"A new husband!" Sidney slammed his cane onto the ground, instantly diverted. "Good heavens, don't tell me. She latched onto one of those Spanish counts who have been paying her court."

"Lady Vye's husband is a German prince," the butler acknowledged.

"A German prince," Sidney echoed, and went off thanking the butler for the news. Surprisingly the fact that Lady Vye was married did not bother him as much as he expected. His feelings for her had never been anything but casual passion, and if she had found a German prince for a husband so much the better.

However, he had been looking forward to spending some of his days with her, and now that route was closed. Musing over this, he walked back to Hill Street. He knew he could take part in Assemblies, breakfasts, and the other entertainments of the Season still in progress in London, but after what had happened to him at Bengal Court he had no taste for idle flirtation much less serious courtship.

Since these activities were for him out of the question, he found his diversion in the gaming rooms of White's and Watier's. Here, surrounded by his cronies, he could for a time and price forget the face and figure of Clarissa Claringdon. He threw himself into the activity with a vengeance, and when the entertainments at White's and Watier's grew too tame for his taste he went off to some of the more disreputable gambling dens that London offered. And it was not uncommon for him to pass a whole night there.

Involved as he was in these nocturnal events, Mr. Sidney Montcrieff was—much to Lady Claringdon's annoyance—not to be found among the guests at the Sefton Ball, but everyone else in the haute ton was. Lady Sefton was one of the ton's leading hostesses and when she beckoned, everyone flocked. Her gatherings, if not noted for the companionship of wits such as those gracing the tables at Lady Jersey's or the Duchess of York's, at least boasted the finest in food, wine, and music.

"And there's no danger of sitting on her mutts," Sir Arthur said, recalling an altercation with a Pekingese at the Duchess of York's.

The Seftons received them graciously, Lady Sefton being too well mannered to inquire after Clarissa's long absence, contented herself with admiring the gown of gold silk and ivory lace that had been Fanchon's latest inspiration. Sir Arthur, his face alight with pride, led his wife and daughter into the grand ballroom.

The ballroom was filled with guests, the women bejeweled and exquisitely gowned. Huge chandeliers overhead were lit with hundreds of candles and swayed in time to the music. Several ladies, flushed with the exertions of the early dances, stood in circles plying their fans. The shimmer of light off their diamonds and echoes of laughter made Clarissa's head swim.

But not for long. Within a minute of her entrance, looking more cool and beautiful than ever, the gentlemen of the ton beat a long-accustomed path to her. To Sir Arthur's amusement and Lady Claringdon's gratification, their daughter was inundated with requests for her hand. With some curiosity Sir Arthur waited to see who would win her hand for the first set. A pleasant surprise awaited. Flashing a saucy smile at her father, Clarissa allowed Colonel Crowne, a good man if a trifle wooden, to lead her onto the floor.

The colonel was nothing at all like Charles Alsgood, who swooped her into the next dance without a greeting and demanded to know why she had saved only one dance for him.

"You arrived too late, Charles," she replied.

"Dash it, Clarissa. How was I to know you'd be here?" he asked with some passion. His green eyes quizzed her. "Carlton never breathed a word of this to me. And where have you been hiding, I long to know."

"I took a holiday at Claring."

"Holiday, my eye," Charles said with acute precision.

She gazed up at Charles, slender, lithe, and possessed of a smile that could melt hearts. Not for the first time Clarissa wondered why her own heart refused to melt in the face of Charles's charm. Perhaps it had something to do with growing up with him. A great pity. Anyway, she reminded herself grimly, it was much too late. Her heart had melted once, and nothing but pain had come of that!

"I say, Clarissa, have you left your hearing at Claring?" Charles asked, looking down at her with some exasperation.

"I beg your pardon?" she asked. "You were saying."

"I was asking if you were promised to anyone for supper."

She nodded. "Bartholemew Brigg was kind enough to ask me."

Amazement spread in Alsgood's eyes. "You are cutting it too thin, my dear. Not like you to encourage the toadeaters."

"Hush, Charles!" she said quickly. "Someone will hear."

"No one will hear us in this crush," he contradicted. "I am shocked at you, my girl. You always had such exquisite taste. But what can any fellow think seeing you dance with Crowne and dine with Brigg?"

"I am also dancing with you," she said demurely.

Charles threw back his head and roared. "Touché. Let's see if we can go and unpromise you to Brigg."

Unhappily this deed was not so easily accomplished as imagined. Mr. Brigg showed a singular distaste for having his invitation usurped by Charles. Only when the two men were recalled to their surroundings by Brigg's bosom friend, William Ledmore—it would never do to come to cuffs at a party of Maria Sefton's—did Clarissa finally sit down to supper with Mr. Brigg.

The table, as always, was laden with the delicacies of the Sefton's French chef, but Clarissa ate with little appetite, merely sampling the turbot and tasting the creamed lobster. The only one who noticed her abstract mood was her mother.

Clarissa's appearance at the ball caused the gentlemen of the ton to renew their battle for her hand. The Claringdon drawing room was again the scene of numerous morning and afternoon callers, not only Mr. Hedges—who seemed, as Lady Claringdon put it, undiscourageable—but also Pedlow, Wentworth, Brigg, Ledmore, and several others. Charles Alsgood, on appearing one day at the threshold and surveying the assembly gathered, remarked under his breath to Clarissa that she seemed bent on founding a menagerie. But his feelings found no favor with Sir Arthur, who glowed with pride and satisfaction each time the knocker sounded. And sound it did!

"Trust me, my dear," he said to his wife, relaxing one evening in her sitting room. "Clarissa is getting accustomed to the idea of marriage."

"So you say," Lady Claringdon agreed skeptically. "But which bridegroom have you selected for her?" Her keen eyes darted from her embroidery to hold his for a long moment. "I trust they have all spoken to you of marriage?"

"Oh, yes," Sir Arthur said, twirling his mustache at both ends. "Pedlow offers her his part of the kingdom, and I know it's riddled with debts, so you mustn't look so worried. I wonder how anyone so dashing can let his estates rot."

"Who else besides Pedlow?" Lady Claringdon asked.

"Oh, Charles, certainly. And that fellow Hedges, and Brigg, and Ledmore. . . ." He broke off in a frown. "Haven't heard from that favorite of yours, Montcrieff."

"Never mind," Lady Claringdon said with great charity. "Whom have you selected for her?"

Sir Arthur sank deeper into the couch. "I don't know," he finally admitted. "I have thought of it. I'm inclined to favor Charles since he's known her since they were children. But I suppose I shall just leave the matter to Clarissa."

Lady Claringdon, who had never dreamed for so much sense in her spouse, quickly agreed. "That is an excellent idea, sir! I just wonder whom she will select."

So, too, did Sir Arthur. After informing their daughter that the choice of bridegroom was hers, he sat back patiently with every expectation of a quick decision. But though Clarissa accepted many invitations extended by her beaux during the ensuing weeks—an excursion to the opera one night with Wentworth and his parents, and a morning drive to Hampton Court with Hedges, who displayed a remarkable talent for getting lost in mazes—she showed no inclination to reach a decision.

In his study Sir Arthur fumed and fretted. *That chit would never get married if left to herself.* When another week had passed without any resultant announcement, he went off in search of his daughter, finding her at long last in a small parlor in the back of the house, frowning over an easel, her paints, and a bowl of peaches and pears.

"Clarissa," he thundered, resolved to bring the matter to a quick close. "I must know your decision."

Clarissa turned a puzzled face from her palette to the figure hovering next to her.

"A decision on what, Papa?"

"On marriage!" Sir Arthur ejaculated, once again doing damage to his intricately arranged neckcloth. "What else have we ever talked about, you and I? You can't keep your suitors on a string forever," he went on. "People shall call you an ape-leader—flighty. We can't have that!"

"No, indeed," Clarissa said, wiping her paintbrush clean with a cloth and emitting a soft sigh. "Were that the case I would be on the shelf forever, wouldn't I?"

Sir Arthur crossed his arms on his chest and stood his ground. "You must reach a decision today. What about Charles? You stand on such good terms with him."

"No," Clarissa said, applying a touch of cobalt to the canvas in front of her. "Not Charles."

"Then who? You have been back in London a fortnight. I know that is not a terribly long time, but surely after five Seasons you must have some idea. . . . And I wish you will attend to me and stop fussing with that blasted painting."

Clarissa took a deep breath and looked her father in the eye.

"Oh, very well, Papa. If it's a decision you *must* have a decision you *shall* have."

"Good." Sir Arthur waited. "Well . . ." he said impatiently.

"I select Mr. Ledmore."

Sir Arthur stared at his daughter, dumbfounded.

"Ledmore?" he croaked when he had found his voice. "Clarissa, if this is another of your tiresome jests . . ."

"Papa, will you stop speaking fustian?" Clarissa pleaded, laying aside her palette in agitation. "You demand a choice from me and when I make one, you stand there gaping at me. I have chosen Mr. *Ledmore.*" She spoke the name slowly as though to a child.

"*William* Ledmore?" Sir Arthur asked, grasping at a straw.

"I believe William is his given name."

Sir Arthur made no attempt to preserve his countenance.

"You have taken leave of your senses," he said, not unkindly. "Why not take Charles? He is so droll. And your mother and I already like him so excessively."

"How wonderful for you and for Charles. But I shall be marrying Mr. Ledmore," Clarissa said in a voice of foreboding.

"Oh, very well," Sir Arthur replied, a grim look forming around his own mouth. He stalked to the door but was unable to resist one last parting shot. "Though why you must have Ledmore, who is the dullest man in the ton, I swear I have no idea!"

He banged the door shut, and Clarissa was alone again with her bowl of fruit. But her mind was no longer engaged in painting, and she laid her brush aside. Her father might be totally bewildered by her choice in husbands, but Ledmore made perfect sense to her. He might very well be the dullest man in the ton, but this was an imperfection she felt willing to tolerate. His lack of wit, grace, and charm—flaws to any other lady—were virtues to her. She wanted a husband who would never remind her in any way of Sidney Montcrieff!

Montcrieff! She grimaced sharply at the name. In vain she had struggled to keep from dwelling on him or his hateful behavior, but her heart would not obey her orders. If Montcrieff had not appeared in her life—for all the world like a flash of lightning on a summer's day—she might very well have chosen Charles and pleased everyone. But now that avenue was closed to her. Charles, sweet dear Charles, deserved better; and he would have soon discovered that he had not won her heart. Whereas Mr. Ledmore, dull-witted to begin with, would never assume from the first that she were marrying him for love.

The following morning Sir Arthur made his way to Mr. Ledmore's bachelor quarters on Green Street to acquaint him with his good fortune. Ushered into the small, cold parlor that served as Ledmore's drawing room, he waited impatiently for his prospective son-in-law to appear. Mr. Ledmore showed no surprise that the prize Beauty Clarissa Claringdon had accepted his offer, and instead, received the news as his just due.

Like a damned popinjay, Sir Arthur thought gloomily, taking the glass of Malaga that Ledmore handed him.

"I think your daughter has shown excellent sense in selecting me over the more frivolous fellows paying her court," Ledmore said.

"Do you indeed," Sir Arthur snapped, sampling what had to be the worst Malaga in creation. He shot Ledmore a measuring look from his chair. What he saw made Clarissa's choice even more incomprehensible. Mr. Ledmore was nothing at all to stare at, being tall, thin, and possessed of a weak, almost Gallic chin. He was, however, well pursed on account of an uncle's timely death a year ago, and it was on account of that purse, Sir Arthur reminded himself as he swirled the vile wine, that he had even entertained Ledmore's suit, never dreaming for a moment that his daughter would accept such a strange specimen.

Sir Arthur tried another sip of the Malaga and found it every bit as bad as the first. Ledmore, perhaps, was not an ugly man, but he was surely no prime article. Bland was the word that Sir Arthur settled on during the course of his visit to Green Street. As bland as bread pudding, which he had never cared for. Come to think of it, neither did his daughter.

"I am certain Clarissa will make me an excellent wife," Ledmore said, sticking out what little chin he possessed and looking down his nose at Sir Arthur.

"And I hope you shall make her an equally excellent husband," Sir Arthur retorted.

Mr. Ledmore smiled his thin smile, offered more Malaga—which was promptly refused—and fixed the arrangement for his proposal to Clarissa. Sir Arthur, his duties done, quickly returned to his curricle and took the long way home to St. James Square.

The day was bright and clear, a rarity in London whatever the season. The streets bustled with crowds and excitement over Alexander, and the usual array of vendors cried out their wares. Sir Arthur paid no notice. His spirits were abysmal, and that perplexed him. Hadn't he wanted Clarissa betrothed? Fought tooth and nail for just such a day? And now that she had chosen a groom he could not find it in his heart to protest. But a broomstick like Ledmore! Bah! Victory was his, but he felt not a groat of satisfaction.

The same, unfortunately, could not be said of Mr. Ledmore, whose consequence was always abnormally large for his modest abilities. Promptly the next morning he paid a duty call on Clarissa, nodding in approval when he saw her figure waiting on the couch in the blue drawing room. At thirty-five Ledmore was a stickler for punctuality in his help, having gone through at least a dozen servants, and any wife of his would be a definite part of the help.

"Good morning, Miss Claringdon," he said politely.

"Good morning, Mr. Ledmore," Clarissa said, extending her hand.

Ledmore took it, puzzled over whether to kiss it, and then gave it the barest of shakes. He sat down on the couch next to her and cleared his bony throat.

"I'm a busy man, Miss Claringdon . . ."

Clarissa's eyes widened. "Indeed, sir."

"So I shall get right to the point. I know you agree with the way I like to do things, and we both know the reason behind my presence. I trust you show no disinclination to becoming my wife?"

Clarissa blinked at this high-handed manner of address. Ledmore might have been ordering a mince pie from his kitchen. But what had she expected? No emotion or passion existed between the two of them. And wasn't that what she had wanted in a husband?

"Miss Claringdon . . ." Ledmore said, sharply breaking into her thoughts.

She started. "Mr. Ledmore, I consider it an honor, and I accept," she said in a voice every bit as cool as his own.

"Good." He rubbed his hands together, pleased. For a moment she grew frightened that he would feel moved to kiss her, but her fears were laid to rest as he merely smiled. "I think you have chosen well."

"Do you indeed," she said with the faintest hauteur.

"Yes, I do. As I told your father yesterday, we shall suit very well." He puffed up his cheeks. "I knew it from the start. You have been headstrong in the past, I know, but a little marriage works a cure of girlish ways."

Two spots of color burned bright on Clarissa's cheeks. She had never heard such odious condescension in her entire life. "I wonder that you would offer for so dissolute a creature!"

Ledmore's face, pinched in annoyance, turned her way. "Dissolute? Surely. . . . Oh, I see. You are offended?" He twisted his lips in another quirky smile. "That too shall change. As my wife, Miss Claringdon, I shall expect you to act in a way that reflects my station."

Clarissa rose majestically from the couch. "I assure you, Mr. Ledmore, I am fully conscious of just what station you command in the ton!"

"Good."

"Now," she said, bringing the proposal to a close, "you must excuse me, for I greatly fear I have the headache!"

19

"And if I had just accepted Ledmore, I should have a headache too!" Lady Claringdon exclaimed the next morning at Mount Street.

Carlton, who had been pleased to find his mother an early morning visitor, had listened in growing astonishment to the events concerning his sister.

"Surely Ledmore is not as odious as all that," he insisted.

Lady Claringdon shrugged, her shoulders moving uneasily under her fox-trimmed pelisse. "Oh, I don't call him odious, Carlton. We would never countenance the match otherwise. But so dull-witted." She appealed to Trixie on the couch. "Duller even than that Mr. Hedges."

"Perhaps that is why Clarissa has selected him," Carlton suggested, placing an arm around his mother for support. The matter must be serious indeed for her to be so agitated. "Clarissa is so sharp-witted herself," he continued, "that she might need some one a little more sober than herself."

"I have always considered sobriety a virtue," Lady Claringdon pronounced. "But Mr. Ledmore has changed my views. You shall see for yourselves on Friday."

"But what happens on Friday, Mama?"

Lady Claringdon hunted for her vinaigrette. "He is coming to dinner. And if you have any other engagements, you shall cry off from them. I want you both near to bear me strength."

Carlton smiled at this inordinate passion in his mother. "And if we disapprove, Mama? Shall Clarissa change her mind?"

Regretfully, Lady Claringdon shook her curly head. "No, that matter is hopeless. She is determined to have him." She sniffed her hartshorn. "Ledmore!"

"Don't distress yourself, Mama," Carlton said. "Clarissa must have some reason for choosing him."

But what that reason was Carlton himself longed to know on Friday evening. Only ten minutes into Ledmore's company, he found himself echoing his parents' stupefaction. What did Clarissa see in the fellow? Not much to look at, and he was hardly the polished sort. Not a Tulip or a Melton Man. A dull dog were the kindest words Carlton could say about Mr. Ledmore.

He gazed across the table at his sister, pushing her food around on her plate with little success. The whole Claringdon family seemed to have come to the table without appetite. Only Mr. Ledmore ate heartily.

"I believe congratulations are in order, Claringdon," Ledmore said when the gentlemen sat alone enjoying their port. The women had withdrawn, and the cloth was removed from the table.

"Congratulations?" Carlton asked politely.

Ledmore favored him with a thin smile. "I did not like

to speak of the matter in front of your wife. Women in their condition are inclined to be nervous."

Carlton sipped his port. "Oh, that. Trixie knows she's expecting. 'Twas she who informed us of the fact."

Sir Arthur, caught with his glass halfway to his lips, narrowly missed chucking it down his shirtfront. Mr. Ledmore swiveled his bony head toward Carlton.

"Do you think it wise that she be out in public at such a time?"

"By all accounts there is more than six months before the babe is due," Carlton said, his eyes narrowing in surprise. "It's civil of you to worry about her, but I assure you you needn't."

"It was the propriety I was concerned with," Ledmore answered, ignoring the dangerous crook of Carlton's brows. "My grandmother stayed her whole term in her own house."

"I should think that devilish boring," Carlton said. "What say you, Papa?"

Sir Arthur, wondering what his son was up to, spoke mildly. "Yes, Trixie wouldn't like it at all."

"Nor would Clarissa."

Ledmore tapped his glass with a fingernail. "When the time is right, Claringdon, Clarissa shall abide by the family traditions. The Ledmore traditions." He turned an indulgent smile at Sir Arthur. "Your daughter is charming, but there are times when a husband must be stricter than a father. Clarissa shall soon mend her ways."

Carlton slapped his port down on the table.

"She is not rag-mannered, sir," he said coldly, thinking that nothing would give him greater pleasure than throttling this prim peacock.

"She is your sister," Ledmore pointed out. "So you are inclined to be more indulgent while I view her dispassionately."

A muscle throbbed in Carlton's left temple. "And what do you find so wanting in Clarissa?" he asked so affably that Sir Arthur felt genuine alarm.

"Her hair, to begin with."

Sir Arthur himself was betrayed into speech. "Her hair!" he barked.

"Yes," Ledmore answered. "All those curls. Most curious."

"She inherited those curious curls from my mother," Carlton said stiffly.

"Yes," Ledmore said hastily. "And on Lady Claringdon they do credit. But I cannot abide such a frivolous-looking wife."

"What do you propose, a wig?"

Mr. Ledmore swallowed some of his port. "I thought she might use a cap."

"A cap?" Carlton howled. The fellow was mad. His laughter turned hollow when he saw that Ledmore was in earnest. "Not even my mother wears a cap, sir."

"It is the custom of our family for married ladies to do so," Ledmore said with composure.

Sir Arthur was no great barometer of feeling, but even he thought it time to switch the topic before Carlton let fall some of his opinions of the Ledmore family. He settled upon politics, but here, too, the attempt was doomed to failure. Mr. Ledmore was a Tory with all of that party's worst excesses, and the Claringdons had always been Whig.

"I don't like this man Ledmore," Carlton said to Trixie as they rode home in their carriage. "He talks of Clarissa as though she were a wall he wanted to redecorate. Criticizing her hair, of all the absurdities, and speaking as though she were left on the shelf for years, when everyone knows she could have had half the men in London."

"Yes," Trixie agreed, a frown puckering her pretty face.

"He did appear to be picking at her throughout the evening."

"And it won't stop," Carlton prophesied. "He'll continue it when they marry."

"It does seem odd that Clarissa would accept him," Trixie said as he helped her down at Mount Street.

Carlton gave a strained laugh. "Odd, my dear? My poor sister has lost all of her wits. Otherwise she would cry off on the instant!"

Back at St. James Square Lady Claringdon was reaching the same conclusion as her son. No sooner did she find her husband alone in his dressing room than she gave full vent to her inner turmoil.

"Arthur, I shall never be able to tolerate that scarecrow as a son-in-law."

Sir Arthur undid his cravat. "Sets one's teeth on edge, doesn't he?"

Lady Claringdon paced wildly. "How could you have accepted his offer?"

"I didn't," Sir Arthur said, stung to the quick by this inaccuracy. "She did."

"Well, she must break the engagement!"

Sir Arthur's face brightened for the first time that evening. "If Clarissa wants to do that, I shall make no objection. I think Charles would be the perfect selection, don't you?"

"I neither know nor care at this point," Lady Claringdon said with rare passion. "As long as she does not marry William Ledmore, I shall be content to count my blessings." She swept out of her husband's room and down the hall with her eyes flashing magnificently.

"My dear, I came to wish you good night," she said, finding Clarissa alone in her bedchamber.

"Thank you, Mama," Clarissa said, fondly embracing her mother.

Lady Claringdon turned her daughter's chin toward the light. "You have been crying!" she exclaimed.

"Oh, no," Clarissa denied. "I am just feeling out of sorts."

"And who can blame you?" Lady Claringdon said, sitting her down on the bed and believing that the time had come for frankness. "I would be feeling out of sorts myself if my betrothed dragged me over the coals so shockingly."

"But he didn't . . ." Clarissa said, drawing away.

"My dear, he pinched and scolded you in that dreary fashion of his until I was certain that Carlton was going to say something." She paused. "I did not care to see that happening."

"Perhaps he shall change when we are married," Clarissa said in a low voice.

"Such men don't change," Lady Claringdon announced, her voice ringing with authority. "And it's obvious that he thinks you shall do all the changing in the marriage."

Clarissa pulled her wrapper closer for comfort. "Perhaps that would not be such a bad notion, Mama."

Lady Claringdon muttered a silent oath. "Clarissa, you must not say such things. You cannot mean to marry that broomstick! Already his influence on you is very bad." She controlled herself for a moment then continued. "I thought his only fault before was his awful dullness. But it's much worse. He's arrogant, and he had nothing whatever to be arrogant about. Clarissa, my dear, your father quite agrees. If you withdraw now, we won't hold it against you. I promise."

Clarissa pressed her mother's hand.

"No, Mama. I must marry someone. Papa was quite

right. It's high time I settled down, and feeling as I do, it might as well be Mr. Ledmore."

Lady Claringdon swallowed hard, and her eyes filled with tears. "My dear, this is not the marriage I dreamed for you!"

Clarissa flung her arms around her mother. "I know, Mama," she said fiercely through her own tears. "But I am well past the age of romance!"

Carlton had intended to ride out early the next morning with Clarissa in the attempt to persuade her to drop her ridiculous choice of a husband, but his departure was delayed by Emily's arrival. She descended upon Trixie and Carlton in a flutter of trunks, apologies and questions, questions that had to do with Clarissa's whereabouts.

"Oh, yes, she's at home in London," Carlton answered. "But she has left all her wits at Claring."

"Good heavens!" Emily said, looking astonished.

"Carlton is exaggerating," Trixie interposed, leading her friend over to the couch. "Clarissa has just accepted an offer of marriage from a Mr. Ledmore . . ."

"Marriage!" Emily said in dismay. "I do beg your pardon for I know she was so highly courted. I suppose he was one of her long-time beaux?"

"No," Carlton declared vehemently. "She never paid him a moment's attention before this."

"Clarissa has not been herself," Trixie said to Emily who was chewing on her lower lip and looking thoughtful. "I confess all of us here in London are perplexed. Can you enlighten us?"

"I suppose I can try," Emily said and quickly sketched in the events that had happened at Claring.

"Sidney Montcrieff offered for Clarissa?" Trixie said, all but riveted by the news. "A love match, you say?"

Emily nodded vigorously. "But then it all came to nought."

Carlton pursed his lips together. "Poor Clarissa. One disappointing offer and then another. I don't know this fellow, Montcrieff, but it stands to reason he can't be any worse than Ledmore and perhaps a good sight better. Where is he now, Emily? Perhaps I can talk to him and patch up their quarrel."

"I don't know where he is," Emily confessed. "I believe Lytton is trying to trace him. I should have arrived here sooner myself, but I was obliged to spend some time with the Boatwrights' friends. I have sent round a letter to Lytton telling him I arrived and giving him this address. I do hope you don't mind."

"Not at all," Trixie said. "We shall be glad to meet him at last. And you must tell me all about him and your marriage plans."

Carlton, however, excused himself from sharing these confidences, explaining that he must be off to Clarissa. But he might have stayed back at Mount Street for all the good his morning drive with his sister came to. Clarissa, as she informed him upon arrival, had had her head filled with objections to Ledmore from both her father and mother, and she was in no mood to tolerate a morning drive filled with more disagreement. Since Carlton loved her too much to make her unhappy, he fell silent on the topic of Ledmore and applied himself to amusing her, telling her all the funniest stories that he knew.

While Emily was regaling Trixie with tales of the earl, and Carlton was attempting to entertain his sister, Lytton was engaged in leading his cousin out of the worst greeking establishments he had ever laid eyes on and was lecturing him at every step.

"Don't you have better sense, Sidney?" he expostulated. "You of all people. If you found *me* in such a place you'd

212

comb my hair. And to lose the Montcrieff diamond to Jack Strange."

Sidney, who had been without sleep for several days, uttered a rude response to his cousin's advice.

"Silliest thing I've seen you do," Lytton said, not taking any notice of what Sidney had said but bullying him into the waiting hack. "Family heirloom. Costs our great-great-grandfather a pretty penny at Rundell and Bridges. Must redeem it immediately before Strange finds himself in a pinch."

"Strange is always in a pinch," Sidney said, rousing himself to respond to this. "And when the devil did you get back to London?"

"Five days ago," Lytton said, giving a sigh of relief as the hack pulled away from the building. "Five days spent hunting you down."

"What a damn nuisance that must have been," Sidney said, surveying his cousin and growing conscious of his own unshaven face and wrinkled clothing. "I dimly recall we came to cuffs at Bengal Court. My apologies. I haven't been myself of late. I even lost to Strange at faro. Most peculiar. I never used to lose," he said reflectively.

Lytton, after dropping his cousin off at Hill Street, returned to his own house feeling travel-stained but relieved that Sidney had not come to any grief. At the entrance hall he found Emily's letter waiting on a silver tray and instantly all trace of fatigue vanished. Racing up the stairs, he called for George, his valet, and gave orders for a bath and shave, for he could not meet Emily looking like this.

An hour later, with his Oriental tie arranged to his scrupulous satisfaction, the earl drove off in his curricle. Carlton was absent, and Trixie was resting comfortably in her rooms when Lytton presented himself. Emily greeted him with what he later told her was a shocking lack of modesty. Undeterred by this she drew him down for an exchange of ardent and enjoyable kisses and consented to a drive, even offering her choice of destination.

"To see Clarissa?" The earl frowned as they got under way. "I don't know if it's such a good idea to impose on her so soon."

"I don't think a visit from two friends can be called a burden," Emily responded as she settled back into the carriage seat. "And I do long to see her, and Sidney as well." Another thought overcame her as the earl settled himself next to her on the seat. "You have found Sidney, I should hope?"

Lytton drove and favored Emily with a carefully doctored account of his cousin's whereabouts. Emily listened in rapt silence, clucking her tongue at the end.

"To think of him wagering that ring and losing it. Do you think it wise to leave him home in such a condition?"

"Sidney shan't suffer," he said ruthlessly. "Even if he does, Bender shall put him to the right."

Emily pressed her face against the earl's arm. "Did he mention Clarissa at all?"

The earl shook his head sadly.

"I wonder what he'll say when he finds out she's engaged."

"Engaged!" Lytton exclaimed, almost colliding with a chaise turning into the street. "Whom is she engaged to?"

"To a quite odious man named William Ledmore," Emily said, her eyes bright as stars.

"How do you know he is so odious, my dear?" Lytton asked, searching his memory for some clue of Ledmore but finding none. "Have you met him?"

Emily smoothed her yellow walking dress. "I don't need to," she asserted primly. "Carlton said so himself, and he is so pleasant that anyone he disapproves of *must* be disagreeable. And Clarissa's parents dislike Ledmore excessively too."

214

The earl mulled this over for a moment. "Not like Clarissa to get betrothed to an ugly customer."

"I know," Emily agreed. "That is why I am determined to find out from her why she is marrying him!"

Unhappily for Emily, she was prevented from asking any questions during the early part of her visit with Clarissa. Lady Claringdon and Sir Arthur had heard the shriek of surprise with which Clarissa had greeted the arrival of her two friends. Both of her parents on entering the drawing room were obliged to meet the newly engaged pair. In short order, however, Sir Arthur and Lady Claringdon withdrew, Lady Claringdon wondering to herself what Sidney Montcrieff must look like since his cousin, the earl, was such a fine figure of a man.

"How nice it is to see you two," Clarissa declared, looking fondly at her two friends on the couch. She had thought that seeing Emily and Lytton would bring back pain, but she was delighted to discover that all she felt was genuine happiness for them.

"When did you arrive?" she demanded.

"Just this morning," Emily said. "And Trixie and Carlton have been so kind. Trixie has told me just who I should patronize and where I should have my dresses made for my trousseau. She insists there is no need to be frightened by the modistes, but I confess to some fear."

"Try Madame Fanchon," Clarissa said kindly. "She is a modiste of the first stare, and she doesn't give herself airs. Should you like me to accompany you?"

Emily clapped her hands. "Oh, would you, Clarissa? If you are certain you are not busy."

"I shall be delighted. And it shall be great fun."

"Trixie and Carlton told me that you are engaged too, Clarissa," Emily said shyly.

Clarissa's mouth curved in a smile. "If I know Carlton, that is not the only thing he had to say about my engagement. But you shall judge for yourselves. Mr. Ledmore will be calling soon. But tell me how were the Boatwrights? And your aunt, Lytton?" With these questions to guide them, the three friends settled down to tea, lemon cakes, and a comfortable cose.

The mood was broken a half hour later when Ledmore was ushered in. The earl, putting down his teacup, looked for some sign of affection between Clarissa and her betrothed. Their greeting, however, was temperate, perhaps even a trifle cold. Ledmore made no move to kiss her on the hand or cheek, merely nodding to her in an offhand way.

"These are friends of mine," Clarissa said, introducing them all. Ledmore bowed to Emily and gave the earl two of the boniest fingers he had ever clutched.

"You are cousin to Sidney Montcrieff, are you not?" Ledmore asked looking down his nose at the earl.

"Yes," Lytton replied, discomposed by this lead. He recovered quickly. "Are you acquainted with Sidney?"

"I met him once," Ledmore confided. "Can't say I enjoyed it. I hope I don't offend with my plain talk."

Clarissa cringed inwardly, and Emily looked astonished, but Lytton had come across mushrooms before. "Not in the least," he said politely. "What did Sidney do to offend?"

"Nearly ran me down with his horse. Driving in some race or other."

"A race!" Lytton exclaimed. "But surely you knew enough to stay off the road at the time . . ."

"I had no notion they would be coming so fast," Ledmore said with some dignity.

"Speed is the essence to any race," the earl said faintly.

He was on the verge of another much ruder comment, but Clarissa adroitly intervened and drew the conversation back to more agreeable routes.

Lytton's first impression of Ledmore remained constant during the visit: a pompous ass. He chafed on the couch, wondering as so many before him had, why Clarissa was marrying the man.

A few minutes later, still unenlightened, he rose with Emily to make their good-byes.

"Don't forget we must go to Madame Fanchon's next week," Clarissa reminded Emily as she embraced her. "Will you be free on Thursday?"

"I am sorry," Ledmore interrupted. "Thursday we are promised to my mother."

"How is this?" Clarissa asked, her eyes kindling. "I was not told."

Ledmore showed no alarm. "I am informing you now."

Emily, quick to sense the rising hostilities in the room, interposed.

"We can visit New Bond Street some other day, Clarissa."

"Let us say Monday," Clarissa suggested. "Then we can see each other sooner."

She hugged her friend again and shook hands warmly with Lytton and felt a sudden emptiness in her heart when she was left alone with Mr. Ledmore.

"Mother is eager to meet you," Mr. Ledmore said, recalling her attention to his presence in the room.

"Is she?" Clarissa said, vaguely distracted. "I'm glad."

"If you are going to the modiste's with your friend, you should make arrangements for fittings for our wedding."

Clarissa nodded obediently, but the very idea of a wedding to Ledmore brought on a fresh supply of despair. Her temples throbbed, and she pressed her fingers to the spot.

"Is anything the matter?" Ledmore asked, growing aware after a few minutes that Clarissa was not listening to his thorough account of the whims of his mother.

"I'm sorry," Clarissa apologized. "I find I have the

headache." She rose to her feet. "I must lie down, and I am sure it will pass, if you excuse me."

"Of course," Ledmore responded. "Though I hope you will be well for Almack's Assembly on Wednesday. They say the czar may look in." He left the room thinking briefly of the last three occasions he had visited Clarissa. On each she had come down with the headache. He took his hat and gloves from Walter, thinking that it was almost as though Clarissa did not relish his company. But that idea was surely absurd! *She was marrying him, wasn't she?*

20

Sidney woke Sunday morning feeling as though his head had been target practice for Wellington's troops. From under tired lids he surveyed his approaching valet and decided to take his fences in a rush.

"Yes, Clemmons, I know I look hellish. But pray do not ring a peal over me."

"Very good, sir," Clemmons responded. "We are all pleased you turned up safely."

"You may thank Lord Lytton for that," Sidney growled as he submitted to Clemmons's shaving brush.

An hour later, dressed to his valet's satisfaction in a new slate blue coat, Sidney descended the stairs. A shudder shook him at Bender's polite mention of breakfast, and he chose to partake modestly of a small piece of toast on which had been spread a dollop of orange marmalade.

Refreshed by this light repast, he decided to call on Strange. It pained him greatly to have to admit, but Larry was correct. An heirloom ought not to be wagered in any match.

Since the day was warm, he strolled over to Grosvenor Square where Strange resided, but to Sidney's annoyance Strange was not receiving callers because he was indisposed. Sidney, who had an accurate idea of the ailment Mr. Strange was afflicted with, scrawled a note of explanation on the back of a gold-embossed card and left it with the butler.

He headed back for Hill Street, pausing now and then to acknowledge sprightly greetings from his friends. His head continued to buzz lightly, and he found a profound sympathy mounting for Jack Strange. At the corner of Mount Street several ladies turned on the arms of their companions, eyelids aflutter and voices atitter. Sidney retained a firm grip on his cane.

A phaeton passed, driven by a curly-headed woman in a gown of heavenly yellow. Her hair danced impudently in the wind, and involuntarily Sidney's step quickened. But it was not Clarissa.

Nor did he wish it to be, he reminded himself, angrily jabbing the cane on the cobblestones as he walked. It was bad enough that she had played him for a fool at Claring, but to pine after her in this ridiculous schoolboy fashion was the height of folly. He scowled as he turned another corner and collided almost immediately with Lytton.

"Good God, Larry! Must you trail me this way?" he complained bitterly as they dusted each other off.

"Trail you?" the earl protested. "Of all the conceits. As though I have nothing better to do with my days but to spend them tracking you down." Aware of the curious looks they received from several of the passersby, he fell into step with Sidney.

"I didn't imagine you would be up so early."

Sidney held a hand gingerly to the side of his head. "If you must speak to me, Larry, I beg you to modulate your voice. I have an aversion to loud noises today."

Lytton grinned. "What are you doing up so early?"

"Paying a call on Strange who was indisposed. You were right, Larry. It doesn't do to lose family heirlooms. I may have use of it myself later on."

"Indeed," the earl murmured politely.

"Certainly. I could always get engaged myself."

"Yes," the earl agreed. "I have heard that Lady Vye herself has gotten married."

Sidney nodded without noticeable emotion. "I have heard the same tale. To a German, of all things. I just hope he has enough funds to support her somewhat fatal addiction to jewelry. But Eleanor was not the only fish in the sea. What think you of Mrs. Lyttle?"

"I'd say she was thought of too often by too many men," Lytton said frankly.

Sidney swung his cane. "I suppose you are right. What of Miss Thomas? I met her at a party several Seasons ago. They say she is still unwed."

Lytton gave a shout of laughter. "All this talk of marriage, Sidney. And to women like those. Are you certain losing the ring to Strange did not also unhinge your mind?"

"I am not so dim-witted," Sidney demurred.

"Speaking of wits, I ran into a chap who has no high opinion of you."

Sidney betrayed a tepid interest. "What enemy can that be, I wonder?"

"Not an enemy," Lytton said. "A chap named Ledmore."

220

His cousin looked puzzled. "Never heard of the fellow."

"He claims you ran him down during a race."

His memory jarred by this tidbit, Sidney slapped his cane down on the street. "My word. That one!" He pushed back his beaver hat. "I should think he'd be dead by now after witnessing his usual folly. And dimwit is too good a word to use on him. Would you believe he wanted me to jaw out an apology while the race was in full tilt?"

"Unbelievable," Lytton murmured.

"It was! And I had ten thousand quid riding on the outcome." Sidney stroked his chin for a moment. "How is it you hang about with Ledmore?"

"I don't! Emily and I made his acquaintance at Clarissa's. She's engaged to him."

In the face of this startling announcement, Sidney maintained a creditable calm. He pulled out an enameled snuffbox and inhaled a choice pinch. When he finally did speak, his words came in a hoarse whisper and made no sense to the earl.

"She lost no time, did she?"

Sidney strode off, thinking hard. But time was of the essence to an unmarried woman in her condition. A woman would settle for anyone, even a skittlebrain like Ledmore. But what would Ledmore say when she presented him with fatherhood in six months' time?

"You needn't bolt away at the mention of Clarissa!" Lytton complained as he hurried to keep up with his cousin's longer stride.

"I don't bolt."

"You must see that it's absurd, someone like Clarissa being attached to a dull dog like Ledmore." He watched his cousin's face intently for some clue. "I met him just once. And that was enough. Not the sort I'd like to cozy up to. And Clarissa's family is in a pelter over the match."

"Clarissa probably has her reasons for the match," Sidney answered coldly.

"So everyone agrees," the earl admitted. "But I should like to hear just one good reason."

Sidney stopped and tapped Lytton lightly with his cane. "Dull dogs don't ask questions, coz."

Grandaunts, however, are not so reticent. Ever since her return to London, Agatha had been trying in vain to piece together the mice feet Sidney had made of his engagement to Clarissa. But all to no avail. Neither Lytton nor Emily knew the cause of the problem, and if Joseph knew, he for once was holding his peace. It was enough, Agatha declared, to drive her to distraction.

However, when Emily quite by chance let fall the news that Clarissa was in the habit of attending Almack's Assemblies, Lady Agatha found herself suddenly with an overwhelming urge to attend Assembly herself.

"And you shall take me," she told Sidney during a visit to his house.

"I, Aunt?" Sidney asked, puzzling over this invitation, if invitation it was since she had delivered it with more the air of command.

"Yes," Agatha said. "Lytton, after all, shall be dancing attendance on Emily, and it wouldn't do for him to have to squire me around and see to my needs."

"You don't seem concerned that I might have a lady to squire around as well," Sidney inquired adroitly.

"Do you?" Agatha asked bluntly.

His eyes met hers fleetingly over the tea tray. But he could read nothing untoward in her countenance. "No," he admitted at last.

"Then you are free to escort me."

"Not only free to do so but delighted as well," Sidney said, giving ground graciously. "Am I to deduce from all this that you find Joseph's company ill suited for Almack's?"

Agatha cackled loudly. "If you think I can abide his fetching and toadying to me in public, Sidney. It's quite bad enough that he fawns over me in private lest I change my mind and throw him and his brats out of the house . . ."

Sidney smiled diffidently. "Joseph has his uses."

"Invite him to live with you for a week and you'll speak differently."

Sidney smiled again and changed the subject. "I take it you are reacquainted with your bosom bows and have returned to town life?"

Agatha shrugged. "I have met some and gone to visit others, but as for meeting them all. . . . That's one reason I'm eager to go to Almack's. They tell me that nothing must do but for dowagers to go there with their granddaughters and nieces who are just out of the schoolrooms." She sighed. "London has changed. It's much noisier than it used to be."

"That's on Alexander's account," Sidney explained. "The crowds are quite eager to see him, and they are just as eager to hiss at poor Prinny if he but dare to show his face. And I would think it shall get worse by the time Wellington arrives. Undoubtedly there will be more fireworks and parades."

"Fireworks and parades," Agatha said half to herself and half to her nephew on the opposite chair. "It's almost like being in love, isn't it, Sidney?"

Sidney's smile never wavered, but his dark eyes gleamed dangerously as he looked at his aunt.

"What would I know of love, Aunt?" he asked politely.

When Clarissa entered the ballroom of Almack's on King Street Wednesday evening, the first person to greet her was Mr. Ledmore. One glance at his pinched face and she uttered a silent oath, wondering to herself why she was marrying him.

"My dear," Ledmore said, frowning. "You must know that I dislike the color pink excessively."

Since her gown was a rose-colored silk with a pink satin underdress, there was no reply that Clarissa could charitably make. Lady Claringdon, however, who was beginning to believe her prospective son-in-law had windmills for brains, entered the fray.

"Pray, how is Clarissa to know what color you despise?" she demanded in a tone every bit as frosty as her silver gown. "Is she a mind reader?"

"A mind reader," Ledmore stuttered. "Good heavens."

"Or perhaps you think she has gypsy blood?"

"No, never that!" Ledmore said, licking his lips and wondering why the amiable Lady Claringdon should rip up so. "It's just that I gave you a precise list of my likes and dislikes, Clarissa."

"Yes, I recall," Clarissa said quickly, not daring to meet her mother's incredulous gaze. The list in question had run fully five pages in length and still gave her the headache to contemplate. "I meant to read it, but I have not had the time," she explained to Ledmore.

"What kind of list is this?" Lady Claringdon demanded. "Do you think my daughter a shopkeeper, sir?"

"Good heavens, no," Ledmore said, feeling thoroughly nonplussed by this inquisition, coming as it did in the sainted grounds of Almack's. "It was a simple matter of convenience. In my family we have a tradition of acquainting the bride and groom on what the family prefers." He turned back to Clarissa. "And I hope you shall look at the list before our wedding. I took particular pains with it."

"Of course I shall," Clarissa said obediently.

Sir Arthur, noticing the frown on his daughter's pretty face, made his own feeble attempt to liven the evening.

"Why don't you two young ones dance?"

Ledmore promptly offered a bony arm, which Clarissa was obliged to take. But the ballroom held no delights for her. Ledmore moved like a mail coach, alternately swaying left and then right and bumping into several august couples on the floor.

"Dancing isn't in my scheme of things," Mr. Ledmore said, struggling to keep time to the music.

"Indeed," Clarissa murmured. "One would never know that!"

Ledmore frowned at this kindly remark. "You must know, Clarissa, that I dislike dancing."

Her eyes flew up. "I must? But how? . . ." She broke off. *That list again, no doubt!* "I suppose it was on your list?" she asked.

"Close to the top."

"Near the color pink?"

"Are you mocking me, Clarissa?" Ledmore asked stiffly.

"No, not at all, sir," Clarissa said, sighing inwardly. The man had no sense of humor at all.

"I took particular pains with that list—"

"So you have said," Clarissa responded. "Since you dislike dancing so much, I can only wonder why you are dancing with me now?"

"Your father made the suggestion plain," Ledmore pointed out with some dignity. "It would seem improper indeed not to have asked you. However, you might have declined politely and made some excuse. Anyone knowing my dislike for dancing would have done just that."

There was no winning this match, Clarissa saw at once, and she gave up the attempt. "I shall keep it in mind for the future," she said mildly. "Shall you wish to stop now?"

Ledmore looked shocked. "Oh, no. That would call attention to ourselves, and I see Lady Jersey herself looking our way. I am determined to see it through to the end."

Fortunately for Clarissa's temperament the dance did come to an end, and Charles Alsgood claimed her almost immediately. But Charles this night was showing as great an aversion to the dance floor as Mr. Ledmore professed. He led her round the perimeter of the room and then quickly into a small anteroom where they could sit in private.

"For we must have a chat, Clarissa!" he said, closing the door and looking very stern.

Clarissa was taken slightly aback by the grimness of his face. "Charles, you are being mysterious and absurd."

"*I* am being absurd!" Charles muttered, casting his eyes imploringly to the chubby water nymphs on the ceiling. "You are the cabbagehead, Clarissa! To think that all these years I believed that you were the only woman in the ton with any brains at all. What must you do but accept William Ledmore!"

"Carlton told you," Clarissa said, mildly piqued as she accepted the Windsor chair he pulled up and arranged the folds of her gown carefully around her. Her devotion to Carlton was complete, but sometimes he overstepped the bounds of brotherly love.

"Of course he told me," Charles expostulated. "He has talked of nothing but you and Ledmore. Is Carlton here tonight?"

Clarissa shook her head. "Trixie was feeling out of sorts, and he didn't wish to leave her. And it's a very good thing he is not here," she said, her steely eyes flashing fire. "For I would give him a thundering scold. He had no right to tell you the news!"

"You are a ninnyhammer, Clarissa. First you dance

226

with Crowne, then you dine with Brigg, and now you see fit to marry Ledmore!"

"Yes," she retorted. "And even he shall notice I am absent from the ballroom and seek us out."

"No, he won't," Charles contradicted. "He won't even notice because of the crush on the floor." He slumped further into his chair. "And I don't think Ledmore has the wit to realize someone might steal his betrothed from under his nose." His green eyes turned pensive. "Clarissa, can you in all honesty prefer that gabblemonger to myself?"

Clarissa made no attempt to argue with this rather accurate opinion of Ledmore.

"No, certainly not," she said impatiently.

"Then why the deuce do you accept him, unless you're foxed!"

"That is hardly the way to speak to a lady," Clarissa said reprovingly.

"You're not a lady. You're my friend." Charles rose to pace under the anxious eye of the water nymphs. "And as my friend I wish you would stop making an ass out of yourself. What sort of hoax is this?"

Clarissa's eyes darkened. "It's no game, Charles. I am in dead earnest."

"Marry Ledmore, my dear, and you'll be dead, period." Charles paused in mid-stride. "By God, Clarissa, you know I'd help you in a minute whatever the situation. And the situation must be pretty desperate for you to agree to Ledmore. My offer still stands. Marry me. We are such good friends, I know our marriage will be a good one."

Clarissa blinked hard. "We are good friends," she agreed. "But you don't love me, or if you do, you love me like a sister. And I love you like a brother."

"Perhaps," Charles conceded. "But even that might be a better bargain than old Ledmore."

"Someday I hope you can meet someone you can love wholeheartedly, Charles," she said quietly.

Charles cocked an eyebrow at her. "Strange advice coming from you, Clarissa, seeing that you are marrying entirely without love."

"Yes, I know. . . ." She managed a rallying tone. "But think how much better for you. You won't be obliged to cope with a strange wife after all. Now we must go back to the floor. You know what gossips people can be!"

Reading in her face that her mind was firm on this matter, Charles returned her to the ballroom, but Clarissa saw immediately that he had been correct about Mr. Ledmore. That gentleman, far from showing any great concern about her whereabouts, was thoroughly engrossed in conversation with Brigg. Probably on horses, Clarissa thought with a sudden flare of wounded pride. Ledmore acted as though he needn't disturb himself any longer with her. But wasn't that exactly how she wanted her husband to act?

"I shall meet his mother tomorrow," Clarissa said mournfully.

"With an announcement to follow in the *Gazette?*" Charles asked sympathetically.

Clarissa gave a tiny shrug. "If all goes well . . ."

"I suppose one may as well wish you happy," Charles said grudgingly. "You must know that once the announcement is made it shall be more difficult to cry off."

"Yes," Clarissa sighed. "I realize that." She gave her head a sudden, defiant shake. The curls danced in the light from the chandeliers. "Let us not talk of such gloomy matters tonight, Charles. For the rest of the evening I want to be reckless and happy and free to enjoy myself!"

"And so you shall," he promised, unable to resist her entreaty. He waltzed her vigorously across the room, so vigorously that they found themselves at the end of the dance breathless with laughter. Charles was leading her through the crowd of other flushed faces when he heard his name called out in greeting.

"Hullo, Alsgood."

The smile on Clarissa's face froze. Sidney Montcrieff stared bemusedly down at her.

"And good evening, Miss Claringdon, isn't it?"

21

The Montcrieff party had entered Almack's some minutes earlier, and Sidney had immediately been shoved to one side as the tide of his aunt's long-lost friends descended upon her with ostrich feathers bristling and much cooing and clucking of the tongues.

Never one to partake in a hen party, Sidney strolled about the ballroom, nodding to a few of the gentlemen, ignoring the more obvious lures launched by the ladies, and raising his quizzing glass to his eyes to observe the dancing assembly. A minute later the glass dropped, the blood drained from his face, and he swore softly and intently.

Clarissa was here! Even as he uttered her name, she had danced out of sight with nary a hair turning on her pretty little head. Sidney's own face took on the look of one about to do murder. And yet . . . he could not resist the advantage of observing her, and he searched the couples on the floor again with his glass before he found her smiling up at her partner, Charles Alsgood. The sight of that shining face brought the blood boiling to his temples.

Not only had he been played the fool by her, but by his own family. One angry look at Lytton—who had taken considerable pains to put the length of the ballroom between himself and Sidney—was sufficient. He had been in on the trick from the first. An escort for Aunt Agatha indeed.

It did not help Sidney's disposition one bit to hear the compliments coming unbidden from Clarissa's admirers close by.

"Clarissa is in her best looks tonight," Wentworth was saying. "A pity it is all wasted on that fool, Ledmore."

"Yes," Lord Pedlow replied. "What is the story there, pray?"

Sidney stepped away. He might have set the quizzes straight on the story if he were anything less than a gentleman, and he could well imagine their reaction. *My good fellows, Miss Claringdon is increasing! The haste of the moment dictates she choose a father for her babe.* By Jove, what he would give to see their faces then. All their professed admiration for her would disappear in a trice.

And yet, watching her, Sidney could not help a flicker of admiration himself. She was not the sort to run shy of the grand hoax. And she looked to be in top form tonight. Sidney muffled his laughter. To be dancing in her condition! And he knew well enough that she was doing more than the waltz. She was actually thumbing her nose at the ton, and the pity was no one could share the joke with him!

"Sidney!" Agatha, having shaken as many hands as she wished to, tapped him lightly on the back with her cane.

"Yes, Aunt?" he asked, smoothly slipping over to her side.

"Is that Miss Claringdon I see dancing on the floor?" she demanded.

Sidney looked into her limpid eyes without any noticeable change of expression.

"My dear Aunt, you must know it is."

"Ask her to come here," Lady Agatha commanded imperiously. "I have a great need to renew my acquaintance with her."

Sidney muttered a silent oath. He was quite content to observe Clarissa at a distance, but to talk to her at close quarters. . . .

"You could send Lytton to bear your message to Miss Claringdon."

Agatha thumped her cane. "Are you afraid of a mere girl, Sidney?"

Montcrieff snapped his jaw shut, and when the music ended he stalked off toward the dancers in the middle of the room.

Now he gazed down at Clarissa, amused that all color had rushed from her cheeks upon seeing him. He felt a glow of satisfaction. She might make sport of the ton and good fellows like Alsgood, but she wouldn't fool Sidney Montcrieff, not for a single moment. And she would learn *that* before the evening was finished.

"Miss Claringdon," he said smoothly. "It is a pleasure to see you again."

"Mr. Montcrieff," Clarissa answered with a meticulous formality that belied the frantic beating of her heart. "It is a surprise to see you here tonight."

"I can see that by your expression," he said, taking her hand and holding it to his lips for a moment. She fought the urge to snatch the hand away.

"I didn't know you two knew each other," Charles said, looking amiably from one to the other.

"Our acquaintanceship dates from the Cotswolds," Sidney explained. "As does my aunt's across the room. She wishes to speak with you, Miss Claringdon. I hope you don't mind, Alsgood."

"I daresay age must have some privileges," Charles said with a cheerful smile. "I shall see you again, Clarissa."

"Yes, Charles, and thank you."

He disappeared into the crowd, leaving her alone with Sidney, who held out his arm to her with exaggerated courtesy. Clarissa, feeling quite faint, took it and walked with her chin high through the whole ballroom, which was now spinning like a child's top. Sidney, expertly steering her through the crush, displayed no such qualms himself.

"Miss Claringdon, I am in raptures at seeing you again," Agatha declared, holding out both hands to Clarissa.

Clarissa embraced the older woman with some relief. "Lady Agatha, I am delighted to see you. Are you enjoying town life?"

"Yes, famously," Agatha replied. "And I am glad that you arrived safely."

Clarissa colored momentarily under the shrewd eyes. "I do apologize for leaving so abruptly and without a word of good-bye to you."

Agatha dismissed the apology. "Tala. In my house we go and come as we please. Sidney, here, also made a bolt for London, did you not?"

"To be sure, Aunt," Sidney replied with the same faint hauteur that Clarissa remembered from their last meeting at Claring. His eyes fell on Clarissa for a fraction of a moment. "I had pressing matters in town."

"Where is your mama?" Agatha asked, briskly taking control of the conversation again before her nephew could make mice feet of it again. "I should like very much to meet her."

"At the moment she is across the room," Clarissa said,

232

singling her out to Lady Agatha. "That is she in the silver gown."

"And the gentleman next to her?" Agatha asked. "Surely he is too young to be your father. So it must be that brother of yours you have spoken of."

Despite herself Clarissa laughed. It was too absurd to compare Ledmore with Carlton. Sidney felt an unexpected pang as her laugh rang out and glared fiercely across the room.

"My brother is home with his wife," Clarissa was explaining to Agatha. "She was not feeling at all the thing, and he chose to remain with her."

"Then who is that gentleman your mama is speaking with?"

"Mr. Ledmore," Clarissa replied. Agatha required further enlightenment and she added, "If all goes well I am to wed him."

"What is this?" Agatha asked, giving such a superb look of shock that Sidney, for one, longed to box her elderly ears. "You are to be married!" She nudged her nephew with the cane. "Did you hear, Sidney?"

"Certainly I heard, Aunt," he replied dutifully as he stepped out of the way of the assaulting cane. "My hearing is in perfect condition, although my back may ail me tomorrow. My felicitations, Miss Claringdon."

"Thank you," she said faintly, unable to meet his scornful eyes. "I am a trifle premature. Our families have not made the announcement yet, but we have every hope of forming a suitable alliance."

"I think you shall make a splendid wife, don't you, Sidney?"

Sidney helped himself to some snuff. Clarissa had grown scarlet with embarrassment. But embarrassed or not, he noted, she was still the most beautiful woman in the room. Motherhood must certainly agree with her.

"Ledmore shall make an excellent husband and a devoted father, I'm sure," he said smoothly.

"Thank you," Clarissa replied, acutely aware of the mockery in his voice. "Although I had not expected you, Mr. Montcrieff, to be such an expert on husbands." She gave him no time to recover from this but turned at once to his aunt. "Are Emily and Lytton in your party tonight, ma'am?"

"They came with us," Agatha explained. "But I have lost sight of them. Oh, there they are on the floor dancing. As Sidney should be." She snorted. "Would you believe it, my dear, my nephew has been standing like a dolt all evening. In my day gentlemen knew how to dance."

"The custom still stands, Aunt."

"This I must endeavor to see for myself," Lady Agatha replied as the musicians struck up a waltz. "Clarissa, you must dance with him. I know you'd rather not, but humor an old woman. Sidney," she ordered trenchantly, "you shall stand up with Miss Claringdon."

Clarissa's face grew even redder. "I cannot," she said, flustered. "My card is quite filled. Colonel Crowne has this waltz."

"I know the Colonel's family intimately," Agatha said, not about to be deterred. "And I shall put the matter right with him. The military, for reasons I have never been able to comprehend, all pay extravagant homage to old ladies." She glared at her nephew still at her elbow. "Well, Sidney, do you mean to stand there like a cake or to dance?"

"Most assuredly, Aunt," Sidney replied grimly. "It shall be to dance."

He held out his arm to Clarissa with a hint of challenge in his eyes. Her own flashed fire as she put her hand on the crook of his arm. Not just an ordinary woman, he reminded himself as he led her out. She would try and brazen it through, and it might be amusing to see how long her masquerade lasted.

"My aunt is incorrigible," he said as they waltzed.

"On the contrary," Clarissa said sharply. "I find her delightful. She cannot be blamed for not knowing we dislike each other so."

"Speak for yourself, Clarissa," Sidney said, gazing down at her face and wondering why the intervening weeks had not turned her into an ugly hag. "I profess a great admiration for you."

"Admiration!"

"Yes," he continued. "But you must realize your scheme won't wash."

She stiffened in his arms. "I beg your pardon?"

"This hoax you are running," he said, looking intently in her eyes. "Your man Ledmore is a fool, I grant you that, but even he shall get wise to you in six months' time."

Clarissa choked on her fury. "Pray, what are you talking about?"

Sidney arched one eyebrow. "Yes, do continue to play the injured lady. It is a role that suits you well. Had you a share of the stage with Kean himself you would far outshine him."

"Now you are calling me an actress," Clarissa said.

"Not just an actress," Sidney corrected. "But one of the best."

"That is a left-handed compliment if ever I heard one."

Sidney dropped his voice. "Heed me well, Clarissa. It doesn't do to flaunt yourself in public. The ton shall remember it, and such vulgarity is never appreciated."

"Vulgarity!" Clarissa's face turned white with rage. "I have never been accused of vulgarity in my life," she said coldly. "And I see nothing vulgar in dancing as I am not as yet formally engaged."

"Have it your own way," Sidney said, breaking in rudely.

"Do you forget to whom you are talking?"

He waltzed her expertly to another corner of the ballroom. "I know exactly to whom I am speaking."

She flinched from the contempt lacing his words. "Oh, why do you dance with me?" she implored.

"My aunt commanded it," he said, keeping his hand on her waist and making it impossible for her to escape. "I always try to keep on her good side, and you promised this dance to me."

"I did no such thing!" she declared hotly.

"There your memory has misled you," he said, glancing at the other dancers close by. "We were in the Cotswolds, and you promised that the next time we met in London you would dance the waltz with me. This is London, we have met, and this is a waltz."

"I remember," Clarissa said, her eyes flying up to his. "But what I said then was given in the spirit of friendship. I hardly think we are such good friends any more that any speech would be other than a severe penance."

"Yes," Sidney agreed. "We do seem to bring out the worst in each other. But save your pretty speeches for the baconbrains like Ledmore. They are quite lost on me."

"I don't know what ails you, sir," Clarissa said with mounting passion. "Or how you can be so mean. I own I should have expected such treatment from you since when we last met you made clear in what loathing you held me. Though why this should be I swear I do not know."

Sidney's ears burned. "Too cute by half, miss."

"You persist in making these hateful remarks to me," Clarissa said, finding relief at last in words. "I doubt that anyone could induce you to stop. But when I first met you I did think you were quite different. I thought you generous and charming and kind." She blinked back tears. "But

I assure you I see you for what you are. You are a villain and a scoundrel, Sidney Montcrieff, and you are definitely not kind. . . ." She stopped, appalled to find her voice breaking on this last syllable, and though the musicians continued to play, she dashed off the floor through the crowd, tears streaking down her cheeks.

22

Clarissa's abrupt departure in tears caused the tongues of the ton to wag. Not a few of the older dowagers laid the blame squarely on the waltz she had been dancing at the time of the incident. It was quite clear to them that this import from Vienna was highly dangerous and that the patronesses of Almack's might do well to ban it hereafter, czar or no czar.

Lady Claringdon, who had no patience with such nacky notions, was not at hand to witness such talk. She had bustled her daughter off at once, ignoring the protests of Mr. Ledmore, who had complained that they would miss seeing Alexander and then more stupidly that Clarissa had seemed prone to all manner of physical ailments.

On reaching home Clarissa was immediately taken upstairs to her room, where she drank down the warm milk that Lady Claringdon prescribed and cried herself to a long and exhausted sleep. No such easy remedy was possible for her parents. Sir Arthur began to be perturbed by his daughter's behavior since her return from Claring and took the opportunity to inform his wife that he had never seen Clarissa act so missish!

Lady Claringdon, her patience sorely tried by Mr. Ledmore's stupidities, grew incensed at hearing her daughter so described and threw aside her legendary placidity and her gloves to give her husband what he described later as a regular trimming.

"For it is your fault, Arthur," she fumed, "that Clarissa has grown missish. You were so eager to see her married. You made all manner of threats, and just see what your precious attempts to marry her off has resulted in. An alliance with Ledmore! I hope you are satisfied!"

"Don't blame me, Constance," he said, mustering a quick defense. "I didn't cause her to fly away from the ball in tears."

"But I do blame you," Lady Claringdon insisted. "Who drove her to Claring? Whose threats have forced her to accept Ledmore, who shall put me to the blush daily?"

"Do you think I am immune there?" Sir Arthur responded, outraged. "I don't like that beanpole any more than you. But it was your fellow Montcrieff, or so they say, who caused Clarissa to bolt the floor. It's not my fault, Constance!"

He was still protesting his innocence to Lord Whalmsey early the next morning as they headed for White's.

"Constance blames me for everything that has happened to Clarissa."

"It is in the nature of women to blame their husbands," Whalmsey replied from his comfortable vantage point as a bachelor. "Though Constance and Clarissa always seemed like top ones to me."

"They are top ones," Sir Arthur replied. "At least Clarissa was before she went to Claring."

"What happened there?"

"How the devil should I know?" Sir Arthur snapped testily. "I was in London."

"But what happened at Almack's?" Lord Whalmsey inquired. He had been absent from the Assembly the night before.

"Now that I do know!" Sir Arthur said as they crossed the street. "Clarissa fell into a quarrel with some dancing partner of hers, and she threw a fit."

"A fit, Arthur?" Whalmsey lifted his shaggy brows. "Hysteria, do you mean?"

"It looked like that," Sir Arthur conceded.

"Ledmore shan't like that."

"All to the good," Sir Arthur said with feeling as they entered the club. "Do you think I care a fig what Ledmore wants or doesn't want? If Clarissa's fit should scare him off, I'd give thanks and so would Constance."

"Who was her dancing partner?" Lord Whalmsey inquired.

"Some fellow named Montcrieff. I never met the chap!"

Sidney had spent a long night at White's, arriving there after quitting Almack's and staying closeted in the gaming rooms until dawn. His string of bad luck had abated. But winning enormous sums of money did not bring him any satisfaction.

When the last of his night's companions had deserted him for their beds he remained alone at the table. But everything he saw—even the queen of hearts—reminded him of Clarissa.

Blast her.

He could still see her eyes, livid with their crystal tears. He could still hear the tongues clucking in the ballroom when she had fled the floor and the well-bred stares that had come his way. He had nearly come to blows with

239

Alsgood after the incident. The lady still had her champions.

And yet try as he might he could not forget her closing words.

You are definitely not kind. . . .

No, he was not! But then neither was she! Damn actress. Her words cut him to the quick. He should not care. But by God he still did.

"And now I am plagued by a guilty conscience," Sidney said, disgusted with himself.

He headed toward the hall. Perhaps the morning papers would take his mind off what had happened. He started to enter the reading room when he noticed two occupants. His eyes narrowed. One of the men he recognized as Lord Whalmsey. Could the other be that good friend of Whalmsey's, Claringdon?

Sidney stood at the door, puzzling over his next move, but when he heard Clarissa's name mentioned, he gave in to his inner devil and stepped across the threshold.

"Who do you mean Clarissa to marry if not Ledmore?" Whalmsey was asking.

"I don't know," Sir Arthur answered gloomily. "Time's growing short."

"Indeed yes," Sidney said, strolling up to the two armchairs. "And if I were you, Sir Arthur, I would not delay so pressing a matter as your daughter's wedding."

Sir Arthur looked up, startled at the figure in front of them. "Who the devil are you?" he asked acidly.

"My name's Montcrieff," Sidney said, extending a hand. "Perhaps you may have heard of me?"

Sir Arthur struggled to his feet, his color bordering on the choleric. "Heard of you?" He choked on his spleen. "You're the very rascal who started this business with Clarissa!"

"Too fast," Sidney murmured. "We both know I had a predecessor."

"I know one thing, sir," Claringdon replied. "I should call you out for what you did to my daughter."

"Arthur!" Whalmsey cried out, alarmed at his friend's expression and knowing too well Montcrieff's own skill with a pistol.

Sidney strolled toward the fire. "Did Clarissa lodge some complaint with you?" he asked.

"Complain? How could she complain? She was too busy crying her eyes out." Sir Arthur drew himself up stiffly. "It's plain to me that you must've insulted her."

Montcrieff yawned. "If it's a duel you want, you may have it, although it's considered bad ton for gentlemen such as ourselves to engage in duels."

"Gentlemen!" Sir Arthur scoffed. "Don't make me laugh, sir."

"Oh, I have no intention of playing the jester," Sidney replied. His voice hardened. "But I am a gentleman, and gentleman enough to hold my tongue."

"About what, pray?" Sir Arthur inquired politely.

Sidney glanced toward the doorway and saw no one else in sight. And Whalmsey was, after all, fully acquainted with the facts. What was the harm in laying open the whole Claringdon hoax?

"Were I not a gentleman, Sir Arthur," he said grimly, seating himself opposite them, "I would congratulate you on becoming a grandfather."

"Now I know you're bosky," Sir Arthur declared, his florid face very red and confused.

Sidney touched a finger to his lips. "Never fear. I shall say nothing outside."

"And why shouldn't you?" Sir Arthur asked. He turned to his friend in the next chair. "Peter, do you know what he is talking about?"

"It's that damn waltz," Whalmsey said, nodding sagely. "People claim all that motion and close contact addles the brain. First Clarissa throws a fit, and now Montcrieff here loses his wits."

Sidney uttered a cold laugh. "You are a brave man, Sir Arthur, to stand up to the wags. However you choose to play this game, I felicitate you."

"Thank you, I think," Sir Arthur replied, uncertainly knitting his forehead. "Though the babe is not yet born."

"I realize that," Sidney said politely.

"And by all rights," Whalmsey added. "It's the father you should congratulate."

Sidney's jaw dropped. "You know the father of the babe?" he hissed, rising to tower over the two men.

Whalmsey, digging deeper into the comfort of his chair, toyed with the idea of the bellpull. Surely no violence would invade the hallowed halls of White's. Watier's perhaps, but not White's.

"You know the father of the babe?" Sidney repeated thickly.

Whalmsey hid his irritation. "Certainly I know him. I've been acquainted with him all my life and why do you look so put out? These things happen."

"Perhaps my sense of propriety is greater than yours," Sidney said, making no effort to conceal his contempt. "And I am disappointed in you, my lord."

Sir Arthur looked as bewildered as his friend. "But see here, Montcrieff, it was you who introduced the topic of the babe. I daresay you're another in Ledmore's ilk who wants nothing more but the family to wait on their hands and never utter a word in public."

A slow flush suffused Sidney's face.

"Ledmore knows?" he quaked.

"He'd be blind not to," Sir Arthur pointed out.

"Your candor does you credit," Sidney said, recovering.

"I take it, Sir Arthur, you know the father of the babe too?"

Sir Arthur blinked hard, his mustache wiggling in exasperation. "Whalmsey, is this man besotted or am I?"

"Oh, it's he, Arthur," Whalmsey quickly assured him. "In all my years, Montcrieff, I've never known you to act so havey-cavey."

"No? I apologize," Sidney roared. "Allow me just a moment's lunacy. Can it be you still see the father of the babe?"

"Naturally we do," Lord Whalmsey said stiffly. "Bad form not to."

"Then I beg you to acquaint me with him immediately," Sidney snapped. "I shall not rest until I deliver my congratulations firsthand."

"Now that would be doing it much too brown," Sir Arthur spoke up.

A brittle smile was etched on Sidney's face. "Would you begrudge me the chance to meet this paragon?"

"Paragon?" Sir Arthur asked, startled. "He's hardly that—"

"I used the word in jest," Sidney said.

"Good. He used to enjoy kicking up scrapes before all this. Sowing his wild oats they called it in our day, eh, Peter? The babe seems to have sobered him."

Sidney felt close to strangulation and tore loose his cravat. "The babe has sobered him, you say," he repeated witheringly. "I would not have known him to possess such sensibility!"

"Sensibility?" Sir Arthur pondered this for a moment. "No, I think Clarissa has more than enough sensibility for the pair of them."

Sidney recoiled as though whipped. "I see! It is too absurd to be speaking any longer to either of you. Sir Arthur, you shall point out this gentleman to me."

"Glad to. But he ain't here," Sir Arthur said cordially. "He's at home where he belongs, with his wife."

Sidney gnashed his teeth. "His wife! He is married?"

Sir Arthur shifted nervously in his chair. Montcrieff was taking on the look of a wild beast.

"That is not so unusual," Sir Arthur went on calmly. "Lots of men are married, Whalmsey to the contrary."

"You shall do me the honor of pointing me toward his house of residence," Sidney said rigidly.

"Why should I?" Sir Arthur asked, affronted. "First you upset Clarissa. Then you pick a quarrel with me, and now you mean to stir up trouble—"

"The trouble is already bestirred," Sidney said. "And if you are not kind enough to tell me his name, I shall find out for myself."

"Well, I hardly think it's worth all that fuss just to shake his hand," Sir Arthur pointed out.

Sidney's lip curled. "I wish to do more than shake his hand."

"Oh, do what he says, Arthur," Whalmsey said. "Then perhaps he shall leave us in peace."

Claringdon drew out his card case. "Very well. Take this to Number 12 Mount Street, if you insist. I daresay Carlton should be up at this hour. Not that you'll get in to see him looking like that!"

Sidney stood thunderstruck, the card in his outstretched hand. Carlton? The lines of print blurred.

"You said Carlton," he said weakly.

Sir Arthur peered into Sidney's face. "Do you mean you don't wish to see him after all? Give me back the card." He snatched it from Sidney's fingers. "I told you he was bosky, Peter."

"No, no." Lord Whalmsey demurred. "It was I who informed you of that."

"First he wants to congratulate the father-to-be and

now he doesn't, and what the devil are you up to now!" Sir Arthur cried out as Sidney lurched around the room muttering a strangled oath.

"I have been a bigger dunce than that poor fool Ledmore!"

"No, how could anyone be that!" Sir Arthur asked.

Sidney whirled to face him. "I have my facts straight finally," he said through clenched teeth. "You are Sir Arthur Claringdon, are you not?"

"Yes," Claringdon said gently, gazing over at Whalmsey who was shaking his head sadly and tapping his right temple.

"Hear me out," Sidney implored. "I know I sound queer in my attic. I have been queer in the attic. You have a son Carlton Claringdon and he and his wife, Trixie—isn't that her name?—are shortly to expect a child. That is the grandchild you have been speaking about all this time!"

"Well, certainly it is," Sir Arthur said. "I've no other grandchildren under way sir." His brows narrowed. "And if you mean to cast any aspersions on my daughter, you shall have a fight on your hands!"

"No, indeed," Sidney leaped to his feet. "I cast no aspersions and as for fighting you, sir, I make it a rule never to fight with any father-in-law of mine!"

Over at St. James Square Lady Claringdon was facing her daughter's early morning visitor with an expression that held civility but no real affection.

"I am afraid, Mr. Ledmore, that my daughter is indisposed."

"But she can't be," Ledmore protested with his thin lips twisted into a pout. "We are going to see my mother. We had it planned for days. It's of the first importance that Clarissa see her and give her an explanation of her behavior at Almack's." He colored somewhat under Lady Claringdon's aghast stare.

"I was of the opinion that your mama did not frequent Almack's," she said now. "How would she know what happened last night at Almack's?"

"I took the liberty of telling her myself," he said. "Felt it best to alert her before the prattle boxes could. They might have caused her to collapse. Her constitution is rather delicate."

"I'm afraid I am not acquainted with either your mama or her constitution," Lady Claringdon responded in her grandest manner. "If her constitution is so ticklish as to fall apart at the idea of a minor misunderstanding at a party, I hardly think she would be able to show her face without falling into hysteria."

"That's why I try to protect her," Ledmore said, beaming at her. "Wouldn't do to get Mama upset. And that's why Clarissa must meet her today and apologize."

"Apologize!" Lady Claringdon abandoned her attempt at civility and glared at him. "Apologize for what?"

"For causing talk, of course," Ledmore said, looking exasperated. "In our family we frown on such behavior."

"Clarissa is not seeing anyone today," Lady Claringdon replied. "Least of all your mother."

"But she must," Ledmore protested. "Do you think you could just tell her that I'm here.".

Lady Claringdon grudgingly admitted that she might do such a thing and exited the room, speeding off to alert her daughter to the problem confronting her.

"Oh, dear, I had forgotten all about him," Clarissa said when her mother had told her of their guest. Reluctantly, she rose from the couch where she had been sitting contemplating the fire. "I had also forgotten about meeting his mother today."

"Clarissa," Lady Claringdon said anxiously, "if you are

feeling unwell, you needn't see either one of them. And had I known he would have called today I would have told Walter that he was not to be allowed in."

"It's not your fault, Mama," Clarissa said with a faint smile. "And I suppose I must see him. There is no point in putting off Mr. Ledmore."

Lady Claringdon, who had her own theories of what one should do with Mr. Ledmore, followed her daughter down the stairs and into the drawing room, resisting his subtle attempts to have a moment alone with Clarissa.

"I'm sorry, Mr. Ledmore," Clarissa was saying now, "but I don't feel up to meeting your mama today."

"After that disgraceful scene last night I don't suppose you are up to seeing anyone," Ledmore scolded. "My dear Clarissa, you must have been mad to run off the dance floor in tears."

Lady Claringdon, who had stiffened immediately at his words, was ready to launch herself into battle again, but she noticed that Clarissa had already risen to address him.

"I regret that you feel that way about the incident," Clarissa said. "I myself wish it had not occurred. But since it did, there is nothing I can do about it. And it is not as disgraceful as you seem to think."

"It was more than disgraceful," Ledmore proclaimed. "That is why you must meet Mama and apologize. And since you can't see her today, perhaps you would write a letter of apology. I will give it to her when I see her."

"Apology!" Clarissa glanced at him wondering how she had ever imagined she could marry such a pompous, narrow-minded man. "I have nothing whatever to apologize to your mama about," she said, feeling more like herself than she had in weeks. "Your mama," she continued to point out, "was not even present at Almack's, and she would undoubtedly think me dim-witted to be apologizing for something she did not witness. And before you begin to tell me what a dutiful wife and daughter-in-law should or should not do, I should like to tell you that I have rethought the matter of our marriage. I am not going to marry you."

"Not marry me!" Ledmore spluttered. "But see here, you can't do such a thing."

His protests, however, were overshadowed by the cry of glee emanating from Lady Claringdon's corner of the room. That good woman, on hearing with her own ears the proof that her daughter had once again regained her senses, leaped up and dashed over to engulf her in a heartfelt embrace.

"My dear Clarissa, I knew you wouldn't marry such a person."

Mr. Ledmore stiffened measurably and vainly sought to make himself heard. That, however, proved impossible since both mother and daughter were occupied in shedding tears of relief and babbling about so joyously that he finally rose in disgust and stalked out of the room, taking his hat from Walter and exiting the establishment just as Carlton and Trixie were about to enter.

Carlton witnessed Ledmore's thundercloud expression and wondered what was in the works. He peered into the drawing room to see his sister and mother.

"Good heavens," he said, pushing back his hat. "What is going on?"

Lady Claringdon wiped her eyes and flew up to greet them. "Clarissa has come to her senses. She is not going to wed that beanpole!"

"Thank God," Carlton ejaculated.

"I'm afraid we weren't very civil to poor Mr. Ledmore," Clarissa said, suddenly stricken by conscience a few minutes later. "I wasn't very tactful in declining his offer, and Mama here almost did a gig."

"If I had been here," Carlton retorted, "I would have

done a gig myself. And so will Papa when he hears the news." He rubbed his hands together in satisfaction and announced that he was starved.

"So am I," his mother agreed. "And I think this calls for a celebration."

So it was that when Sir Arthur finally returned home from his visit to White's he found a celebration in progress. Discovering the reason behind the festive mood, he did not break into a gig, but he did order a bottle of his finest champagne to be broken out.

"For I never could stomach that broomstick," he said succinctly.

Clarissa giggled and kissed him on the cheek. "Poor Papa, but perhaps you have not realized that I am still on the shelf."

"But not for long, I warrant," he said cheerfully, and looked at her in such a way that she could not help wondering whom he would attempt to match her with next.

"A visitor, Walter?" Clarissa sighed and looked up from her embroidery with a frown. The afternoon had grown quiet with both Sir Arthur and Lady Claringdon on a round of afternoon calls. "It's not Mr. Ledmore?" she asked quickly. "I left strict orders that I would be unavailable to him."

"Oh, no, miss," Walter hastened to assure her. "It is not Mr. Ledmore. It's the Earl of Lytton, miss."

Lytton? Frowning, she followed the butler into the drawing room and found the earl pacing back and forth. "Lytton? What are you doing here, sir?" she asked.

"I have come to beg your help, Clarissa," he said urgently. "It's Emily. She has flown up into the boughs and insists that our wedding be called off."

"Oh, no!" Clarissa exclaimed.

"Oh, yes," the earl ejaculated and threw up his hands.

"It is the stupidest thing. We fell into a quarrel in the carriage on the way to see you. She insists she will not even come in. She must be the most stubborn creature on earth. Would you please talk to her, Clarissa? Perhaps you can coax her out of her pet."

Clarissa shook her head. "I think it's you she really wishes to see. Emily tells you to go away because she wants you near. That's the nature of lover's quarrels."

"You are the only one she will listen to, Clarissa," the earl said, unconvinced. "Would you just go and speak to her? You can talk in the carriage. I promise you I wouldn't ask if the matter were not desperate!"

"Very well," Clarissa agreed. She moved toward the door, glancing back at Lytton expectantly.

"I shall remain here," Lytton explained. "I fear she will erupt in hysteria if she sees my face."

"She cannot be such a goose," Clarissa muttered but went out of the room and the house alone. It took only a moment for her to step toward the carriage, a closed carriage she noticed with some surprise. Lytton's footman opened the door to her, and she stepped up and in. The door slammed behind her, and, as if on cue, horses and coachmen roared away. Clarissa was thrown back hard against the carriage seat.

"Emily?" she asked in some confusion.

"Emily's not here," a voice answered.

Clarissa's eyes widened in the dim light. She knew that voice!

"Sidney!" she exclaimed, making out his countenance finally. "This is monstrous, no infamous. Odious, odious creature. Stop this carriage at once," she ordered.

"I am sorry, my darling Clarissa, but I cannot," Sidney said, appearing unperturbed by her words. He put his arm about her shoulder.

With all her might she pushed him away. "I am not your darling, and what do you mean you cannot?"

"Lytton gave his man direct orders," Sidney explained with a chuckle. "And he answers only to the earl. Anything I might say is quite useless. We are on our way to St. Albans, says his lordship. And we are not to stop until we arrive there."

"To St. Albans," Clarissa said incredulously. "What's at St. Albans?"

"A church, I believe," Sidney said softly. "Complete with minister to, er, perform the duties."

"I am not going to St. Albans," Clarissa declared. "And I am certainly not going to be married to you. I know what this is," she said, setting her lips grimly together. "This is another of your abominable hoaxes. But I warn you, Sidney, I shall not keep silent on this score. You have treated me shabbily for the last time. I shall not stand for this."

"Nor should you," he answered, ruthlessly pulling her into his arms. "I have been a gudgeon, Clarissa. How large a fool I am prepared to let you know in just a little while, but for now I promise I do love you," and he bent his head and kissed her fiercely.

Clarissa's head swam, and she returned his kiss passionately before she realized what was happening. Then she struggled away. He had talked just as lovingly at Claring when he was playing his hoax. She would not be fooled twice by the same trick.

"You are more than abominable," she cried out now with tears springing unbidden from her eyes. "You have treated me like a veritable mawworm, and if you don't stop this coach I shall scream."

"Clarissa," Sidney entreated as he took possession of her hands. "My actions, odious though they were, were due to a mistake. A misunderstanding. I thought. . . ." He paused. "Good heavens, there is no right way to say this and I do apologize beforehand if it gives offense for undoubtedly it shall, and I could strangle Joseph for making such a mull of things. I thought," he said with a gulp, "that you were expecting a child."

"Expecting a child?!" Clarissa stared at him aghast, wondering if her ears were playing tricks on her. "How could you have come to such a conclusion?"

"Joseph overheard Lord Whalmsey at White's telling someone that your father was unhappy despite the fact that he was going to be a grandfather. He was unhappy with you. His mind, blast it, put that tidbit together with the fact that you were at Claring in the middle of Season and came up with the suspicion that you were increasing. He thought that you had been sent to the country to have the babe quietly."

Clarissa stared at Sidney coldly. "And you agreed—"

"Oh, Clarissa, I know it sounds so illogical now. But when Joseph told me what he had heard from the mouth of Lord Whalmsey, I did not stop to think it could be your sister-in-law who was to have the babe shortly, and that your father was displeased with you for not being at hand in London to enjoy the occasion with them."

"You thought I was no more than a cheap trollop," Clarissa said. "Oh, how could you have believed anything so vulgar?"

"I don't know," Sidney admitted, his words coming with difficulty but showing no attempt to escape his just punishment. "It was only this morning at White's that I finally confronted your father. I was in a devil of a mood after meeting you last night, as you can imagine. I ironically congratulated him on being a grandfather, expecting that he would poker up. Instead he quite frankly told me I was bosky. It didn't take much after that to discover that it was Carlton's wife who was to have the child and that you had nothing to do with it."

Clarissa could not stop a giggle from spurting out. "You actually went up to Papa and told him?" Her eyes widened as she imagined the scene.

"Yes," Sidney admitted. "And it was all I could do not to bolt away to your home and propose to you then and there. But I felt that you might not see me if I did come round to call. And there were plans to be made. Arrangements."

She shot him a quick measuring look. "Arrangements?"

He nodded. "First I had to find a bishop who would draw up a special license so we could be wed, and then I had to go over to Lytton to persuade him to help me. And I had to contend with Aunt Agatha, who was certain that after last night I was making a mull of my life. And not the least, I had to convince your father that I wasn't out to ruin you, and he of course would deliver the message to your mother."

"You spoke with Papa about marriage?"

He grinned widely. "Oh, yes. In fact at this very moment they are awaiting us at St. Albans along with Trixie and Carlton and Emily and, if he is quick enough on a horse, Lytton might beat us to the church."

"Everyone was in on this plan!" she said, growing angry.

"Not everyone," he denied. "Not the most important person in the plan. You, my darling." He hesitated for a moment as though groping for words. "I am truly sorry, Clarissa, for all I have said and done to hurt you. I was everything that was cruel and heartless and, as you reminded me so aptly last night, I was certainly not kind to you. But do you know in the weeks that I have been away from you, never once did I stop thinking of you or dreaming of you? And if you forgive me, I swear I shall spend the rest of my days atoning for ever doubting you." He fumbled for a moment in his coat and took out the Montcrieff diamond.

"It has always belonged here," he said simply, slipping it onto her finger. "I must say I had a devil of a time finding Jack Strange. He had it."

Clarissa gazed down at the diamond on her finger and then looked up at him in bewilderment. "You gave the diamond to Jack Strange?"

Sidney gave a shaky laugh. "I shall explain later. But for now you must tell me how you feel for me."

"How should I feel for you?" Clarissa demanded coldly. "You were a villain and a scoundrel and no man ever treated a woman so shabbily. And as for your precious Montcrieff diamond, perhaps you had better take it and return it to Jack Strange, for I don't care for it in the least."

"Perhaps not," he said with a nod. "But you do care for me just a trifle, do you not? Oh, you cannot have changed that much in such a short time. Last night when we danced at Almack's I still sensed something between us."

She turned away, but he had already caught her up abruptly in his arms. "Speak, Clarissa, I beg of you. You were ready to marry Ledmore without love. Don't you love me even a little?"

Her silence filled the carriage.

"Clarissa," he said wretchedly. "If you don't speak to me I shall do something desperate."

"Such as?" she inquired with a challenge in her eyes.

"Such as this," he said, responding by pulling her into his arms once more and kissing her more wildly than before. Clarissa, breathless in the tide of his emotion and hers, buried herself with a laugh and a sob against his coat of Bath blue superfine.

"You do love me, you do love me," he said as she rested her head on his shoulder. "Don't you?"